CHECKMATE

This is Love

Kennedy Fox

Checkmate: This is Love
Checkmate Duet, Book 2

Cover Design & Photography by Sara Eirew Photography

Copy editors: Keizha at Librum Artis Editorial Services and Mitzi Carroll

Proofreader: Marisa Nichols

Checkmate

/ˈCHekˌmāt/

Noun

(Chess)

1. A position in which a player's king is in check and the player has no legal move (i.e. cannot move out of or escape the check). A player whose king is checkmated loses the game.

2. Utter defeat

TO OUR BOOKSTAGRAM FAM

We are so grateful for you and all your enthusiasm over the Checkmate Duet! You've showed Travis King and his princess so much love these past few months, and we're forever humbled by your love!

TABLE OF CONTENTS

CHAPTER ONE

TRAVIS

Ten hours earlier...

I press my palms into my eyes and exhale deeply.

I cannot lose control. I cannot lose control.

I wish I'd told Viola what happened at work and talked to her about it instead of shutting down. Not that there'd be anything she could do, but she's always been a great listener, even when she was being the biggest pain in my ass. When we were kids, she always made time to listen to my ramblings. I didn't speak to my parents much, about anything, and had learned to keep most of my feelings buried inside. Being real and open felt natural with Viola.

That was before I fucked it all up and hurt her.

I should just call it a night and go to bed, but I'm too restless, thinking about that bitch, Alyssa. Which makes me think of fucking Blake, who ripped my dream of moving up in the company away from me, but I won't go down without a fight.

I decide I should probably eat something, but I hadn't gone grocery shopping since before Drew left and he isn't home tonight, so that leaves me with limited options.

Ramen noodles or PB&J on moldy bread.

Wrinkling my nose, I shut the cupboard and grab my car keys. I need to clear my head.

I take a drive down the highway, heading out of town, blaring my stereo with the windows rolled down. The evening breeze feels good, and the music numbs my mind. I allow the pavement to lead the way.

Hours later, I end up just outside of Sacramento and stop at a diner that's open twenty-four hours. It looks old and run-down, but I'm ready to chew my damn arm off so I can't be too picky.

Once I find a booth, I order a cup of coffee and some water. The sounds of clanking silverware and late night chatter fill the diner. There are only a handful of people at the counter—who look to be truck drivers—and a few couples sitting in the other booths. I shouldn't be surprised at this time of night, though.

The waitress comes back with my drinks and then takes my order of pancakes and bacon. She barely looks up from her writing pad as she scribbles it down, and walks away before I can hand back the menu.

Tempted to text Viola and make sure she's okay, I stop myself and decide I'd rather talk to her in person about it all. I don't know what we're going to do now that Drew is home early, and although I've broken the bro code by banging my best friend's little sister, I don't want him to find out from anyone besides me. Knowing I owe him that, at least, we need to figure out how we're going to tell him. *Or what I'm going to tell him.*

The truth is, Viola and I aren't a couple. We have a history—a damaged one—but nevertheless, a history that has bound us together since we were kids. The more I think about it, the more I want to punch myself for every sting I blew her way. She hadn't deserved it, *most of the time,* but she made sure to give it right back.

That's what I love most about her. She's never taken my shit, and she's the only girl to challenge me at every damn opportunity. Perhaps that's what kept the fire burning all these years, but I'm done playing those games. I lost her as one of my best friends all those years ago, and I'll be damned if I lose her again.

The waitress drops my plates in front of me and mutters that she'll be back to refill my coffee. I pour the syrup over my pancakes and begin cutting into them when I hear a familiar voice behind me.

I turn my head slightly, listening again. It can't be.

"You jackass! You can't just leave me here!"

"Get off me, you crazy bitch!"

The voice is definitely one I've heard before. Panic sets in as I set my fork down and slide out of the booth. Then I see her familiar face and curse under my breath.

Mia *Fucking* Montgomery.

She's arguing with a guy as she pulls on his leather jacket. She's crying and pleading with him, but he just pushes her off and walks out the door. I'm shocked to see her here, especially with someone else. It flat-out bothers the shit out of me, considering she and Drew broke up only days ago.

"You're a fucking asshole, Will!" she calls out, rushing behind him through the door in a skimpy little dress.

I'm quick to follow as I call out her name. "Mia, stop!" I grab her elbow and turn her around. "What the hell are you doing here?"

"Travis?" Her eyes widen. "Holy shit! Thank God you're here!" She wraps her body around my arm and cries even harder. It's awkward as hell, but I don't push her away.

"Oh, look. It took you less than thirty seconds to latch onto another guy," Will yells. "Enjoy her, dude. She's as easy as she looks."

"Screw you, motherfucker!" she shouts, and it takes me a moment to recognize the guy she's screaming at. *Will Tamer.*

"All right, man. That's enough. Just go. I'll make sure she gets back safely."

He laughs. "Don't fucking care."

I see red again at the way he's yelling at her; it takes every ounce of my being to keep my feet planted on the ground. The way he's treating her is way too reminiscent of how my father treated my mother all those years. Regardless of how much of a bitch Mia's been to Drew, I'm not okay with any guy talking to a woman like that.

"She's just another typical attention whore. Just wanted to use me as a way to get her fifteen minutes of fame."

"Oh right, Will, because a sex tape is so unusual today. That's *exactly* what I was doing because I definitely didn't sleep with you for your three-inch dick. Would be such a shame for the entire world to know that the only thing Will Tamer is packing is sugar-free gum and expired condoms."

"Mia," I hiss, warning her to shut her mouth. The sooner he leaves, the sooner I can get her out of here.

"What did you say, bitch?" He takes a step toward us, ready to get in her face, but I don't care who he is, there's no way I'm letting him touch her. The vile way he's talking to her makes my fists clench.

"Just let it go, man." I hold my hand up, blocking Mia behind me. "She runs her mouth a lot, but she's harmless." I try to diffuse the situation. The last thing I need is to get into another fight, but he's not taking the bait.

"Fuck off, little mama's boy." He pushes a finger directly into my chest, and now I'm seething. Will Tamer isn't someone I'd want to fight on one of my best days. He's a world champion fighter, and he's built like a fucking rock. Everyone in Northern California knows about Will Tamer, and only a dumbass would throw the first punch.

"Mia, go back inside," I say, keeping my eyes locked on him. He's a ticking time bomb.

"But Travis..." she argues.

"Go," I say firmer. "Get inside."

"I'd listen to your new little fuck toy if I were you," Will tells her, stretching his arms out in front of his chest and cracking his knuckles. "Unless you want to get blood on your fake designer shoes."

His words hit me like a ton of bricks. He could snap me like a twig in less than two seconds. I work out and lift weights, but there's absolutely no comparison. His biceps are as big as my head.

She gasps. "They aren't fake!"

"Jesus Christ, Mia!" I snap. "Get in the fucking diner."

"We have some unresolved issues to discuss," Will's voice is thick with amusement. He obviously gets a rush from fighting, in or out of the ring.

We both stay standing as we hear her shoes click against the pavement as she heads back inside. I don't want to fight this guy, or rather, get pummeled into the ground, but somehow I welcomed myself in her damn mess.

"Before you assume anything, Mia's just a friend..."

He takes a step closer.

"She was actually my best friend's girlfriend. So, whatever your tiff with her is, let's just drop it. She's a hot mess even on her best days."

"You think I care about any of that shit?" He steps forward again. "She took a video of us, and unless she gives it back, it's your face I'm going to be punching in."

"Okay, I'll tell her to give it back."

"It's on her cell. I want it."

"All right. No problem."

"You have five minutes. She either gives it back, or I crush your skull."

Fuck, and I thought *I* had anger issues. He's on a totally different spectrum.

I pinch my lips together and slowly take a step back toward the diner again. Once I'm inside, I grab Mia and tell her his demands.

"I need it, Mia. Just hand it over, and you can get another one."

"I *don't* have it!" She crosses her arms. "I've been telling him that for the past thirty miles."

"Where the hell is it?"

She shrugs. "Somewhere on I-50 between Riverton and Cedar Grove. I threw it out the car window."

I inhale sharply, brushing my hand through my hair and turn slightly to see he's watching our every move.

"Why the hell did you do that?" Now I'm annoyed.

"Because he was being an asshole! He kept telling me to give it to him, so I said 'fine, go get it,' and then threw it out the window."

"Fuck, Mia," I hiss under my breath.

"Well, I didn't know he was going to lose his shit over it."

"You recorded you guys having sex?" I whisper. "That's not exactly something a guy like him wants leaked."

She shrugs and her indifference feeds my anger even more.

Reluctantly, I walk back outside and face him. "She says she threw it out the window, which means there's no way it can go viral."

His jaw ticks, and I watch as his hands ball into tight fists. "Bullshit. I know she uploaded it to the iCloud."

Dammit, Mia, I mutter to myself.

"She won't upload it. I know Mia. She's all talk."

"You think I'm going to take your word?"

Before I can respond, Mia flies out the door and begins swearing at him. I can see people inside the diner watching us from the windows. Mia is all fired up, and Will is a second away from losing his shit.

"What are you so afraid of? Worried that people are going to wonder why I had to *fake* every single orgasm? Or maybe you're worried what people will think when they see you crying after you come?"

She storms past me, and I'm quick to grab her arm, pulling her back. For a petite girl, she's pretty determined when she's pissed.

"You fucking cunt," Will hisses. His body unleashes, and before he can make contact with Mia, I push her out of his way and take the hit.

I immediately lose my footing, and I can hear Mia shouting in the distance. His hands are on me before I even collide with the ground. Thankfully, the punch he served to my gut makes my head veer forward instead of slamming against the cement.

I block his next hit, but just barely. There's commotion and screaming around me, but I can't open my eyes long enough to find a way out. It's obvious this guy feeds off anger, and he won't stop till I'm a lifeless lump. It's engraved into him, so I do the only thing I can to break his fog.

It's a bitch move, I know, but I lift a knee up and kick him right between the legs with every inch of strength I have left.

As soon as I feel his weight lift off me, I roll out from under him and pull myself up. He's muttering a variety of curse words as he cups his junk and struggles to breathe.

"Oh my God, Travis!" Mia runs toward me, a handful of customers now outside watching behind her. "Are you—"

"Get in the car," I shout.

"What?" she asks as she runs behind me.

"Get in the fucking car! We're getting out of here."

I grab my keys from my pocket and unlock the doors as fast as I can. I know he's probably going to be down for a while, but I can't risk someone calling the cops on me. I'm already in deep shit at work; I don't need to add a misdemeanor charge of disturbing the peace on top of that. They could lock my ass up in the county jail, fine me, or both.

We both slide in and I rev the engine, shifting it into reverse and back into drive again. My heart is hammering in my chest as we make our way out of the parking lot, tires squealing and dust kicking up in our wake.

"What the actual fuck?" I'm so pissed to be in this position, that all I can do is drive faster and hold the steering wheel tighter. I'm so angry; I can't even look at her. The ounce of control that I've worked so hard to keep all day is slowly slipping, but she doesn't dare say a word, which I'm thankful for because I'm on the edge of losing my shit. Honestly, I think she understands what she's done, and I hope she feels a small sliver of regret, but as I glance over, I'm not sure if that's even possible. I already know what kind of girl Mia is; she's trouble.

"You just had to go piss off one of the strongest guys in the country?" I yell once we've cleared the area and are cruising back on the highway. The next time I turn and look at her, she's pale, and I can see her chest rapidly moving up and down.

"Mia?" I reach over and shake her knee, trying to grab her attention. "You all right?"

She shakes her head without looking at me. "I think I'm going to be sick."

She's going into shock, and there's no shoulder on the highway for me to pull over.

"Mia, listen to me," I say softly, trying to change my tone. "Your adrenaline is decreasing, and you need to try and stay calm. Listen to my voice. Inhale through your nose and exhale through your mouth."

She abides and grips my hand that's still resting on her knee. I want to pull it away, but I don't because she's in shock and I'm genuinely concerned.

"I can't believe that just happened." She begins choking on her sobs, and I realize I'm going to have to take the next exit before she pukes everywhere.

"Stay with me, Mia," I say evenly.

"I can't."

"It's okay. We're going to be okay."

She finally turns and looks at me. "You're not."

The stiffness in my body is evident, but I won't admit it—not right now at least. "I'll be fine."

"He could've killed you, Travis! I've never seen him act that way outside of the ring."

"Well, he didn't." I try to sound confident, but we both know had he pinned me down long enough, he certainly could've. My entire body is bruising already, and I just hope I'm able to move tomorrow.

I take the exit ahead and pull into a gas station that's nearly empty. It's after one in the morning, but the street lamps paint the parking lot in a mysterious orange glow. I can see the fear in her eyes as she stares off into the cloudy night sky.

"I can't believe that after everything, you'd do all that for me, Travis," she says moments later. Her voice is soft and sincere, her breathing finally regulating.

I shrug, not really wanting to get into the details of why I interfered. "Men shouldn't yell at women that way." As much as she probably deserved it, the moment I heard him raise his voice and get in her face, I snapped. If it'd been any other woman, I probably would've done the same thing, but the fact that it's Drew's ex, ignoring it wasn't an option.

She slowly exhales, bowing her head. "I'm such an idiot."

"Yeah," I say with a low chuckle, her hand still gripping mine. "You are."

Her jaw drops as she turns, eyes wide as she chokes out a laugh, too. "You weren't supposed to agree with me, jerk."

"Well, I don't sugarcoat shit. If you're being a pain in the ass, I'll tell you."

She laughs, her shoulders finally relaxing. "That's actually a quality most girls like about you, I bet." The look on her face causes me to release my grip, and she releases my hand. Mia and I haven't spent that much time together, considering Drew went to visit her more than she visited him. Being with her feels awkward, even for me. The mood shifts and I don't care for how she's looking at me.

"Most don't stick around long enough to find out," I mutter a bit too honestly.

"Why's that? Not the relationship type?"

I cock a brow. "Are you really one to be asking me that question?"

"What? You think I'm like a horrible person now?"

"I never said that, but given your current situation, you might not be the right person to be talking about relationships with."

She sighs. "I didn't cheat on him, if that's what you're thinking."

"I wasn't thinking anything."

"I doubt that. I can only imagine the things Drew has said about me." Her lips turn down, and I can tell she's in a vulnerable place right now, but she brought this onto herself.

"He loves you," I say. "He thinks the world of you."

She nods, avoiding my eye contact.

"Long-distance relationships are hard. I didn't think it'd be this hard, but with Drew's crazy work schedule and my school schedule, things just got way more complicated than I imagined they could. Even when he came up to visit me for a weekend, he'd be on his phone all the time checking in at work, or he'd be talking about work."

She sighs and continues without waiting for me to respond.

"He's married to his job, and I got lonely, but then when we are together and things are great, it gives me hope that things will stay great until they aren't again."

The way she's rambling on is making my head spin. I don't talk relationship crap with anyone, so I should get extra credit just for listening to her babble on now.

"Well, maybe it's best you both make a clean break. Sometimes you have to let go even when it hurts, because you know it's what's best."

"Wow," she says with a smile, turning toward me. "Who knew Travis King was so poetic?"

I laugh and shake my head. "Don't tell anyone."

She flashes a genuine smile, placing her hand on my cheek. "I won't tell. This secret will be ours. You're not as bad as you want everyone to think you are."

My lips turn down. "I don't know about that."

She reaches for my hand and squeezes it. "Well, I do."

Mia stares into my eyes. "You're just the distraction I need..."

CHAPTER TWO

VIOLA

Present Day

Mia *Fucking* Montgomery.

What the hell was Travis doing with her? Why the hell were they *together*? And why was she naked?

All questions I probably won't get answers to, at least for a while. I want to trust Travis. I want to believe nothing happened between him and Mia, but the circumstances aren't looking good right now.

Courtney offers to drive me once she sees how badly my knees are shaking. I call Drew as we walk to the Jeep, to find out which hospital they were sent to.

"Placerville?" I gasp. "Why the hell did they transfer them up there?"

"Closest hospital to the scene of the accident," he informs me. He's already up there, in full cop mode, but they haven't allowed him to see them yet.

"What was he doing up there?" *And with her?*

"I don't know, Vi. You know everything I do." I hear the concern in his voice and try to stay calm for both of our sakes.

"Okay, sorry. I'm just worried is all."

Courtney gives me a look, knowing I'm full of shit. As we climb into the Jeep, she quietly suggests I just tell Drew and get it over with, but until there's something to tell, I'm keeping my lips sealed. If he was hanging out with Mia and something happened between the two of them, there'd be no secret to keep. There'd be no *us*. But I have to try to give him the benefit of the doubt before jumping to conclusions, regardless of how easy that is.

I can't deny how the thought of it makes my throat dry. I'm not naïve enough to think that sleeping with Travis changes things. It doesn't change who he is or who I am. In fact, until I know what happened between us this past week meant something, and where we stand, it may be better to pretend it never happened. Even I know that's easier said than done.

I'm losing myself in my thoughts when I hear Drew yelling my name through the phone. "Viola!"

"Sorry, I'm here."

"You don't have to come up here, you know? I can keep you updated on Mia."

I roll my eyes. "What about Travis?"

"I figured you probably didn't care."

"Drew!" I scold. "I'm not a robot. Of course I care."

"Well, most days you two are at each other's throats."

"That doesn't mean I want him to be hurt...or worse." I rest my head against the headrest of the Jeep and inhale, trying to focus on the white line on the side of the road. *Maybe I should just tell him...* "Listen, Drew. There's something—"

"Oh hey, the doctor is coming out. I'll call you right back." He hangs up before I can respond.

"Well, that has to be a sign," I mutter to myself.

"What?" Courtney asks, driving onto the highway. It's about an hour drive, which means my mind has fifty-nine minutes to overthink everything.

"I was going to tell him, and he cut me off as soon as he saw the doctor."

"What exactly were you going to say?"

I shrug, knowing I hadn't thought it through. "I don't know. That Travis and I hatefucked all over the house, so I have a reason to be worried, although now I'm wondering if he screwed Mia and if I should go back to hating his fucking guts again."

She widens her eyes and grips the steering wheel tighter. "Perhaps it's a good thing he hung up then. No matter what, everything is going to be okay. Got it?" She gives me a hopeful smile, and we ride in silence the rest of the way.

Finally arriving at the hospital, anxious butterflies swarm my belly, and I have no idea what to expect. Courtney grabs my hand as we walk through the entrance and find Drew waiting for us.

She leans in and whispers, "Would this be a bad time to mention how hot your brother looks right now?"

I look at her and scowl.

"You guys made it," Drew says as he walks toward us. He wraps an arm around my shoulder and squeezes. He notices Courtney and flashes her a small smile. Of course, she melts, and I nudge her.

"Nurse said we could go in and see them soon," Drew continues.

"Do you know what happened yet? Or how bad they're hurt?" I search his face for a reaction, but he's calm and calculated with his words and movements. Drew is worried shitless right now.

"Mia didn't have her seatbelt on, so she's banged up pretty bad. Her lung collapsed, and she slammed her head pretty hard. They're keeping her overnight for observation, so I'm not sure when she'll be released."

"Glad to hear she'll survive," I say dryly between gritted teeth, but it's lost on him.

"What about Travis?" Courtney fills the silence, and I'm so grateful she asks.

"The airbags deployed, causing some burns, and he smacked his head on the driver's side window during impact. He had his seatbelt on, but the force of the impact broke a few ribs. He's bruised, but he'll survive."

I'm finally able to exhale the breath I've been holding since I received the call. To say I'm relieved to hear he's going to be okay is an understatement.

"He'll stay in ICU for observation to make sure there's no swelling in his brain, but knowing Travis, his head was already swelled up as big as his ego," he cracks, getting a small smile out of me.

"So, what happened exactly? Do they know?" I'm impatient as I ask, but I try to stay calm.

"The sheriff told me bits and pieces, but until they do a full accident reconstruction, they only know from what the witnesses told them. Basically, he was driving down the ramp and a semi in the right lane wasn't moving over, so he slowed down to get behind it. However, the car behind them wasn't paying attention and rammed right into the back of them at full speed, pushing them forward into traffic. Luckily, there weren't many cars were on the highway at two in the morning."

Jesus.

My heart hammers in my chest as I picture Travis going through something like that. He could've been hurt a lot worse had there been more traffic or the semi driver suddenly slowed down or the car that hit him was going faster or...

"Viola," Drew's voice breaks me out of my thoughts that were pulling me away. "He'll be okay."

"What about his precious Challenger?" Courtney asks with a mock smile.

"It's in bad shape."

"Priorities, Courtney!" I scold.

Drew looks at her, holding back a smile. It's the most attention he's paid to any girl since his breakup. Courtney instantly lights up.

"What? It's not like I asked about the car first!"

He glances over at her again, and I wonder what he's thinking because his face isn't giving him away.

I roll my eyes at her comment and follow Drew as he finds us a spot in the waiting area, but I'm glad she took the attention away from me.

We sit and stare at the TV, knowing damn well none of us can focus on whatever courtroom reality show is on. I hate this.

I hate waiting.

I hate not knowing.

I hate being left in the dark.

It's eating me up inside; I have to speak up. "So, any idea why Travis would be with Mia in the first place?"

Courtney's eyes widen as she looks to Drew for a reaction, but he doesn't give one.

"None that make any sense." He shrugs, keeping his eyes locked on the screen, paying us no attention at all. It's such a dude reaction.

"You don't seem too concerned that your friend was in a car with your girlfriend or that she was naked in his backseat."

He cracks a weak smile. "Well, I know he wasn't fooling around with her, so I'm not that concerned."

He pauses a moment. "And technically, she's my *ex*-girlfriend now, unless she magically changed her mind again." The sadness in his tone doesn't go unnoticed.

I ignore the ex-girlfriend comment, but Courtney perks up at the mention of it.

"Travis may be a lot of things, but he'd never betray me like that," he states with certainty.

"Bro-code," Courtney adds, and I glare at her without Drew noticing.

"There are just certain people you don't fool around with, and he'd never do something like that behind my back."

Certain people like an ex-girlfriend or little sister…?

A dagger shoots right into my chest as I hear about Drew talking about the strong friendship and bond he has with Travis.

Courtney flashes me a look, and I know we're both thinking it. If we weren't all sitting together, Courtney would be swooning over Drew a lot harder. He's clueless as to how he affects girls, especially Courtney. Even though she was with Toby, and Drew's been on and off with Mia, she's always had a little thing for him. And takes every opportunity to remind me.

Even before Toby and she were on the path to breakup city, Courtney had crushed hard on him. Shortly after we first met, she came with me to his house and nearly walked into a beam the first time she saw him.

"Are you all right?" he asked her, genuinely concerned.

She blinked a few times, and Drew took a step toward her.

"Fine," she finally said. "Just wasn't looking where I was going."

He nodded and flashed one of his infamous charming smiles. Drew doesn't have to do much to get a girl's attention, with his dark, shaggy hair and tattoos lining his arms and chest. He's built like a rock and was the reason guys wouldn't come to the house back in high school. He looked terrifying, but I knew he had a soft side, too.

"Stop looking at my brother like you want to rip off his clothes!" I groaned once Drew was out of hearing distance. My friends swooning over him was something I had gotten used to in high school, and somehow it continued to happen in college.

Her eyes remained locked on him as he walked down the hall to his bedroom. "I want to do a lot more than that..." Her lips tilted up. "And those handcuffs— "

"All right, I get it," I said, cutting her off. "You want to go all Fifty Shades on his ass."

She chuckled. "Hot cop fantasy." She shrugged unapologetically.

I smile, remembering the moment. She'd been completely devoted to Toby, and would never act on anything outside of their relationship, but now that there was no relationship, I hope she'd finally allow herself to go out and have some fun. She needs to meet people and see what life is like without a relationship status determining her every move. With Drew being available, it might take her mind off the dirty breakup.

"Are you the friends of Mia Montgomery?" a doctor walks up to us, and we all look up.

"Yes," Drew says, standing up. Courtney and I both stand up next to him.

"She's pretty drowsy from the pain medication we gave her, but you can see her one at a time for a few minutes."

"What about the driver, Travis King?" I ask before he can walk away.

"He's on some pretty heavy painkillers as well, but a few minutes should be okay."

"Just enough time for you to put a pillow over his head," Drew teases. The doctor gives a disapproving look but doesn't comment.

"That's pretty harsh," I say, following behind him.

He chuckles. "Sorry, I didn't know you two became best friends since I left."

Courtney snorts behind me, and I turn around, flashing her a glare.

"Um, definitely not. Doesn't mean I'd want him dead."

"All right, go check on him while I check on Mia."

"Okay."

"Mia Montgomery is in 707, and Travis King is in 713, just down that hall." The doctor directs us. We both thank him. "Just a few minutes," he reminds us.

Courtney walks with me to Travis' room but doesn't follow me inside.

"I'll wait out here so you two can be alone."

I purse my lips and exhale. "Okay."

I knock softly on the door before slowly opening it. I'm not sure what to expect, but I just need to visually confirm that he's okay.

"Travis?" I walk quietly up to his bed, taking in his closed eyes and the bandage over his forehead. "Can you hear me?" I take his hand, feeling the warmth against mine, and wait for a response.

He has an IV in his other hand, his left knee is propped up on pillows under the sheets, and his face is bruised and swollen. I've never seen him like this before, and for the first time, he looks vulnerable. My chest aches, seeing his body lying almost lifeless, his chest slowly rising and falling, and I can't help but want to kiss every bruised part of him.

Sitting on the edge of his bed, I keep his hand in mine and hope he can hear what I'm about to say.

"I don't know if you can hear me, but it's V." I choke down tears and laughter. "I can't believe I just called myself that."

I wait, hoping he'll respond and join in on our inside joke, but he doesn't flinch. I watch his chest move up and down, as the sounds of the machines fill the room.

"You look pretty awful, but the doctor says you should be back to your normal self in no time. Truthfully, seeing you like this is tearing me apart."

I swallow and catch my breath, and then I begin to ramble. "I don't know why you and Mia were together, and I honestly don't think I want to know. I'm going to try to trust you, Travis. It'll be hard because of our past, but I'm going to try to be more like Drew. It doesn't faze him at all that you were with Mia, and it reminded me that although you're an asshole most of the time, you wouldn't do anything like that to Drew. Apparently, there's some sort of bro code." I shake my head at the thought.

"To be honest, I hope you wouldn't do that to me either, but I don't know where we stand and what we're doing. When you get out of here, and you're not hooked to machines like Darth Vader, we're going to have to talk—like a real talk—about us. I need to know that we're on the same page and where we should go from here. I want to trust you, Travis, and I'm going to try really hard. Please don't make me regret wearing my heart on my sleeve."

I sit next to him for a few more minutes, watching him sleep. Realizing I've been in his room way too long, I squeeze his hand, wishing he'd squeeze it back, but he never does. I stand up and lean over him, careful not to touch or put weight on his chest and press my lips to his.

"Bye, Travis," I whisper.

I walk toward the door, wiping my face as tears begin falling down my cheeks. I can't stand to see him so vulnerable and broken; it's tearing me apart. Before I can open the door, a nurse walks in and immediately studies my face.

"Oh, it's okay, sweetie." She flashes me a genuine smile. "Mr. King will have a full recovery in a few weeks. He's pretty drugged up on painkillers right now, but I'll let him know you were here."

All I can do is nod and reach for the door.

I really hope this isn't *game over*.

CHAPTER THREE

TRAVIS

The constant beep pulls me back to a harsh reality with whitewashed walls and numbing pain that coats my body from head to toe. I force my eyes open, and it's hard to pinpoint what hurts the most. My throat is painfully dry, and the thick head fog I'm swimming in makes it hard to focus in the bland room. I glance down at the countless tubes attached to my arm and broken memories cut through the confusion like shards of glass I can't piece together.

The rhythmic tone of the machine I'm attached to, and the low sound of the television, pulls my limited attention to the corner of the room. I can't make out the words, and it takes everything I have just to turn my head toward the noise. Once I'm able to focus, I hear rustling and watch as Drew sits up from the chair. He rubs a hand over his face and flashes a small grin. He's wearing his blues and badge, and it somewhat confuses me.

"The King lives."

It hurts when I try to laugh and end up coughing instead. "Barely."

"You look rough."

He does too, but I don't tell him that. He must've been sitting here a while.

He looks me over, concern written on his face. "How do you feel?"

"Like shit," I admit. "What happened? What day is it?"

A bandage is wrapped around my head, and I realize I've got one wrapped around my leg too. Nausea overtakes me for a second, and I try to reposition my body, but it's a lost cause. The bed is raised up so high; I'm basically sitting up straight, which is uncomfortable as hell. My neck is tight, and the loud pounding in my head continues on the beat, making it harder to focus on anything but the intense pain. I try reaching for the plastic cup of water that's on a silver tray next to my bed, but it's out of reach.

"I'll get it," Drew says, grabbing it and handing it to me. "It's Tuesday morning."

I take it, hating that I need his help. I end up drinking it so fast, I gasp for air afterward, and even that hurts. His words finally register with me. Tuesday? I know I've been in and out of it, but four days of my life has evaporated into what seemed like hours.

Drew takes a deep breath before he starts explaining the technicality of the accident in cop lingo. I give him a look, letting him know I have no fucking idea what he's talking about, so he begins again, explaining it more slowly and without as much detail so I can comprehend it all.

"You were rear-ended at a high rate of speed and pushed into oncoming traffic. A few fractured ribs, a concussion, bruises, cuts, and lots of pain meds, from what I've been told. The airbag went off and caused a lot of damage. But they said you'd live, and that your thick skull will be okay." He forces out a laugh. "I was worried, though, man. They said you both could've died, and you were really lucky. I thought the worst. I've seen way too many accidents like this where people aren't as fortunate." He inhales a deep breath, his eyes glassing over. "And Mia..."

Shit. I'd almost forgotten she was with me. Bits and pieces of that night start to flash by, but when I try to remember the accident, my mind goes blank. I can't remember a damn thing after leaving the gas station.

The selfish part of me is grateful Viola wasn't in the car with me. I could never forgive myself if anything happened to her on my watch.

"How's Mia?" My heart thumps hard in my chest at the realization I was responsible for another person in the car.

"She's doing okay. She got lucky; you both did. She could've easily been ejected from the car because she wasn't wearing a seatbelt. She smacked her head and has a lot of bruises," Drew explains.

The pain on his face is evident as he talks about her. Their relationship has been toxic since day one, but for some reason, he loves her unconditionally. I've never second-guessed that, but he deserves someone a lot better than her. Even after everything, I know he still cares about her well-being.

"I'm sorry, man," I begin, relieved she's not hurt worse. "I wish I could remember what happened, but I can explain why she was with me." He hadn't asked why, but even being high as a kite on pain meds, I know I owe him that much. "Mia and I—," I start to explain, but he's quick to cut me off.

"Travis, stop. I trust you more than anyone. You need to rest and shouldn't waste your strength explaining anything to me."

I want to argue, tell him that I *do* have to explain the circumstances that brought Mia and I together on Thursday night, but between the meds and the truth of his words ripping through me, I'm left speechless.

"As crazy as it sounds, I miss her so fucking much. She won't let me be there for her, and even after what she said to me the last night we were together, I want to be there for her more than anything."

"Because you're a good man," I choke out. He truly is, and as much as it would hurt for him to hear, Mia doesn't deserve him. Drew deserves better.

He shrugs. "Her parents came up right away, so I gave them privacy. I don't know what Mia told them about us, so I figured it was best to stay away and let her rest."

"I'm sorry," I say softly, not having the strength to tell him about Will Tamer. *Damn her.* I'd like to have forgotten those details, but they are as clear as a California summer sky.

"Your mom was here on Saturday," he says, changing the subject. I arch my brows, surprised to hear she came. "Stayed for hours, but the nurse said you probably wouldn't be coherent for a few days, so I told her to go home and get some rest, and I'd call her when you were up for visitors."

I swallow hard and guilt washes over me. I haven't called and checked on her recently. Life got in the way is not a good enough excuse. I can't find my words and all I want to do is go back to sleep, but my mind won't stop wandering and thinking *what if*.

"Viola checked in on you, too," Drew continues. "Surprised she didn't set a spell to put you in a permanent coma." He chuckles, making me smile at the thought of her being here.

Viola.

I feel like shit for the way things were left between us. God, I miss her. I can't imagine what she's thinking about me being with Mia, but I know it can't be good. Drew continues talking, filling the room with words, and I keep trying to listen, but with every passing minute, it becomes harder. Focus slips through my fingers like water.

"Bad news, though," he says, his words bringing me back to him, "the Challenger is totaled."

"Fucking hell," I curse, exhaustion completely covering me like a warm blanket. My eyes are heavy, and I'm fighting to stay awake, but I'm drifting farther and farther away from Drew's voice. Soon everything goes black.

CHECKMATE: THIS IS LOVE

I wake up to a dark room and am completely disoriented on what time it is or if it's even the same day. I have no fucking idea anymore. I glance around and see a tray of food with green Jell-O and two plastic cups of liquid. I don't have an appetite, but my throat is still dry.

I'm able to reach over and grab one of the cups. As I finish off the apple juice, I realize I have to piss. I don't know if there's a catheter in me or not, so I shift to the end of the bed to find my way to the bathroom.

Within seconds, I realize the pain is too much, and I can't lift myself up. *Jesus*. This fucking sucks. I feel like a pathetic, weak pansy.

I see the remote on the side of my bed with a big red button and press it for help.

"Nurses' station."

"Uh, yeah… I think I need some help."

The woman clears her throat. "What can I help you with, Mr. King?"

My voice drops to a whisper, and I'm humiliated even asking. "Uh, bathroom."

"What was that? Speak up, honey. I can barely hear you."

I groan, curling my fingers into fists. Fuck it; I'll do it myself. As I try to stand again, my body screams out in protest and frustration gets the best of me.

Surrendering, I respond, "*Pissing*. I need to piss, okay?"

"I'll send someone in."

At least ten minutes pass and my bladder feels like it's going to explode. They've been pumping me full of fluids and medicine for hours, and it's finally caught up to me. I'm two seconds away from pissing on the floor when a gray-haired woman walks in.

"Glad to see you're awake." She smiles. "I'm Nancy."

All I can offer her is an impatient smile. She pulls the blankets further back and adjusts her body in front of me to help my balance.

"It hurts to breathe," I tell her before attempting to stand once again.

"Fractured ribs will do that. You'll probably be stiff from being in bed for so long, so it's even more important to start walking around now that you're out of the haze." She gives me her arm, and I feel guilty for leaning against her small frame. It takes everything I have not to scream out in pain when I get to my feet. Dizziness surrounds me, my head feels like it splitting in two, and I grab the woman like she's my saving grace.

We take small steps all the way to the bathroom, which isn't that far, but somehow it feels like we'll never get there. She pulls the machine and fluids behind me and keeps one arm around my waist.

"Do you want me to walk in with you?" she asks in a casual tone.

"No," I say before she follows me in. "Thanks, but I should be fine." I spot the metal railing along the wall and hold onto it for balance.

"I'll be right outside the door," she informs me, turning her back.

This is fucking humiliating.

I need the added stability, so I hold on—my knuckles white from the tight grip. Once I'm finished, I rub antibacterial foam in my hands and walk out to where she's waiting for me. She places her arm around me, and we make our long journey back to the bed. A breeze brushes across my bare ass, and I realize there's nothing underneath the thin hospital gown. I'm sure the nurse has seen an eyeful already while walking me to the bathroom, but I don't have the energy to care.

She must notice my discomfort, because as soon as I turn to sit back down on the bed, I'm quick to cover back up. "Don't worry, hon. I've seen it all in my thirty years of being a nurse." She grins, but that doesn't help ease my concern.

I'm a proud man and not shy about my body, but this woman is old enough to be my grandmother.

She helps me settle back into the bed, covering me up and pushing the tray closer to me.

"You should try to eat something," she says.

I nod, not wanting to tackle that feat just yet, but I don't argue with her.

"This is for your morphine drip." She places the cord across my lap, along with the remote that has a call button. "If you feel more pain coming on, push this button. You can get another dose every seventeen minutes if you need it."

I tell her thank you, and she reminds me to press the call button if I need anything else. *Is liquor an option?*

"The doctor will go over your file and check in on you around seven or eight. As long as your stats are stable, you should have no issue getting discharged within a day or two." Her smile is genuine, and she has a sweet demeanor, just like my mother.

"And today is what day exactly?"

"Thursday, honey. We started giving you less pain medication and removed your catheter, so things should start feeling back to normal soon."

I knew it felt like I was pissing fire. As I lift my legs and lean back onto the pillow, I look over and see my cell phone sitting on the counter. Nancy notices and hands them over. I try to turn my phone on, but it's dead. I let out a frustrated groan.

"Is that an iPhone?"

"Yes, ma'am."

Nancy smiles then winks. "I've got a charger for you back at the nurses' station. You probably want to get in touch with that girl that's been calling to check on you several times a day."

She smiles and finishes entering the updates into the computer before quietly walking out and shutting the door behind her. I glance at the clock and see it's just after 3:00 a.m. I probably won't get much sleep at this point, but my body is begging for it. I've never felt so drained in my entire life.

When I close my eyes, images of Viola fill my mind. I can almost taste her lips on mine, and I cringe as I remember the look on her face when she left the house. I wish we didn't leave things the way we did, but I'm determined more than ever to make it right again. The door opens and closes before I hear Nancy plug in my phone. If I weren't so exhausted, and it wasn't so late, I'd call Viola right now just to hear her voice.

Before falling back asleep, I think about Mia, and how she's a complete fucking mess. Drew needs to know the truth, but I know it'll hurt him more than anything. If their relationship is truly over, there's no point in digging the knife deeper.

I think about how Mia was starting to freak out, so I pulled off the highway and into a parking lot to help calm her down. She was nearly in tears and knowing Drew wouldn't want her to be upset; I tried comforting her the best that I could.

Before I can think about what happened after that, I'm ripped away from my thoughts of her to the thoughts of my car. Memories of the sounds of breaking glass and crashing metal start to surface, but I can't visualize any of it, which almost makes it worse. Maybe it's for the best, but I wish I could erase all the memories of what happened from my mind.

Sharp pain stabs me in the chest as I linger on my thoughts. Before they can transform into nightmares, I push the miracle button to erase it all, and soon enough, I'm drifting into nothingness.

VIOLA

I've been completely out of it since I saw Travis in his hospital bed on Friday morning. It's been eight grueling days and the fact that school starts back tomorrow doesn't help. *Where did the time go?* Most of it was spent trying to work out the scenario that led Travis and Mia together. I don't know the circumstances, but I'm going to *try* to give him the benefit of the doubt. Not knowing has been torture, but I won't allow myself to jump to conclusions until we talk. I don't know what I should be thinking or doing right now, but one thing is for certain: I can't handle another broken heart because of him.

At the beginning of spring break, I said I didn't want to be around Travis. Now, it's torture being away from him. I wake up Sunday morning to the ringing of my phone. My heart races when I see Travis' name flash across the screen. I quickly answer, and butterflies mixed with an anxious feeling swarm my entire body.

"Princess..."

"Travis?"

"I've missed you." He sounds weak, and his throat is raspy.

My heart thumps hard in my chest, and I choke back tears. "I've been calling every day to get updates. I've been so worried."

"I know. I'm being released today, though, and then we can talk. The doctor's walking in. I'll see you soon."

"Okay," I add just before the call ends.

My head is a bit clearer now, knowing he's finally being released, but I won't be at ease until Travis is home. Finding out he was with a girl—Mia, of all people—still makes my chest clench with a sharp ache. Will there always be a *Mia* in the picture? Or *Sarah from the Bar* or a *Rachel*? I can't remember a time in Travis King's life where he didn't have a long line of conquests at his beck and call. That old nagging feeling returns in the pit of my stomach, but I force it away.

I drag myself out of bed and head to the kitchen for some coffee. While I wait for it to brew, I begin collecting my things from around the house, because class starts back tomorrow and I need to get back to my dorm. It feels like a different lifetime from who I was when I left the dorm two weeks ago.

Once I've placed my crap by the door, I pour a cup of steaming hot coffee, add a splash of milk and a spoonful of sugar. As I'm stirring my liquid magic, Drew speaks from behind me, scaring the living shit out of me. I jump, nearly spilling my perfect concoction of caffeine.

"What the hell?" I gasp, glaring at him. "Warn a girl before you creep up on her."

"Someone's jumpy this morning." He moves around me and grabs a mug for himself.

I watch as he pours it and instantly takes a sip.

"Gross." I make a gagging noise. "How can you drink that black?"

"I can't drink basic bitch coffee, Vi." He takes another sip just to taunt me.

"At least add some sugar."

He wrinkles his nose and shakes his head. "What's up with your crap by the door? Did you finally get your letter to Hogwarts?"

I glare at him. "He's got jokes," I say with mock amusement.

"So, which house will you be sorted in? Slytherin or Gryffindor? Actually, now I'm thinking you're more of a Hufflepuff." His lips curl into a cocky smirk.

"You're such a jerk!" I playfully swing at him, but he's all muscles and barely flinches. "You better take that back!" I try to hold back laughter, but the way he dodges my hits makes it hard.

"You hit like a girl," he quips, smirking over his mug.

I roll my eyes. "I *am* a girl," I say. "A girl who used to kick your ass, too."

He snorts. "You mean, *I let you* kick my ass."

"You're such a liar!"

He tilts his head at me, daring me to challenge him.

"You know, for someone who mocks Harry Potter all the time, you sure do know a lot about it." I cross my arms and give him an evil grin because I know he's just as nerdy as I am. He just likes to hide it behind his big muscles, inked arms, and shiny badge.

"I've seen the movies a hundred times, thanks to you. Only nerds read the books."

I snarl. "Are you trying to piss me off this early in the morning?"

He finishes his coffee with a smirk on his face, even though I've only taken a single sip of mine. After pouring another cup of coffee and chugging it, he speaks up again. "I'm picking Travis up from the hospital in a few. I asked the Chief if I could come in a little later today because he's being discharged any minute. Wanna ride up there with me?"

"Nah, I'm good." I try to put on my best poker face, but I'm not sure how convincing I look. I didn't dare mention I already knew. I hide my excitement and put up my front. I pretend to feel indifferent about him coming home, though my heart instantly races at the sound of his name and I still have a million questions.

"All right. Well, I should be back in a few hours then."

"Okay." I avoid eye contact, taking another drink of the best coffee in the world, hoping it will cover my emotions that are ready to boil over. I exhale and look at Drew. He's staring at me intently, and for a moment I wonder what the hell he's going to ask me. Does he know? No. He's not smiling or anything, and I begin to freak out.

"What?" I ask, reluctantly.

Drew sets his empty cup down.

"It's about you and Travis."

My heart races and I instantly shake my head at the way he's looking at me. I fight the urge to say anything in case I'm being paranoid.

"Ask me anything," I lie, channeling my inner *Travis King is an asshole* act that I've perfected over the years. I swallow hard, watching and waiting for him to speak. Damn Drew. The anticipation eats me alive.

"I need a favor."

"Class starts tomorrow, and I won't really be around to do any more *favors*."

I nod my head toward my bags that are waiting for me at the front door.

"Well, see… that's not really going to work for me. Or Travis."

My mouth falls open. He's way smarter than he looks, and I know whatever he's about to say has already been worked out in his head. Even when we were kids, he was a negotiator, and not much has changed since then.

"This week between classes, do you think you could come over and check on him?" He flashes a genuine smile, one of those charming smirks that make girls like Courtney swoon. Being his sister, I have a genetic immunity to his charm.

"I won't have time," I say with certainty, hoping I sound convincing, but I know I can make it work.

All he does is laugh, not believing my words.

"I won't be around to help him, but since you're right down the road..."

"Don't act like you don't goof off when you're on patrol. All those donuts..."

"Number one: I don't eat that shit, and you know it. Number two: You already survived him during spring break, so what're a few hours between classes?"

Focusing on my coffee, I don't have any words. At least not any I can say aloud. All sorts of thoughts are running through my mind, but Drew's voice brings me back to reality.

"Look, I know you can't stand to be in the same room as him, and you'll probably poison him by the weekend, but he really needs you, and you're a little genius, so you don't need to study as much as you do."

My heart feels like it may beat out of my chest. My palms are sweaty, and Drew is enjoying putting me on the spot a little too much.

"Please, Vi. I'll even have Starbucks waiting for you after class."

Fighting a smile, I say, "Wow, you really are desperate." I almost feel bad for playing him like this.

"I'd do anything for Travis," he states so genuinely. "But I can't be late to work even if I begged. The Chief will have my head, and my partner won't take my shit."

I let out a deep breath, *acting* defeated. "All right, fine. But you owe me *huge*. Any favor that I can use at any time I want."

Drew holds out his hand, and we shake on it. "Deal. I'll allow you to cash in on one *reasonable* favor. I'm a cop, not a millionaire."

I smile. "Venti White Mocha."

"What the hell does that mean?" He looks utterly confused, and I chuckle at his expense.

"My Starbucks order. I want a Venti White Mocha with an extra shot and a blueberry muffin."

"Wait, I didn't agree on the muffin—"

I shoot him a look, challenging him to fall back on our deal.

"*Fine,*" he states between gritted teeth. "You play to bust balls."

"It's one of my best qualities," I say with a cheesy grin.

"You have to actually be helpful, though, Vi. He's going to be sore and on pain meds. Just make him some lunch and make sure he stays hydrated."

"So, play Betty Crocker and greet his one-night stands at the door?" The words leave my mouth before I can stop myself.

He shakes his head at me with a knowing grin. "If I didn't know any better, I'd say you two were secretly in love with each other."

I nearly choke on my saliva.

"Relax, I was just kidding." He pats me on the back. "Anyway, I gotta head out. The Chief about had an aneurysm when I asked for a half-day."

He walks over and wraps his big arms around me, squeezing me so tight it hurts. I squeal and try to wiggle out of his tight grip. He's always been so much bigger than me, and he knows how much I hate it when he hugs me like that because it's painful. "Drew, stop!"

"You're the best little sister ever." He releases me, and before he walks out of the kitchen, he turns and smiles. "Thanks again. It means a lot to me, and I know it'll mean a lot to him. He'll appreciate the help, even if he doesn't say it."

When I hear the door click shut, I let out a deep sigh. As much as I should be keeping my distance while Travis is in this condition, I can't fathom the thought of him being alone all week while he's recovering.

I reach for my phone and text Courtney, letting her know the new plan. I'll invite her over and allow her to drool over Drew one night this week.

V: **Drew gave me his stupid begging eyes and bribed me with Starbucks. I've been voluntold to take care of Travis all week, but I'm not complaining.**

C: **I could stare into Drew's gorgeous eyes for hours. I can't wait to come over and "visit." It's almost as if Drew is setting you up for "success" ... if you know what I mean.**

V: **Focus, Court. And gross. I'll text you once he's home.**

I grab my bags and boxes and carry them out to my car. Returning to school tomorrow is almost bittersweet. After I place everything in my trunk, I head back to Drew's room and wait. I sit on the edge of the bed, and fall back and stare at the ceiling. The realization that I'm going to be here between classes makes me feel more nervous than before about being around Travis. But seeing him bruised and broken is going to kill me.

I startle from the bed at the sound of the front door closing. I look around and realize I must've fallen asleep. I check my phone and see a few messages Drew sent letting me know they were on the way and they were almost home.

I can hear the faint sound of Drew's voice followed by the muffled sounds of Travis' voice. Moments later a light knock taps against the door, and I sit straight up, hair a mess, and yell that it's open.

Drew cracks open the door. "Travis is in bed. He's pretty tired, and I have to get to work. If he wakes up and needs something, can you help?"

"Does this mean house arrest begins now?"

"That's a great idea. Maybe I can see about getting you one of those ankle bracelets for convicts so I can track your every move."

I roll my eyes at him.

"Thanks, sis! You're the best." Drew winks before he shuts the door.

I try to concentrate on my breathing, but all I can hear are the hard beats of my heart. Standing up, I brush my fingers through my hair, then adjust my shirt and make sure I look completely unaffected before slipping out of Drew's room. I walk the short distance down the hall to Travis' room but stop before opening it.

I can't believe how anxious I feel right now, seeing him for the first time since the hospital. I have no idea what he remembers or if he remembers me being there at all. I don't know what to expect, considering our phone conversation was so short. The unknown has been and continues, driving me crazy.

Swallowing hard, I softly knock on the door.

"Come in." I hear the weakness in his voice, and it takes everything in me to move my feet.

I push open the door and see Travis propped up on pillows. His face is slightly swollen and bruised, and it looks like he hasn't slept in days, though that's all he's been doing for a week. I cringe when I study the bandages on his head where it smacked into the glass.

He watches my expression. "You should see the other guy." His lips turn up in a cocky smirk.

I shake my head and lick my lips that suddenly feel dry. "I'm sure it was an unfair match."

"Well, four thousand pounds of badass muscle car against an eighty-thousand-pound semi wasn't exactly a fair fight, but hey, I live to tell the tale." He smiles as if he's trying to make me laugh and bring light to the situation, which it partially does, given the awkward circumstances.

"Well, I was really worried about you," I say, taking a step inside but not getting too close. "I'm really glad you're okay." The concern is evident in my tone, and my poker face is quickly fading the more I look at him.

"Princess, come here." His eyes are hooded, his voice sounding pained from my distance. My heart sinks, and I want to run to him and talk to him about everything, but my expression doesn't change. My feet feel like they are glued to the floor and I can't move, not with his eyes on me, looking at me so intensely that it makes me weak.

"Is it safe?" I tilt my lips up slightly.

"I won't break," he insists.

"Clearly."

He pats his palm on the bed next to him.

"I don't want to hurt you, though," I say, hesitating.

"Trust me. The only thing keeping me going the past couple of days was knowing I'd get to see your beautiful face and kiss your soft lips."

"Well, I see the accident didn't affect your ability to charm."

"It'd take a lot more than that." He winks.

I give in and sit on the edge of the bed next to him, careful to keep my distance.

"I know we should probably talk," I begin, "but when you're feeling better. You should be resting so you can get back to your cocky-ass self."

"Let's talk now," he insists, pushing himself up higher on the pillows, but I can tell by the way he cringes that his body is still sore.

I shake my head. "When you feel better, we will. You're all drugged up on pain meds."

"It doesn't have to wait, I'm fine," he tries to brush off the pain, but I can see right through his bullshit.

"Really?" I give him a pointed look. "How many elements are in the periodic table?"

He furrows his brows. "Seventy-five?"

"Wrong. It's one hundred and fourteen!" I respond confidently. "See, you're not in the right state of mind."

He leans his head back and laughs. I watch as his throat moves and think about the last time we were together in his bed. "To be fair, I wouldn't know the answer to that question, either way, you little nerd."

I narrow my eyes at him and hold back a smile.

"Look at us—having an actual conversation without arguing," he says, covering his hand over mine.

"Don't get cocky," I tease. "When the drugs are all out of your system, you'll be back to pissing me off, I'm sure."

"I can do that while I'm on drugs," he mocks.

I laugh because this is the first time in years Travis and I have had a normal conversation.

"Glad to see nothing's changed then."

"Princess, come on. I might be bruised in places I didn't even know could bruise, and my ribs might be fractured and hurt like a motherfucker, but I can see the questions written all over your face. So, just ask me. You know you can ask me anything."

I pull my lips into my mouth and exhale through my nose. "Fine. Why was Mia naked in your backseat?"

"Going right for the jugular," he teases.

Maybe I shouldn't have blurted that out.

"Never mind." I start shifting off the bed.

"Wait...Viola, please don't go," he pleads, and I wait. "There's a lot we need to talk about. I've been lying in bed the last week, and the physical pain is nothing compared to having you walk away from me, knowing I can't chase you."

"Then just tell me, because the thought of you with someone else makes me sick."

"Viola, it's not what you're thinking."

I exhale, staring intently at him. "So, girls just magically end up naked in the backseat of your car?"

"Well, I recall you in the backseat of my car not so long ago…" He smirks, and I hate that the memory sends shivers down my spine. "But why don't you ask me what you really want to know."

Heat rushes through me, and I'm too scared to ask if they had sex. The truth is, I want to know everything, every detail. But I'm afraid it will break my heart into a million little pieces, and I'm not sure if I can handle that again.

I shrug, not sure where to even start. I like this side of Travis—sweet and vulnerable, even though I know it won't last long. "I don't think I can handle knowing right now."

"You want to know for the same reason I wanted to punch Axel's face in."

"Andrew," I correct.

He rolls his eyes. "So, just say whatever it is you're so busy overthinking about."

I slide farther onto the bed, leaning my back against the wall and crossing my legs. "Which part? Why you were in such a shitty mood when you got home from work? Why did you even leave the house? Why wouldn't you talk to me? How did you end up out of the city, with Drew's crazy ex-girlfriend? I mean, I don't even know if I want to know the answers to the questions swirling around in my mind."

"And why she was naked in the backseat of my car?" He arches a brow, knowing damn well it's driving me insane.

"Well, I can do the math in my head," I say shyly, bowing my head because I don't think I'm strong enough to hear it.

"You really think that?" I hear the pain in his voice, and I cringe at the way his words cut through me.

"Well, your track history isn't very promising. Like when you asked my friend, Heather McNeil, out and promised her a good time, only to ditch her at the movie theater when you ran into Betsy St. Clair and ended up making out with her in the parking lot."

"I was a dumb kid," he says, "running on hormones."

I chuckle, agreeing. "Well, I'm not so sure much has changed." I know my words catch him off guard, but he reaches for my hand and ignores my comments. I don't know if this is going to be the end of whatever we had, or…

"You know you're going to have to learn to trust me, now that we're together."

His words stop my thoughts, and I'm immediately silenced.

I look up and see a smile spread across his face, his fingers gripping mine tighter.

"Oh?" My brows rise. "We're together now?"

"Well, yeah. Do you see any other girls walking around here?"

I burst out in easy laughter. "Give it a few days. I'm sure they'll be here in no time."

"Guess I deserved that." He grins, rubbing the pad of his thumb over my hand. "You know you can trust me, Viola." His voice sounds sincere. "I may be a lot of things, but I've never lied to you."

He's right. Travis King may be a lot of things, but he's not a liar. He's always been honest and straightforward about everything. Even when his honest words weren't what I wanted to hear.

"So, Mia being naked in your backseat?" I cringe at saying the words aloud again. "Nothing happened between you two?"

"Viola?" He places his finger under my chin and locks his eyes on mine. "Do you trust me?"

He's not exactly answering the question, but deep inside, I do trust him. Remembering what Drew said back at the hospital, Travis would never betray him.

I nod.

"Good, because I'm not sharing you with anyone else."

"You can't just be a caveman and claim me," I tease as his thumb lingers over my bottom lip.

"Sure, I can. You're mine."

Goose bumps.

His words send shivers down my spine at how genuine his words sound. It's everything I've ever wanted to hear him say.

But I won't give in that easy. At least not right away.

"Come closer," he says.

"You aren't the boss of me, Travis King."

He smirks, knowing damn well I'm full of shit. "I think we both know that's not true. I've had you counting until you lost your voice." His lips turn up, obviously very impressed with himself.

"So arrogant." I sigh. "Some things never change." I shake my head, trying to hold back a smile.

"And some things do," he says, cupping my face. "No more games." He rubs the pad of his thumb over my cheek, and I nearly melt into him. If he weren't injured, I'd be ready to strip all his clothes off.

I nod in agreement. "No more games."

I know we'll eventually need to have a conversation about that night and talk about what all happened, but I also know I trust him. Even after all the hurt, anger, and heartache, Travis King will always be the boy I loved as a child.

He pulls me toward him, pressing his lips to mine. It's nothing like our previous kisses. This one is slow, soft, and passionate. I don't push for more because I know he's using every ounce of energy to kiss me.

I pull back, even though I don't want to. Sitting next to Travis, I make sure to avoid touching or putting pressure on him.

"Since I'll be dropping by between classes, there need to be some rules."

He grins slightly. “There’s the V I’m used to.”

I roll my eyes at the V comment. “We have to act like nothing’s changed in front of Drew. And while you’re hurt, no sex or sexual innuendos or making sexual comments.”

He groans. “You're just like the nurses at the hospital. No fun.”

“You mean they didn’t turn to mush at the Travis King charm?”

“Nope. Wouldn’t even let me get to second base.”

I roll my eyes again and fight the urge to curse and kiss him. “How rude of them.”

“But at least I’m back home with my own private nurse.” He winks. “If there’s going to be this no sex rule, can you at least provide other accommodations for your patient?”

I throw my head back and laugh at his ridiculousness. “I’m starting to wonder if they missed something when they did your brain scan.”

He pulls me closer again, but winces before our lips meet.

“You need to rest.” I press a hand softly against his chest. “Take some meds and get some sleep. I’ll be here when you wake up.” I smile, and he smiles, too.

I watch as he grabs his medicine bottle off his nightstand and takes out a couple of pills. He swallows them down with some water and settles against the pillows, adjusting his ice pack before finally settling in. Once his eyes flutter closed, I carefully scoot off the bed and lean down to kiss his cheek. Just as I'm walking toward the door, he speaks up, stopping me in my tracks. "I love you, Viola Fisher."

CHAPTER FOUR

TRAVIS

Waking up hours later, hunger and soreness both fight for my attention. My phone says it's three in the afternoon. My body says I need out of this bed. I need to eat, but more importantly I *need* Viola.

I hate asking for help, but I'm in no position to allow my pride to rule. But first, I'll try. After managing to roll myself out of bed, I stand with the help of a few choice words. I showered at the hospital before I was discharged and it was the most humiliating thing I've experienced in my life. Nancy and I had formed a decent relationship at night, but once her shift ended, Helen took over; let's just say she was much less patient with me. She was a nurse sent straight from the pits of hell.

Once I'm out of my room, I walk down the hall to where I hear the TV and Viola's sweet laughter. Yes, *this* is home. I instantly smile when I hear her.

I pause for a second and take a deep breath, watching her, curled up in the corner of the couch with a blanket tossed over her legs. She's focused on some chick flick, and I'm focused on her. I clear my throat after a moment, and she turns and looks at me, concern on her face.

"You feeling okay?" She moves over slightly, giving me room that I wish she didn't feel she needs to give me. I want her as close as possible.

I sit on the couch next to her, and she watches me.

"Never felt better."

She smiles.

"You mind if I watch this with you?" I nod toward the TV.

She flashes me a look. "You want to watch *Bridget Jones' Diary* with me?"

I swallow my words of disdain and plaster on a cocky grin. "Yeah, of course. BJ's my homegirl."

She bursts out laughing, her head falling back as a sweet roar releases from her throat. "Oh, my God," she says between tears. "I should be recording this."

"Recording what?" I furrow my brows.

"You." She wipes under her eyes. "You're as high as the Empire State Building."

I snort. "Get your mind out of the gutter, princess. BJ is Bridget Jones, not—"

"Okay!" she interrupts before I can continue, a faint blush covering her cheeks.

I roll my eyes at her expense, getting another chuckle out of her.

I try to focus, but I can't. "Are you going to catch me up on whatever the hell is happening?"

"I thought BJ was your homegirl?" she throws back, the corner of her lips turning up as she continues watching the movie. This is the Viola I adore—simple, funny, cute. *God*. I wish I weren't in pain. I wish Thursday night would've never happened and I could pull her into my lap.

"She is; I mean, she reminds me of a cornier, klutzier you."

"Rude!" She playfully smacks me on the arm before realization hits that I'm already bruised. "Shit! I'm sorry!" She closes her eyes for a moment. "I didn't mean to hit you."

"Just a natural twitch?" I smirk, not wanting her to feel too bad.

She cocks her head.

"Lighten up, princess."

"Are you hungry?" she asks sincerely, changing the subject.

"Yes."

"What are you hungry for?"

My eyes widen as my lips tilt up in a cocky pout. "Well…"

"*Food,*" she clarifies. "I meant, what kind of food are you hungry for?"

"Why do you assume I was going to say something else?"

She rolls her eyes, shifting her body toward me. "Because I know you. You have a dirty mind."

"And you're going to deny a broken man his dying wish?" I arch a brow.

"You aren't dying, but you are definitely being overly dramatic." My eyes follow her as she stands up and walks toward the kitchen. "My mother always told me a man is the biggest baby when hurt or sick. Guess she was right."

I laugh, knowing her mother well enough to know she would say something like that.

"Are you calling me baby?" I shout, hoping to get a reaction out of her.

"*A* baby, yes." She peeks her head around the wall with a lifted eyebrow.

"Fine, I'll make my own food." I shift off the couch, trying to prop myself up.

She walks back in and points her finger at me. "Sit back down. Drew will have my head if he thinks I'm not helping."

"Still afraid of your big brother, huh?" I ask in amusement.

She crosses her arms. "*No*. But I don't want to hear about it from either of you."

"Whatever you say, princess." I sit back on the couch as she walks toward the kitchen.

"Don't make me poison your sandwich, King," she shouts loud enough to be heard, but I can hear the smile in her tone.

"I've assumed you've been doing that all along, *V*."

She saunters in with two sandwiches and a bag of chips, and I'm grateful for something other than Jell-O and juice.

"Enjoy," she says, picking up her sandwich and taking a bite with a side of an evil grin.

After a very tasty *unpoisoned* sandwich and finishing up a second chick flick, Viola falls asleep against the arm of the couch. I desperately want to lie next to her and wrap my arms around her, but I know that'd be playing with fire. Drew's been gone for hours, and I can only imagine that the moment I'm too close to Viola, he'd come prancing back in.

Instead, I grab the blanket that's fallen from her body and cover her back up. She looks absolutely breathtaking. Her chest rises and falls evenly, and her lips are lined in a soft pout. I miss the taste of her lips, and I desperately want to kiss them again.

But I *can't*.

If I'm going to prove myself to her, that she can trust me and that I'm all in, I need to change the game.

After turning off the TV, I slowly make my way back to my room and sleep off another round of pain meds. They make me so damn drowsy that I can barely see straight. As I sink into the sheets and my body goes numb, my thoughts drift to Viola and the girl who sat up on the rooftop with me when we were just kids.

"What's your favorite movie?" she asked me, twirling her dark hair around her fingers.

"Hmm…" I thought about it for a moment. "Lord of the Rings, probably. I've seen it over a dozen times now."

She rolled her eyes and sighed. "That's boring."

"Well then tell me yours, if you think it's so much better than mine."

She smiled and looked up at the sky that was fading to black. "No laughing," she warned, and I flashed her a devious smile.

"No promises."

She glared back at me. "Then I'm not telling you."

"C'mon, I'm just kidding. What is it?"

She shook her head no and pretended to zip up her lips.

I reached over and poked her in the side where I knew she was ticklish.

"Stop it!" she squealed, her feet kicking toward me. "Fine! I'll tell you!"

I released her, but the touch of her warm skin on mine doesn't go unnoticed.

"All right, spill it."

"13 Going on 30," she said with a shy look in her eyes. I'd seen her watching that several times since it came out, so I'm not surprised, but that didn't stop me from teasing her about it.

"That's because you have a huge crush on Mark Ruffalo!"

"Is not!" She pushed both hands against me, and I laughed.

I snorted. "Typical chick flick."

"Oh really, Lord of the Rings? That's a typical guy flick."

"Men don't have guy flicks," I corrected. "We have action movies."

She rolled her eyes again. "Boring."

"So are chick flicks," I countered.

"So, you'd never watch a chick flick then?"

"No way. I'd lose my man card."

The only reason I knew the term 'man card' was because Drew had said it several times to me. He mocked me for hanging out with Viola, but I tried to ignore it.

The sound of the front door closing shakes the house and wakes me. I think about the memory and how close Viola and I once were. We had formed a friendship that was bonded and full of trust. I want to feel that again. Most importantly, I want *her* to feel that again.

"Travis, are you awake?" Drew's voice comes from the hallway as he knocks quietly on my door.

"Yeah, come on in." I push myself up and lean against the headboard. "What's with all the commotion?" I ask once he steps inside.

"Oh, sorry. I went to the gym for a couple of hours after work, and then I did some grocery shopping and bought you a few things."

I raise my brows. "Really? Getting all domestic for me?"

"You wish," he spits back. "But I figured you'd get sick of Viola's PB&J specialty sandwiches pretty soon, so I grabbed you some cans of soup, ramen noodles, and chips."

"Bon appétit," I tease.

"I'll bring dinner home after work tomorrow, but you guys are on your own for breakfast and lunch."

"Thanks, man. Appreciate it."

"Hopefully Viola doesn't strangle you before the week's over."

I shrug, hoping he doesn't see right through me. "I think my charm is starting to win her over."

He laughs. "Right. That'll be the day."

VIOLA

Thumping from the kitchen startles me awake, making me nearly fall off the couch before I realize where I am. A blanket is over me, and I vaguely remember Travis covering me up before I fell deeper.

"Jesus, Drew!" I scold, looking over my shoulder to where the racket is coming from.

He pops his head around the kitchen wall and frowns. "Sorry, I didn't realize you were catnapping on the *couch* that you hate sleeping on."

"Maybe you two should think about getting an upgrade. You've had this couch since you were freshmen." I stand and fold the blanket and throw it over the back. "What the hell are you doing anyway?"

"Unpacking groceries. I figured it was the least I could do for making you help this week."

"It's fine. He'll probably sleep most of the time anyway." I walk toward the kitchen and see bags covering the counter. "Did you buy out the whole store, or what?"

"Well, I wasn't sure what you wanted or what you could make without burning it, so I got a little of everything."

I arch a brow and pout. "Funny."

He shrugs, unapologetically. "I know."

I help unpack everything and put it away, although I have no idea where he wants all this stuff, so I just randomly put them in the pantry.

"I'm going to check on Travis," he says as we finish unpacking. "I have three more bags in the car...if you don't mind grabbing them?" He flashes a wide grin my direction, knowing I can't say no.

I groan. "Fine. You better have bought ice cream."

He winks before walking away and heading down the hall to Travis' room. I grab the rest of the bags and unload them all before I hear Drew waltz back in. "That was fast."

"Well I wasn't sure where everything went, so I just stuffed them all into the same cupboard." I flash him an evil smile as I toss the empty bags in the recycling bin. "But I did manage to put the cold items in the fridge."

"Why do you enjoying messing with my OCD?" I can almost see the twitch in his eyes and laugh.

"Because it's just too damn easy."

He groans and begins opening the doors to the cupboards and pantry. "Jesus, Vi."

"That's what you get."

"For what?" he asks with genuine confusion.

"For making me drop by between classes and cutting into my study time," I throw back in his face even though I don't mind it that much.

"Well, according to Travis, you're coming around to his charm."

My heart begins to race in panic. "*What?*" I gasp, turning to read his expression. "What's that mean?"

"Relax," he says, chuckling at my expense. "You're so jumpy today."

"Am not!" I argue, although it's a childish move.

"Man, I hope Travis lives to see this weekend." He cracks a grin. "Should've warned him he'd be rooming with Aunt Flo, too."

"Oh, my God!" I squeal, throwing the first thing I can reach off the counter.

A banana.

"You're such an ass sometimes!" The words come out in between laughter, so I'm not too convincing. "I am not PMS-ing!"

"Could've fooled me," he teases, throwing the banana back at me.

"Is this some kind of weird family tradition I'm unaware of?" Travis' question comes from behind me, and the closeness of his body to mine sends a thrill down my spine.

Drew chuckles and shifts around me. "Need anything?"

"Nah, man. I'm fine."

Travis glances to me, giving me a look that makes me want to ask what he's thinking, but with Drew around us, I know I have to act as I had pre-hatefuck.

"Would you like me to reserve your daily one-night stand before or after your dinner?" The words shoot out of my mouth before I can stop them, and the sly grin that spreads across Travis' face isn't missed. I swallow down my words. I don't want to say crass things, but I've been on defense mode around Travis for so long that it comes out whether I mean it to or not.

He sinks his teeth into his bottom lip before releasing it and replacing his expression with a cocky grin. "That depends. Are you offering to be my appetizer or my dessert?" He leans against the wall with his arms crossed, both brows raised. It's easy for him to throw words back at me—lots of practice.

My jaw drops at his audacity, especially in front of Drew. I know it's a game I have to play, but that doesn't mean I'm going to let him make all the moves without a fight.

"Well, you know what they say. Save the best for last."

"Then I'll choose to eat dessert first." His smug look burns into me, and it takes all the willpower in the world to walk away.

"You two shouldn't be left in the same room together," Drew interrupts our stare down. "And dude," he says, turning to Travis, "you fracture your ribs, and you're still hitting on my sister?"

He shrugs with a smirk.

"You're lucky you're already hurt, or I'd break the rest of your ribs." I know he's joking, but the way he says it sounds like a genuine threat. Travis may be his best friend, but he's made it known he'd never approve of Travis making a move on me.

"I bet I could take you, broken ribs and all," Travis teases, pushing him with his good shoulder.

Drew flashes him a look that says otherwise. "Oh, please." He goes back to reorganizing the cupboards as Travis and I stand awkwardly. He's looking intently at me like he wants to say something, but there's nothing else to say—especially with Drew around.

"Well, I need to make sure I didn't forget anything around the house before I go. I've got class bright and early."

I begin walking away before Drew speaks up again. "Ten in the morning isn't early. Join the Academy if you want to understand early."

I scoff and glance at Travis, desperately needing to put distance between us before things look suspicious.

As I walk out of the kitchen, I hear footsteps behind me. Before I make it to Drew's room, Travis grabs my elbow and turns me around.

"What are you doing?" I whisper, feeling the beat of my racing heart in my neck, knowing that Drew is in the next room and could round the corner at any second.

"You make me want to do really bad things to you."

"Travis!" I hiss between gritted teeth. "We can't do this. We have to keep up the act around Drew until he's in the loop. He really will break your other ribs if he walks in on something." I look into his eyes, and then past them, to make sure we're still in the clear. My nerves are on edge, and my emotions are going haywire. As his mouth dips in close to my ear, a bolt of electricity forces its way through my veins. Travis is my drug, and when I'm getting my fix, it's hard to concentrate on anything at all, but I know I have to.

"You know I don't mean any of those bitchy things I say, right?"

He gives me a side grin. "I know it's just an act. It always has been."

His words bring me back to reality.

"Princess...I want to be the one to tell him. I owe him that."

I swallow hard and nod in agreement. "What are you going to say exactly?"

"I'm going to say, 'Oh, hey Drew. Your sister and I have been having dirty raw sex for the past week, and we want to keep doing it.'"

I smile and slap his arm. Travis winces.

"Shit, I'm sorry. It's a reflex."

"I'll let you make it up to me later."

CHAPTER FIVE

TRAVIS

Locking eyes with her, I find the strength to wrap an arm around her waist and pull her to my chest. It's dangerous, and I know we have to keep our secret for now, but I have to touch her. Her breath hitches as she feels the warmth of our bodies, and it's the first time I've had her this close since before the accident. If I didn't feel like I'd just gotten hit by a truck, I wouldn't be so gentle.

She lowers her eyes so I can't look into them, and I squeeze her hip to grab her attention.

"Viola, I'm going to tell him the truth," I whisper, and she looks up at me.

I know the risk of the game we're playing. I know what we have to lose, but there's so much more to win. Viola Fisher has always been mine, and finally being together is the endgame.

"I'm going to tell him I can't live without you, and I'd like his blessing," I whisper, brushing my thumb across her cheek. My touch forces her eyes to mine, and I don't let her go. I'll never let her go again. Fuck that.

"You mean that?"

"Yes." I don't miss a beat with my response.

She takes a deep breath and rests her head against my chest before breaking the electric current of our bodies being so close. A smile fills her face, and it's everything I need to know. I want to kiss the fuck out of her, but I know it's too risky.

She bites her lower lip and releases it before speaking. "Just know, if you break my heart again, Travis King, I'll break your balls."

"That's my firecracker," I smirk. Though my face is bruised and broken, it still causes her body to react. I press my lips against the softness of her neck, and she sighs.

Knowing it'll drive her mad, I place a soft kiss on her cheek and release her. Stepping away, I walk toward my room, feeling her eyes burn holes in the back of my head. We've been standing in the hallway for way too long. Viola's right, though; Drew can't find out by walking in on us. I have to find the right time to tell him.

As I walk to my room, I focus on taking small, calculated steps. Before I can make it to my bed, Viola enters, and she's all worked up. Slowly, I manage to climb into bed and lie down. With my hands behind my head, I smile at her. She's so predictable. I love that about her.

I look at her nipples. *Hard. As. A. Rock.* As my eyes roam down the rest of her, she notices and crosses her arms and huffs.

"It's going to be really hard pretending to hate you when you look at me like that."

I can tell she's fighting back a laugh.

"So, does that mean you don't hate me anymore, princess?"

She groans loudly and finally cracks a smile.

On cue, the door barely opens and Drew steps in. "What the hell?"

Viola turns and glares at him with her hands on her hips.

"What damage did he manage to do already?"

Without a beat, she responds, "He knocked my toothbrush off the counter, and it fell into the toilet."

My eyes widen at the story she creates. I know she wouldn't lie to Drew normally, but she's good at playing the part, so he doesn't get suspicious before I have the chance to tell him.

"Dude..." He looks behind Viola and stares right at me.

"Genuine accident," I say, knowing he'll think I'm full of bullshit.

Viola turns to scowl at me, knowing Drew is watching our every move. "Was it a genuine accident when you didn't tell me until *after* I brushed my teeth?"

I hear Drew snort behind her, and I can't help cracking a smile at her performance.

"Sorry, man. Can't help you out of this one," he says to me, and then shuts the door, leaving us to rip each other apart, or at least that's what it looks like. In any other circumstance, it might seem odd to him that Viola's in my room, but considering her reaction, it just looks typical.

"Great acting. You really should have pursued that theater degree," I say.

She scoffs. "I'm much better at reading words than reciting them."

Patting my hand on the bed, I motion for her to come closer. Hesitantly, Viola comes closer and sits on the edge. Her voice drops to a whisper, and she leans into me. "I have to go, but I'll be back tomorrow after my morning class."

I cup her cheek and brush my lips across hers. "You better."

After grabbing my bottom lip in her mouth and tugging, she forces herself to stand before I'm able to take it any further.

"So, tomorrow," I begin, "I'm going to need some help taking a shower." I lift my eyebrows hoping she gets the hint.

I know she wants us to work as much as I do, and I'm determined to spend as much time with her as I can. Fuck the rules. I've never been one to follow them anyway.

"I'm sure Drew can help," she teases.

I smile at her sweetly and lift an eyebrow. "Don't think so, princess."

She's contemplating it, and I wish I could read her thoughts right now. When she breaks a small smile, I know she's on board. "I don't really have a choice, do I?"

"So, it's a date?"

She fights back laughter. "You're ridiculous."

"And you're beautiful."

The mood shifts and she stills. Viola searches my face as if she's memorizing it and I can't seem to take my eyes from hers.

"If you're trying to win me over..."

"I've been trying for years," I said, cutting her off. "Nothing's going to stop me now." I wink, knowing it'll drive her nuts.

"You're relentless," she says before flashing a quick smile. After a moment, she glances over at the clock, then back at me. I know it's time for her to leave, and I'm half-tempted to beg her to stay and climb in bed with me. But that's a horrible idea.

"Goodnight, Travis," she says as she walks across the room.

Before turning off the light, Viola turns and smiles at me. The door clicks shut, and as I close my eyes, the only image I can see is her.

The sun peeking through the blinds wakes me up sooner than I'd like. Sleeping in the same position all night sucks ass. My neck is stiff, and my back is tight. With all my strength, I move my legs to the floor and try to stand. Once I'm finally up, I slowly make my way to the bathroom. I didn't realize something as natural as pissing could be so difficult and painful.

When I step out, I hear music echoing down the hall, and as I walk toward the kitchen, it gets louder. Rounding the corner, I see Viola dancing around the kitchen in a t-shirt that says *Dumbledore is my Homeboy* on the back. I hold in laughter as I watch her shake her hips and bob her head. She's holding a bowl and stirring it as she sings along with the music blaring from her phone.

I lean against the wall, balancing myself while silently watching her. She's so distracted by what's she's doing, she doesn't even notice me. This is the Viola I love. The one that's wild and free, who doesn't give a shit about anything. Her hair is up in a messy bun, and she's wearing her black-rimmed glasses.

I clear my throat, letting her know I'm behind her. She goes frigid, and the smile fades from her face. I can see her pulse beating rapidly in her neck.

"I wouldn't mind waking up to this every day." I offer a smile, and she blushes.

She swallows hard. We're alone at last, and she notices it, too.

"I'm baking banana bread. Thought you might be hungry for something besides Jell-O." She pulls in her bottom lip before releasing it and flashing a small smile.

There's a shift between us, and I can tell she feels it as well. No longer at each other's throats, the sexual tension is more intense than ever before.

"Starving," I reply, gently pushing off the wall and walking toward her.

She licks her lips as she watches my every step. I cup her face and press a soft kiss on her lips. Her breath hitches as she anticipates more, but I don't give in. "How'd you sleep?"

She blinks. "Uh, fine, but Drew's bed is way more comfortable than my dorm bed. You?" She turns and shuts off the stove before sliding the pan from the burner.

"Like shit, but at least the pain meds helped knock me out for a few hours."

She turns and offers a sincere smile. "Well, good thing the only items on your agenda today are to eat and rest."

"Oh, don't forget my daily required lap dance."

She points a finger at me, trying to act strong. "Breaking the rules before breakfast?"

"Rules? What rules?" I tease, knowing it'll get her riled up and maybe she'll loosen up a bit.

"You know exactly which rules I'm talking about. The ones we discussed when we had our little chat in your bed yesterday morning."

"You were in my bed yesterday? We had a discussion?"

"Yes, after you got home from the hospital." She looks at me, waiting for me to tell her I remember. She sighs. "Quit playing." Her shoulders tense, and she's staring intently at me.

"Viola, I'm sorry, but I don't remember talking to you yesterday morning. I was on a ton of painkillers when I left the hospital. The last thing I remember is Drew waking me up sometime in the afternoon and saying he went grocery shopping."

She studies me, waiting to see if I'll crack. "Then why'd you kiss me just now?"

I shrug. "Habit, I guess. Gorgeous girl in my kitchen baking seems like it requires a morning kiss."

"Are you freaking kidding me right now?" I can see her lips trembling, and I know I'm going straight to hell for this.

"What? Why'd you kiss me back?" I try my damnedest to keep my stance, but the fire brewing in her eyes is just too fucking much to keep my stance.

She sees me cracking, my lips fighting the smile that soon appears.

Realization sets in and soon there's a wooden spoon pointing right in front of my face. "I'm going to murder you!" she says between gritted teeth.

I burst out in laughter, taking a step back to avoid her murder weapon.

"You don't mean that." I flash her a charming smile, and she glares at me in return.

I watch as she pours the mixture into a bread pan, carefully scraping the bowl and leveling the batter out evenly.

I'm grateful Drew bought food for the week, but I'd much rather wake up to Viola baking in my kitchen.

She grabs a coffee cup from the counter and sips it.

"You went to Starbucks and didn't bring me anything?" I arch a brow, knowing damn well I don't drink her fancy lattes and whatever.

She glares while flashing a crooked smile. "No. Drew's paying for my services."

"All it takes is Starbucks?" I smirk. "Duly noted."

She playfully rolls her eyes at me, and I laugh. The oven beeps and she places the bread pan inside, which gives me a nice view of her ass as she bends over.

She notices and immediately frowns. "No mischief," she warns.

"I never agreed to that."

"I'm here to help you with your recovery, and that's all," she states in a firm tone, but I don't believe a word of it. I know her way too well. She's only saying it aloud to convince herself.

"You're the worst liar I've ever met."

She furrows her brows, keeping a safe distance from me, knowing damn well that if I were able, I'd show her exactly what I mean.

"How is it that you bruise your ribs and get all cut up, and you're still unable to behave yourself?"

I step toward her, trying to ignore the pain in my rib cage, and wrap my arms around her waist. She watches my every move, her breath hitching the closer I lean into her. My lips brush against hers, tasting the sweet coffee flavor against mine.

I hear her groan as I deepen the kiss, but pull away before going any further.

"Nothing could come between my lips and your body, princess. Bruised ribs or not, I'll suffer through just to be close to you."

She smiles up at me, but it's soon replaced with a frown. "I bet you were the worst patient ever."

"Only around the hot nurses." I wink.

She groans again. "You aren't going to make this easy for me, are you?"

I press my lips to hers again. "And what fun would that be?"

After the banana bread is done, she sets it down to cool. It smells fucking amazing, and I'm tempted to start eating it right out of the pan.

"You have to wait," she warns. "It tastes best when it's just the right temperature. Warm, but not hot."

"That's torture," I whine as we sit on the couch together, only a small throw pillow between us. "Coming in here, smelling up my house with banana bread and coffee and you, and I can't have any of it." I pout, getting a laugh out of her.

"I guess it's time you learn one of life's hard lessons." She puckers her lips. "Travis King doesn't always win."

I toss the pillow at her; her laughter brings a smile to my face. "The king always wins, princess."

"I'm not so sure..." She pinches her lips and taps a finger against her bottom lip. "But making you work for it just might be what you need to shrink that big head of yours."

"Never had an issue with working for what I want." I grab her hand and kiss the finger she was just tapping against her mouth. "But I was hoping we were done playing games now that..." I let the words rest on my lips in hopes she gets what I'm trying to say.

"That what?"

"That we can be in the same room together without the urge to kill one another."

"Just because you kissed me doesn't mean the urge went away." She spits it out so quickly, without a beat, making me smile at her words.

"Well, I guess some things never change." I pull her closer, forcing her to be right next to me. We're both on the couch, facing each other, neither caring what's on the TV anymore. "Like my feelings for you, Viola. Since I was twelve years old. I always knew there was something between us, even before I wasn't old enough to understand what those feelings meant."

"Yeah, I had feelings for you, too." She pauses with a grin. "Feelings of hate."

"Viola..." I hiss under my breath, knowing damn well she's making this much harder than it has to be. "Why are you being so difficult?"

"Because it's fun to see you sweating for once," she answers honestly, flashing a victorious smile.

"Well, mission accomplished, smartass. Now would you drop the act and just listen to me?"

She exhales and then smiles, her eyes softening. "Are you asking me to go steady?" Her voice is high pitched like an overly exaggerated cheerleader on those ridiculous chick flicks she watched when she was in high school.

I drop her hand and sigh. "I give up."

She licks her lips, holding in a smirk. "Defeated the King! Finally!"

"You've been waiting twelve years to say that, haven't you?"

"Pretty much." She flashes a smug grin. "In fact, everything in my life has led up to this very moment."

"Fuck, you're a sassy thing today. What happened to the sweet little girl I first met?"

"You corrupted her," she says matter-of-factly.

"Can't say I'm sorry about that."

She looks at me as if she's in deep thought, and I try to read her. I know I have a lot of proving to do, but I'll do whatever it takes to gain her trust again.

"I don't want anyone else, Viola," I say genuinely, knowing she needs to hear it. "I never truly did. It's always been you."

"I want to trust you," she says softly. "But I'm scared."

"What are you scared of?" I ask, hoping I can ease some of her fears.

"I'm scared of getting hurt again. Scared Drew will throw you across the room. Scared I'll never fully be able to trust you."

"Viola, listen to me. I'll do whatever it takes to take those fears away. Don't worry about Drew. I'll talk to him and do whatever it takes to gain his trust, too. But don't be scared of getting hurt. I can't promise there won't be times I fuck up, but I would never intentionally hurt you." I take her head in mine again. "But I will promise you one thing. I won't be like those guys you read about in your romance novels. I won't feather the bed with red rose petals, make love to you under the stars, or write an original song and sing it to you on top of Butternut Hill."

She chuckles, tilting her head to look deeper into my eyes.

"Because I'm not like those guys in your romance novels. I'm the guy that'll fuck you against the wall, wrap my hand around your throat, and pull your hair as you scream out my name. I'm the guy that'll have you waking up on a bare mattress because we fucked the sheets off it in the middle of the night. I'm the guy that can't sing a tune to save my soul, but I'd tell you every single day of my life how much you mean to me. So, before you make your decision, you need to know everything it entails."

I watch as her throat moves, her tongue running along her lips as she wets them. She blinks and looks back up at me; her eyes are glassy.

"I don't want you to be those guys in my romance novels," she states. "They're usually flawless with perfect abs and hair and they always say the right things, and they're always hung even when they're soft…"

I put a hand up, making her stop so I can make sure I'm hearing her correctly. "Wait a minute…"

She ignores me and continues. "I don't want perfect, Travis. I don't expect a relationship where everything is always smooth and happy. I want us to continue challenging one another, testing the limits, and growing as one. I'd get bored being with a perfect guy. I'd feel inadequate, and I'd rather have an imperfect relationship than a perfect one."

Her words are music to my ears. My heart beats harder in my chest. "So, are you saying you're all in?" I ask, desperate to hear her say the words.

She sucks in her lips and nods. "Yes. I am."

Her eyes are glassing over again. I press my thumb over her cheek, catching a tear that drops down. "I hope those are tears of happiness," I smirk, cupping her face.

"Tears of regret," she spits out.

"Dammit, Viola," I hiss, trying to hold in annoyed laughter. "Are you always going to be this difficult to seduce?"

"You have a lot to learn, King." She winks.

"Trust me. I know, princess." I bring our mouths together and push her lips apart with my tongue. "Just know that if I weren't on bed rest, I'd have both your legs above your head right now."

"Clearly it was your charm that won me over."

"I thought it was my ability to make you count to ten with your head buried in the pillow?"

She playfully slaps my arm and scowls. "If I didn't know any better, I'd say I'd just agreed to be with a horny fifteen-year-old boy."

"Twenty-four-year-old man," I clarify with a shrug. "Not much has really changed."

She laughs and before I can stop her, she leans in, brings both hands around my neck and pulls me in for a deep, greedy-as-fuck kiss. She has my body all kinds of fired up. My ribs may be broken, but my cock sure isn't.

"Goddammit, Viola," I growl, needing her to stop. I press my forehead against hers, our pants mixing in the air as we try to catch our breaths. "I think I need to go take that shower now." *A fucking cold one.*

"Are you sure that's a good idea?"

"Well, it was suggested I either sit in the shower or have someone nearby to help in case I slip or get drowsy from the meds and since we don't exactly have a shower chair, you'll have to be my on-duty nurse."

"Should I put the uniform on for you and everything? Give you the full nurse experience?" The corner of her lips tilts up.

I smile. I fucking love her smart mouth.

VIOLA

Following Travis to the bathroom, I'm already drooling at the thought of seeing him naked again. I stare at him, admiring the way his jeans hug his ass. He glances over his shoulder and catches me.

"Eyes up here, nurse."

I blink my eyes back up to his and blush as if I'd been caught getting into trouble. A cocky grin forms over his face, and I know he's enjoying every second of my ogling.

Once inside the bathroom, I reach into the shower and turn on the water. Travis watches me as he begins unbuttoning his jeans. I watch as he pushes them down, but they get stuck at his knees. I step in and pull them down the rest of the way so he can kick them off. I slide my hand over his waist and grip the end of his shirt. I know he's in more pain than he's letting on, so I slowly lift his shirt so he can pull his arms out one by one. He winces slightly and I cringe at the way raising his arms over his head causes pain.

"Are you okay?" I ask, fearing that he's not going to be able to shower alone.

"A hot nurse undressing me? I'm more than fine." He grins, and I roll my eyes at his inability to answer a serious question.

"Don't get any ideas," I scold. "This is strictly for medical purposes only."

"We'll see about that." He nods his head down to his boxers, which is the only clothing left on him.

I nod, knowing damn well he can take his boxer shorts off. But if that's how he wants to play it, I'm all in.

Looping my fingers underneath the waistband, I slowly pull them down his body. I kneel, but I keep my eyes locked on his. As soon as I have them down far enough, his cock frees and is saluting to the ceiling. I swallow, fighting the urge to taste him, but I know I can't start anything right now—as much as I *desperately* want to.

Making eye contact with him, I watch as a smug expression forms over his face, and he stands with both hands on his hips.

"Are you sure you're up for this, princess?"

Blinking, I clear my throat and flash a forced smile. I stand up and watch as he finally kicks his shorts to the side. "You really think you're going to win this game?" I challenge, knowing exactly what he's trying to do.

I will not cave. I will not cave.

"I *know* I will."

"You'll never learn, will you?" I smirk.

He shrugs.

I'm not above needing to prove myself to him when I need to. I bring my fingers down to my jeans and unbutton them. He watches me intently as I remove them, and then I bring my hands to the bottom of my shirt and pull it over my head.

"What the hell are you doing?" he finally asks.

"Getting undressed." I reach behind my back and unclasp my bra.

He watches as it slides down my arms and falls to the floor.

"Why?"

"Well, I don't normally shower with my clothes on…" I lower my hands to the fabric of my panties and begin pulling them down.

"Wait," he says eagerly, stopping me. "Don't you think you being naked is a safety hazard? I mean, you're supposed to make sure I don't stumble or some shit."

I smile, ignoring his hand and push my panties the rest of the way down. "Good thing you have your very own personal nurse, willing to go the distance."

Stepping toward me, he closes the gap between us. I feel his cock throbbing against my skin and my body shivers. He cups my face and brings his mouth to mine. Slowly, he kisses me and parts my lips with his tongue, giving me a torturous taste of exactly what I want.

"You forget who you're playing with, princess?" he asks, breaking the kiss.

I swallow, keeping my eyes closed as I try to compose myself and not give into the temptation my body so deeply wants.

"Viola," he whispers, his breath vibrating against my lips. "Viola, look at me."

I hear the desperation in his voice, the eagerness in his tone, and I fight obeying with every part of my body. "No," I say, exhaling. "I don't trust myself with you."

I hear a soft chuckle release from his lips, and it brings me comfort. "I don't blame you."

His words make me laugh, and I shake my head in protest. "Arrogance isn't a flattering trait, you know."

"Your body seems to disagree." He pinches my nipple between his fingers and releases a deep, satisfied hum. "In fact, every part of you disagrees."

I can feel myself getting wet as the ache intensifies between my legs. It's as if he has pussy radar or something. He knows exactly what he's doing to me.

"My body needs a cold shower," I admit, needing to diminish the tension in the air. I need the shock of the cold water on my skin to wake me from this spell Travis has cast on me.

"You're the boss, nurse."

I peel my eyes back open and see the amused grin on his face. "Sometimes I really want to smack you." I put my hand under the shower to test the temperature of the water.

"You wouldn't be the first to say that."

"Not surprising." I roll my eyes with a grin and step inside the shower. "Ready?"

"Ready if you are," he says, taking a step in. "Just don't forget the real reason you're in here, princess," he warns with fake authority.

"Yes," I say, closing the shower curtain. "To make sure you don't slip and break that big head of yours."

"Oh." He turns to face me, handing me a bar of soap. "I'm not supposed to move my arms behind my back, so it looks like you'll have to soap me up, too."

"And who helped you when you were in the hospital?" I ask, grabbing it from him.

"Nancy. She had grabby hands, so watch yourself. I had to remind her to keep her eyes up quite often. I think she enjoyed the show." He lowers his eyes to his still-hard cock.

I shake my head and hold back a smile. "You're ridiculous."

He chuckles. "She was also old enough to be my grandmother, and I'm pretty sure she was blind in one eye."

Rolling my eyes, I lather the soap in my palms and wait as it foams between my hands. I begin rubbing circles over his chest and massaging the soap into his chest hair and then carefully over his ribs and stomach. He's watching me intently, studying my every move. A comfortable silence hangs between us as I continue lathering and washing him. My hand slides around his waist and down to his hips. I'm tempted to wrap my hands around his cock and torture him the same way he does to me, but then I decide not touching him would bring him more agony.

"Turn around."

He obeys, and I repeat the process. I rub my palms over his shoulders, neck, and down his back. Although the water is hot, I can feel goose bumps prick his skin when I touch him. Feeling bold, I slide my hand lower and rub the soap down his spine, all the way down to his ass. I feel his body tighten and decide to keep going.

Once I've thoroughly cleaned down the back of his legs and his perfect, tight ass, I make my way back up and wash his shoulders and arms.

"You're very thorough," he says in amusement, turning back around to face me.

"I take pride in my work," I say, weaving my fingers through his and making sure every finger gets clean.

He watches me for a few more moments and then grabs my hand and wraps it around his cock. "You missed a spot."

I swallow, taken off guard by his boldness. "Well, I figured it was an area you could reach yourself."

"Doctor's orders," he says with a lazy shrug. "I can't risk getting dizzy and slipping to my death with my dick in my hand."

I resist the urge to roll my eyes again. God, he's too much sometimes. "I bet the nurses had a party the day you were discharged."

"Nah, they enjoyed my antics. Kept them on their toes."

"I bet," I say dryly. I slathered more soap between my hands and wrapped my fingers around his erection that never seems to go down, rubbing the suds up and down his length. With my other hand, I massage his balls, making sure to be as gentle as I can. I'll give him the satisfaction that he won this round, but I won't finish him off, as much as I'd love to.

As soon as his head falls back and his body begins to tighten, I release my hands and rinse them underneath the water. "All done, Mr. King," I say in a professional tone. "Can I help you with anything else?"

His throat moves and his chest rises and falls quickly. "Yes, as a matter of fact." His tone is sharp. "Put your hands back on me right now." He lowers his face and locks eyes with me. "You're going to give me blue balls."

"Sorry, Mr. King, but that's not in the paperwork. Any pleasuring will have to be done on your own time." I flash a witty smile, and I can tell he's brewing inside.

"I should've known your smart mouth would come out to play." The corner of his lips tilt up, and I know he's up to something. He grabs the soap and smirks at me. "My turn."

I furrow my brows, but he stays silent as he circles a finger in the air, motioning for me to turn around. After a few moments, I feel his hands on my shoulders, and it's the most amazing feeling in the world. His hands are so big and strong, and even though they're covered in soap, I want his hands on me—*everywhere*.

A moan releases from my throat as he makes his way down my back and ass, thoroughly covering every inch of me. I miss his body on mine, touching me, kissing me, pushing my every limit. I want everything this man has to offer, and I'm not sure how much longer I can wait.

"Put your hands up on the wall," he says over my ear, pressing his body into mine and feeling his erection against the small of my back. "Spread your legs apart."

I do as he says, and am just about to ask what he's doing when he wraps both arms around my waist, holding onto me. His legs are spread behind mine, keeping his balance, and before I can make a comment about how I'm supposed to be the one keeping an eye on him, he lowers his hand down my stomach and palms my pussy. Every thought vanishes and the only thing I need in this world is for his hands never to stop touching me.

His other hand slides up and covers my breast, massaging it in rhythm as he rubs his thumb over my clit. A soft moan releases, and I'm no longer in control.

"I've missed you," he says, his words vibrating over my ear. My entire body shivers. The water cascades down his back, leaving me naked and cold. "You have goose bumps."

I swallow as his fingers slide along my slit, building up the ache that I was already fighting. I can't concentrate on anything beyond his hand on my breast and his fingers sliding inside me, building up the pressure I so desperately want to release.

My head falls back against his chest and rests on his shoulder. "I think this is a safety hazard, Mr. King. I can't be liable for any injuries due to your wandering hands."

His teeth scrape along the lobe of my ear, and he groans. "Any injuries would be worth it." I can feel his lips forming into a smirk. "And I'm not really in that much pain anymore."

Although his words take me off guard, I don't believe him. After hearing about his injuries, I looked them up, and know for a fact that fractured ribs can take up to six weeks to recover or sometimes even longer. I know Travis takes good care of his body and health, but I can't imagine he wouldn't still be in pain after less than two weeks.

"You're still supposed to be resting and taking it easy," I manage to say in between his thumb rubbing circles on me and his fingers sliding deeper inside me.

"Trust me, princess, this is me taking it easy," he growls and flashbacks of our first time surface. "You'd be holding onto your ankles as I bent you over and gave you every-fucking-thing you're begging for right now, so trust me when I say that this is as *easy* as I'll be taking it."

God. Why does he do this to me? *How,* after all these years, can my body crave him this much?

He speeds up his fingers, making me unable to respond to him, and even if I could, I don't know that I'd be able to say anything that made any sense right now.

"Are you ready to count, princess?" He kisses under my ear and sends more shivers down my spine.

I begin shaking my head, because I know I can't control myself around him, especially with his body pressed up against mine and his magic fingers driving me wild.

"I'm so fucking hard for you, Viola. God, it's driving me insane."

I begin panting, losing the strength to deny him, so I give in and practically beg him for it. "I need more," I say between heavy breaths. "Harder."

One hand slides up my body and fists my hair as his other hand pushes two fingers deep inside me and finds a rhythm that nearly has my knees buckling. If he keeps this up, we'll both be on the shower floor with broken ribs.

"You're going to make me fall," I say, pushing my hips harder into his palm, desperately needing a release. My hands on the shower wall are barely holding me up anymore.

He speeds up his fingers, giving me no room for protests, as his other hand slides back down my body and presses into my stomach, fusing our bodies together even tighter. "I've already fallen, princess, but trust me when I tell you that I'd never let you get hurt."

My heart skips a beat, or maybe even two because the way he speaks is so raw and genuine that I almost forget to breathe. My mind flashes back to the other day when I could've sworn I heard him say *'I love you,'* but I figured that was the effects of the pain meds he's been taking. I don't know how to react to his words now because I'm not even certain he meant it that way, and now I'm so lost in my thoughts that when my body tightens, and his fingers fuck me into complete oblivion, so much so that I nearly pass out, I don't see it coming.

"Princess?" His lips press against my ear, and I know exactly what he's after.

"One," I finally whimper, catching my breath as his thumb continues rubbing over my clit. Once I'm able to control my breathing, I slowly turn around and face him. "You broke the rules," I say, wrapping an arm around his waist.

He cups my face and leans down, his lips lingering over mine. "You're damn right I did." The smile he flashes makes me want to melt right into him. "There's no fucking way I'm waiting six weeks. Hell, the doctor should be impressed if I manage to wait six days."

I chuckle, hating that his words make me want to smile like a love-struck teen. But my heart knows exactly who Travis King is, and it hasn't been able to let him go since the first day we met.

"Are you ready to get the hell out of here so I can warm you up in my bed?"

"I have a feeling the doctor's orders didn't even stand a chance." I grin, slicking my ice-cold wet hair back.

"Not one fucking bit."

CHAPTER SIX

TRAVIS

I place my hand against the wall and slowly step out of the shower behind Viola, watching water drip down her back and perfect tight ass. Good thing I haven't experienced any side effects from the meds, because I'm definitely distracted enough to slip and bust my face. Fortunately, she turns around and hands me a towel, breaking me out of my trance.

Grabbing the towel, I close the space between us as Viola looks up at me with hooded eyes, and we both know that was only the beginning. Instead of drying myself off, I take the opportunity to touch her and rub the soft cotton over her face, neck, shoulders, chest, and arms.

I motion for her to turn around so I can dry the rest of her, and when she does, I take my time as I touch her. I lean forward, kissing then biting each shoulder, as my fingertips trace down her torso, memorizing her body. My chest rests against her back, and she leans against me as I guide my hand over a breast, pinching her hard nipple before moving lower. With each ragged breath, she melts into my touch, and I drop to my knees in front of her. At first, she gives me a worried look, but I shake my head as I rest one of her legs over my shoulder. She doesn't fully put her weight on me but gives me what I want. I have to fucking taste her.

Viola closes her eyes, sinking deeper into my tongue as I flick her clit. The way she tastes, and the way her skin smells so sweetly, makes my cock throb. She leans against the door, steadying herself, taking her nipples between her fingers and pinching and pulling them. It's almost too much for me to watch. I dip my tongue inside, listening to her pants as I tongue fuck her to oblivion. I can taste the edge of her orgasm, and as much as she wants it right then, I slow down my movements, allowing her to enjoy it even more.

"Please," she begs, but I don't listen.

As her leg shakes in anticipation, I guide a finger in, then another, and after a few more swirls on her hard nub, Viola moans my name again and whispers '*two*' like it's a prayer.

"You're so goddamn greedy," I tell her as I place a finger in my mouth, tasting her sweetness again.

"You've created a monster," she says playfully.

"Mm. Love the sound of that. My little sex monster."

After we're both dry, she laces her fingers with mine and leads the way, taking full control. She turns and looks at me as we walk down the hallway, and it's a moment I never want to forget.

Viola in the raw.

Viola happy.

Viola with *me*.

Fuck me, maybe all that Mickey Mouse shit is real and dreams really do come true.

Once the bedroom door shuts, I can't keep my hands from her. I grab her face and brush my lips against hers. Light moans escape from her as our tongues tangle together, fighting a war that neither of us will win. She stands on her tiptoes and wraps her arms around my neck, pulling deeper into the kiss.

"You're so goddamn beautiful," I whisper against her lips. All inhibitions roll from her shoulders, and when she looks into my eyes, I know there's no other woman in the world that can make me feel this way. Fuck, if this is a game, I'll gladly lose if it means having her exactly like this.

Grabbing her chin between my fingers, I search her face as her eyes flutter open. "I want to fuck you until you can't walk."

She cracks a smile. "You were worrying me for a second. Didn't know if that smart mouth was still in there."

"I may have left it in your sweet little pussy."

"Oh, my God, Travis. You're so vile."

"I love riling you up. Makes me hard as fuck."

She looks down at my cock, which is at full attention, and smirks. "Obviously."

"And you like it, so…"

She drops down to her knees and licks the precum from the tip, then takes her time licking me. I grab fists of her hair as she manages to put most of me in her mouth. My eyes practically roll in the back of my head when she cups my ass in her hands and shoves me deeper down her throat.

"Mm," I say, knowing that if she keeps up this rhythm, I won't be able to last much longer. It's been too long since I've felt her. It's been too long since I've felt this overwhelming need. And though I'm known for my stamina, right now, it's complete bullshit. I watch her every movement as she slows her pace, paying attention to every inch. Before she brings me to the edge, she looks up at me and places my balls in her mouth, teasing me, while she strokes me. *Holy. Fuck.*

"Viola." I look into her eyes, and she knows. Our gaze isn't broken as I come, and she swallows it all.

"King," she says, smiling.

I take her hand and lead her to the bed, kissing the fuck out of her before she falls back against my pillows. Taking my time, I sit on the edge and position myself beside her. The pain is a motherfucker, but it's nothing more than an inconvenience when Viola's naked body is pressed against me, practically begging me with every blink of her eyes.

I run my fingers through her hair before our kisses transform into pure greed.

"Jesus, you're ready to go again?"

"Don't look so surprised, princess."

She bends down and grabs my nipple between her teeth and tugs.

"Keep doing that, and you might not walk for a week."

"Challenge accepted." Viola doesn't wait another second before she's straddling me and taking full control. This confident, sexually charged side of her is sexy as fuck. She eases all of me in and closes her eyes, letting out a deep throaty moan as our ends meet.

Once she begins rolling her hips, taking me from the shaft to the tip then back down again, I feel like a goddamn virgin on prom night. Especially with her greedy little pussy wrapped around me so tightly, taking every inch like she owns it. Maybe she does.

"Viola," I say as I dig my fingers in her hips, slowing her down. For once, I want to enjoy it, enjoy *her*.

She leans over, concern written on her face. "Are you okay? I'm not hurting you, am I?"

I laugh and wrap my arms around her back and pull her closer until her face is inches from mine. "The only thing that hurts is knowing we can't do this whenever we want."

She kisses me, and every emotion of hers floods straight through me. It's want and need mixed with lust. It's hate and love and every pent-up aggression we've shared over the years. All of it trickles away and is replaced with something else, something different. It feels like pure fucking perfection. Once her orgasm builds, she counts to three, then four, and eventually five. Before I lose myself completely, I realize that we're no longer fucking. No, for the first time, Viola and I are making love. And the look on her face, before she whispers six, tells me that she feels it, too.

Seconds turn into minutes as I hold her in my arms.

"I have to read a chapter for my Strategic Management class before I go," she whispers, leaning her head against my chest.

"I'm sure you've read it several times already." I gently trace circles on her arm with my thumb. She perks up and gives me a look confirming my suspicion, but it doesn't surprise me.

"Being here is just too comfortable," she says with her naked body against mine, pouting.

For a second, I stop everything and listen. And the fear on Viola's face, tells all.

"Up, out, hurry," I say, as Viola frantically rushes out of my room. I pull the blankets up over my body and close my eyes.

My door cracks open. "Dude, you awake?" Drew asks.

My heart is racing as I pretend to be groggy.

"What's up?" I ask.

"Is Viola here?"

The memory of what we had done still lingers in the room.

"Not sure," I answer, hating to lie, but hoping she was able to make it back to the bathroom where our clothes were.

"What do you want, Drew? And what are you doing here?" I hear Viola question him from behind. "Making sure I'm doing what I'm told?"

He turns and looks at her. "I live here, remember? Yeah, I'm making sure you're not slacking."

Viola is burning holes through his head by the way she's looking at him.

"Actually, I forgot my wallet and it's my turn to buy lunch today. Why are you being so weird?"

"I'm not being weird." She storms into the kitchen with a groan. I hear the refrigerator door open then slam closed.

"Yeah, she's been weird for days," I tell Drew just loud enough for Viola to hear, knowing it will aggravate the shit out of her, but we have to keep this up.

"She's about to start her period," Drew says with a laugh.

"Oh, that's what it is? Makes sense. Thanks for the warning." I chuckle, making sure to keep the blanket over my naked body.

"You're an asshole. Actually, you're both assholes," she yells from the kitchen.

"Dude, told you. Aunt Flo." He looks at his phone then back at me. "Is everything going okay so far?"

I think back to the shower, and then to the moment when Viola melted in my hands, the taste of her, and how my name fell from her lips as if she was claiming me as her own.

"Yeah, *perfect,*" I add a hint of sarcasm, which isn't lost on him.

"I was hoping she'd warm up to you. I guess it's going to take a few more days."

I laugh. "Yeah, looks like it."

"Might take the rest of time, though."

If he only knew.

"So, Mia texted me."

I can't tell if he's excited about it or not, so I stay neutral, but it makes me uneasy when I think about her.

"She's been released from the hospital," he adds.

"Well, that's good news." I focus on him, trying to read him.

"She wants to come over and talk about what happened after she finishes up some school projects."

I'm not sure what my reaction should be at this moment. He doesn't know the circumstances and hasn't asked me one question, but I put on a fake smile because I know he loves her, even though she doesn't deserve him.

"That's great." But I know her being here is not a good idea. She's playing my best friend, and I don't like that one fucking bit.

"Shit. I've gotta go. I left Logan in the car. You two play nice, okay?"

I give him a nod, and he leaves me to my thoughts.

Mia is acting out, begging for attention, and she knows Drew will give it to her. I thought she'd learned a lesson, but clearly, I was mistaken.

VIOLA

Once Drew leaves, I make my way back to Travis' room, where he's getting dressed.

"I'm not being weird," I say matter-of-factly.

Travis smiles at me. "It's okay. It's all of the dirty sex you've been having."

"What just happened cannot happen again. One moment longer and Drew could've caught us. He will kill you and me both."

I lean against the doorway, and Travis walks toward me.

"I'd happily die for you," he says, kissing me sweetly.

"Seriously. We have to be smarter about this." Knowing that Drew could barge in at any minute and find us together makes me jittery and nervous.

He waits a long time before he responds. "I agree, but don't be so paranoid around him. I'll tell him right now if you want me to." He turns and looks at me with an arched eyebrow and a cheesy grin as he picks up his phone and pretends to call Drew.

"Travis!" Heat rushes to my cheeks, and I'm two seconds from tackling him, but I know that would lead to round two. So, I reel it back, regardless of what my body wants.

A ding rings out, and I pull my phone from my pocket. Immediately I start smiling and laughing. It dings again and again. Travis studies me, watching me bite my lip as I respond. I can tell he wants to ask me who I'm talking to, but it's not his business, as much as he wants to make it his business. I glance up at him, and he drops the smile, which only causes me to laugh again.

"Don't worry," I say, watching him tense, almost as if he's jealous. I turn the phone around and flash him a picture of a flaccid dick on the screen. "Courtney sends me dick pics randomly, but they're all weird and have issues."

"That's the most fucked-up thing I've seen in a long time. Is it wrapped around his balls?"

I laugh again. "I don't know what it's doing, but it shouldn't bend that way. I'm so glad you don't have a messed up one."

"You mean you wouldn't give me a chance if I had a weird dick?"

"No. Weird dicks are a hard limit for me," I say with a smile.

The dick pics flood in and I go back to my phone. Tears stream down my face because I'm laughing so hard. I swear she has a folder of these gross pictures reserved just to torture me.

C: **SO PLEASE COME OVER AFTER CLASS!**

V: **Okay! Geez.**

C: **I promise to make it worth your while ;)**

I roll my eyes because I don't think I want to know what she's talking about. With her, there's really no telling.

"Courtney has too much time on her hands. And shouldn't you be reading that chapter?" Travis reminds me, dropping down on the couch and turning on the television. He stops on some old western where the gunshots sound like ricochets and everything on the screen looks brown—the horses, the hats, the shirts, and even the mesa in the background are the same color. I sit down next to him and begin speed-reading.

An alarm on my phone goes off, and I know it's time to go. "Shit. Class. I'll be back later."

"There's no way I could tempt you into staying, is there?" Travis lifts his shirt, and his abs beg me to stay. But I shake my head and stand, throwing my bag over my shoulder. I force myself to take a few steps forward.

As I walk past him, he grabs my hand and pulls me to him, causing me to stumble. My body lands next to him on the edge of the couch, and our faces are so close that the warmth of his breath brushes against my cheek. Tucking loose strands of hair behind my ear, Travis leans in and kisses me so sweetly that he practically steals my breath away. I feel like I'm floating, suspended above reality, as I experience him in a different way. Over the years, he's whittled away at my heart and has finally carved a path straight through the middle. I hope to God this never ends. My hands thread through his hair and our movements become wilder, daring, almost animalistic in all aspects; it takes everything I have not to give into him again.

"The things I'd do to you right now," Travis says in a low rasp, with his eyes closed, before he pulls away.

"The things you've already done to me."

"You're never enough, princess."

"And sometimes you're too much." I smile against his lips. My heart is fluttering, and I'm practically gasping for air. The intensity of that single kiss lights my body on fire, and it's so hard to leave, but I muster the strength to stand.

"You almost cast a spell on me, King," I say, before leaning down and giving him another smack on the lips.

I walk to my car and sit in the driveway for a few moments, trying to process it all. Being with Travis felt different today. It felt real and meaningful, as if our souls touched for the first time since we were kids. For the first time in years, I saw the boy I fell in love with. And I hope he never leaves again.

Once I start the car, I realize how late I am. *Shit!*

Hurriedly, I park at my dorm and run across campus, arriving to class late. I sit down, hair a mess, with swollen lips. I try to listen to my professor speak about managing projects with a focus on long-term strategies instead of day-to-day issues, but my mind goes to Travis.

After class I text him.

V: **Courtney is begging me to come over. Do you need anything?**

His response is immediate, and I instantly smile.

T: **Just you.**

V: **You should be resting.**

T: **You should be sitting on my face.**

V: **OMG! Now your phone is evidence. It must be destroyed.**

I'm half tempted to send him some of those crazy dick pics, but I refrain—for once.

T: **I'm taking a nap now. Nurse's orders :)**

V: **Sweet dreams.**

I send the text quickly as I throw my bag in the back of my car.

T: Only if you're in them.

V: **Gag. You're laying it on thick.**

T: **You like it thick.**

Shaking my head, I should've anticipated that response from him.

V: **Shut it and go to sleep! Your meds have made you delirious.**

I respond before starting the car and driving to Courtney's in complete silence. My mind is racing a million miles per hour as I replay everything that's happened.

"I guess my bribe texts and dick pics worked," she says with a wide smile when she opens the door.

"Of course! Nothing like soft penises that hang over balls like waterfalls!" I lay on the sarcasm, laughing at the thought of those horrific pictures.

"I needed someone else to be scarred for life, too. Just sharing the *love*."

"What would I ever do without you?" I ask.

"Study twenty-four hours a day, seven days a week, probably." She stuffs her phone inside her pocket and smiles back at me. She's in a much better mood than last week. Court's almost herself again, and I'm so happy to have her back.

"Come on; we have somewhere to be."

I narrow my eyes at her as we walk out of her apartment toward the Jeep. After unlocking it, she pulls her long blonde hair into a high ponytail. Before she reverses, Courtney gives me a wink then slams on the gas, causing the wheels to squeal out in protest. Soon we're cruising through neighborhoods, and she turns down the music and begins with her questions.

"So…" She wiggles her eyebrows at me.

"Things are great," I say with a big smile.

"You've already had sex, haven't you?"

My mouth drops open. "Well…"

"I love the two of you together. Did he ever say why Mia was with him?" She looks over at me, hoping I'll give her all the dirty gossip, but there's nothing to say.

"He said nothing happened, so I'm choosing to believe him."

Courtney pulls into the mall parking lot. "Where is Viola Fisher and what have you done with her?"

"If Drew trusts him and believes nothing happened, and Travis says nothing happened, all I can do is follow my heart and trust him, too."

She gives me a big smile. "Good. Because I saw the way he looked at you last week. He's got it bad. Almost lovesick puppy love shit. Plus, he'd be an idiot to mess that up. You're a ten, Lola."

I roll my eyes at her and shake my head, and she gives me a quick wink.

"Now let's go buy tons of sexy lingerie. It always makes me feel better."

I laugh. "I can't afford it. It's too expensive."

She smiles and flashes her credit card. "My treat. Well, my parent's treat, but the same thing. You're the Selena to my Taylor."

We walk through the mall and stop inside Victoria's Secret. The lace is so pretty and soft, and it's been way too long since I've splurged on myself. Between tutoring, paying for what groceries I can afford, and my ridiculous Starbucks habit, I'm just a broke college student, scraping by. Courtney doesn't act entitled like some of the other rich girls at school, but her parents do support her shopping habits. I pray to the retail gods that she finds a job that pays her well or she marries a man with deep pockets. I laugh at the thought.

Courtney starts picking up pretty bras and panties in all sorts of colors and shoves them into my arms.

She's lost her damn mind, and I'm not complaining, but I feel guilty. It's too much to accept.

"Court, you don't have to do this."

"Shut it, sister." She finds some scandalous thongs and adds them to my things. "You can't look like a frump for Travis."

If I didn't know better, I'd say she and Travis were on the same team.

"Whose side are you on, anyway?" I ask her as she snatches up more panties.

"What do you mean?" She's not even really listening to me. She has this wild look in her eyes like she's unstoppable.

"I'm team Traviola. Ha! All the Hollywood power couples have nicknames, so we'll have to work on that. Bennifer, Brangelina, Kimye, Jelena..." She drops the panties in a wire basket, not even paying attention to my reaction.

I can't stop laughing. Courtney's crazy. But it makes me feel good to know she's on our side. Before dragging me to the counter, she grabs a few bottles of perfume. The woman at the checkout gives us a smile.

"I'm a sucker for a panties sale," Courtney says, leaning against the counter like she just bought the place, which she practically did by the amount of clothes that's piled up high.

The woman smiles. "Your total is five hundred forty-two dollars and thirty-six cents."

"Courtney, seriously," I whisper, but she brushes me off.

She hands over her credit card without batting an eye and signs the screen. "Oh, can we have two separate bags?"

The woman hands us their signature pink bags with Victoria's Secret written across the front in shiny, silver letters, and I'm so excited about my new things.

Completely giddy, I take a quick picture of the pink bag and send it to Travis.

T: **Damn!**

I read his text message and shove my phone back in my pocket.

"I think I love you. Thanks, Court."

She gives me a hug. "I love you too, Lola."

We walk out of the store, and all I can do is smile.

"Buying lingerie always makes me happy. And my mom totally supports my habit. She's a firm believer that a woman should splurge on panties and bras. But I'm sure it's going to trigger a phone call when the statement comes in. It's a dead giveaway that I'm upset about something, and I haven't told her about Toby yet." Courtney laughs it off but her voice slightly cracks, and I can tell she's thinking about it, which upsets her. I try to change the subject before she gets lost in Toby thoughts.

"When I'm a millionaire, you're getting tons of gifts."

She perks up. "The only gift I want is your brother wrapped in nothing but a bow."

I playfully nudge her.

"Hey, I'm just being honest." She smiles.

On the way back to her townhouse, I look down at my phone as another text message from Travis flashes across.

T: **Drew's home a little early, and he's stinking up the kitchen with his special tofu recipe.**

I reply knowing exactly what Drew's making. It's this Asian dish with broccoli and soy sauce. For some reason, he thinks it's the most delicious thing on the planet, although we all tell him it's disgusting.

V: **Gross. Enjoy that.**

T: **I'll smile and pretend it's chicken, like always.**

I laugh because I do the same thing.

T: **So about that lingerie? When will I see?**

I can't wait to show him.

V: **I dunno. I like keeping you on edge.**

T: **Tomorrow?**

V: **Tuesdays and Thursdays are usually booked to the max with tutoring and classes, so I'm stressing just a little.**

T: **Don't worry about me, princess. I'll be just fine. Drew's making enough of this crap that I'll be eating it until my ribs heal.**

I feel bad for not being there for him, but I don't see how I could work it in. I'll have to make it up to him.

V: **If you need anything, I'll be your on-call nurse.**

T: **Anything? :)**

V: **Well not anything, but you know!**

T: **Damn. I'll keep you in the loop. Promise.**

V: **Sounds good :)**

T: **I'll be thinking about you naked all day tomorrow.**

I read his message over and over again. Sometimes, seeing this side of Travis doesn't seem real.

But I have to remind myself that it is, and for once, I'm getting exactly what I've always wanted.

V: **Shut up! :)**

CHAPTER SEVEN

TRAVIS

Knowing Viola wouldn't be around to keep me company made Tuesday drag by extra slow, and my night was just as restless. Wednesday arrives, and I wake up exhausted even though I've been lying around for days. I'm not used to this laid-back lifestyle, and while I'm mentally ready to get back to the gym—and even back to work—it's physically not an option. On top of the meds that kick my ass anytime I do decide to take them, I wouldn't be able to sit in an office chair for longer than an hour.

The doctor has refused to release me for an indefinite amount of time, and I'm worried Crawford Marketing will find a reason to let me go, but luckily, I'm covered by short-term disability. Though it's only been two weeks since the accident, Alyssa has already threatened to have her daddy fire me, but she's not stupid and knows she'll face a lawsuit, which is bad PR for the firm. Thankfully, I'm not dealing with Blake and Alyssa's bullshit for ten hours a day on top of the pain, but the stress of working there still haunts me daily. I'm sure my work is stacking up, waiting for when I'm able to return. I'm positive it'll be Blake's way of legally retaliating against me for being out of the office. If it weren't for that place, I would've never gone on that drive, and I'm not sure I can ever forgive or respect Blake and Alyssa for that. My body aches just thinking about it.

However, the biggest reason for being extra sore today is a five-foot-five sassy know-it-all who's been making every ounce of pain worth it. Although those are moments I'll never forget, my body is kicking my ass for it.

The rain pounding against my bedroom window makes me want to stay in bed all day, but the growling in my stomach lets me know it's time to get up and eat something. The gloomy sky makes it extra hard to get up, but knowing I'll be seeing Viola today gives me strength to get moving.

I make a pot of coffee regardless of how hard it is to lift my arms and sit on the couch while it brews. I've had no appetite, and I know I need to eat before I wither away. Once the coffeemaker beeps, I shuffle to the kitchen and pop two pieces of toast into the toaster.

The smell of that fucking tofu is still lingering in the house, and I'm a little pissed I ate it. Never again.

As soon as the toast pops up, I smear butter and strawberry jelly on top and throw it on a plate. As I'm walking out of the kitchen, the front door opens and slams closed. Viola comes in, drenched, her hair flat and sticking to her forehead, while the rest is up in a messy ponytail. Her jacket and pants are wet. My eyes widen as soon as she looks at me. She's sexy as fuck regardless of how she looks, but today she's in hot mess mode.

"I hate it when it rains! My damn umbrella broke! Gah!" She drops her bag, and it makes a loud thud on the floor.

"Did you feel that?" I joke with her, trying to lighten the mood.

"Feel what?" She stops and looks around.

"I think your bag of books just tripped the Richter scale." I sit at the table, take two bites of toast, and I'm done. I seriously need to get over this bullshit.

She sits in front of me, exhaustion covering her.

I study her face. "Everything okay?"

"I'm having a small freak-out. There are only five more weeks of class left. Finals are coming up. I have to keep up my GPA. I'm not ahead with my reading, and I've been showing up late. Everyone that I'm tutoring thinks I can guarantee them an A when they aren't putting in the work to make that shit happen. I'm concerned about telling Drew about us, and I'm worried about you and–"

"Whoa, whoa, whoa. Princess, don't add me or us to your list of worries. Okay?"

She doesn't look me in the eyes.

"Viola," I say sternly, and she finally looks up at me. The stress is written across her face.

"It's just..." She sighs. "School and graduation. It's a lot to think about. My life afterward. A job. Moving out of the dorms. It's a huge change. School has consumed my life for so long that I'm not sure I know who I am without my books and class, so I'm freaking out just a little bit."

I lean across the table and grab her hand, offering her some comfort. "It's a normal reaction. When I graduated, I didn't know what I would do afterward. I didn't have a plan—just a piece of paper, a shitty job, and average grades. You're *so* smart and have nothing to worry about. Opportunities will fall in your lap when you least expect them. Don't worry about life after school yet. Just be concerned with what's going on *right now*. I'm always going to be here for you, okay?

Not sure if you realize this or not, but I'm not going anywhere. So, if you need to focus on school and yourself, I understand. We can tell Drew closer to graduation, so then you don't have that extra stress. Don't worry about us. Don't worry about me. I've waited over a decade for you, so five weeks is nothing. It will fly by, and when you're walking across that stage with your perfect grade point average, you'll laugh at how you feel right now. Trust me, princess."

She sighs and her shoulders relax slightly. "Thank you."

"And I have the perfect remedy to get rid of that extra stress," I say slyly, taking a drink of coffee, and she smiles for the first time since she opened the front door.

"Actually," she says with a cute little smirk, "I have a surprise for you."

I lick my lips, intrigued by her words. "A surprise?"

She nods her head, stands, and walks to me. Leaning over, she grabs my face and kisses me. It takes everything I have not to bend her over the kitchen table and fuck her right there. My body says no, but my dick says *now*. I stand, meeting her intensity, and she wraps her arms around my neck. I wince, and she pulls away.

"Are you feeling okay?"

"Actually, all the *gymnastics* have caught up to me."

She smiles. "Then my surprise is perfect for you."

Viola takes my hand and leads the way to my bedroom. I already love where this is going.

"Sit here," she demands and pulls the office chair from under my desk. I don't even argue and just follow her directions. She turns on the lamp in the corner of the room and sets her phone on the docking station on my nightstand. She smiles before she presses play. After a second, she flips the light switch. Since it's rainy and gray outside, a warm glow fills the space. I don't know what the song is, and give absolutely no fucks about it until Viola starts slowly moving her hips to the beat of the music.

Her eyes don't leave mine as she slips her jacket off her shoulders and drops it to the floor. One by one, she unbuttons her shirt, turning and teasing me with her perfect little ass in those tight jeans. A few moments pass and she drops her long-sleeved shirt to the floor next to her jacket. If ever I thought Viola had cast a spell on me, it's right now at this very moment, because I can't take my eyes from her.

Slowly, she unbuttons and then unzips her jeans, taking her time as she moves them down her hips and off her legs. She makes sure to bend over, showing me her ass in a black thong that matches the bra that barely covers her beautiful tits.

"*Sweet Jesus,*" I growl, and all she does is smile, taking her wet hair out of that high ponytail and allowing it to cascade around her face. Viola is a vixen, a little sex kitten, who has her fingers hooked at the edge of her panties, but she doesn't remove them. I'm on edge, watching as she spins in circles, showing me that bare ass. She moves closer, rubbing her ass against my dick, but still dancing to the beat of the music.

She rolls her head on her shoulders and stands right in front of me before she places her finger in her mouth and sucks. One bra strap slides off her shoulder, then the other. Moving her hands behind her back, she unhooks the black bra and allows it to fall to the floor. Her breasts are perfect, and her nipples are at full attention. She's standing in only a black thong, with eyes closed, dancing to the slow erotic music—just for me. I swallow hard, and I'm not sure how much longer I can watch. Surprise is an understatement; this was a fucking gift.

The song finally ends, and she opens her eyes, looking at me with a burning desire. She strides toward me and straddles me in the office chair. I grab her face right before our lips crash together. It's as if we're both lost at sea, being pulled and pushed together by the undercurrent of one another, and there's no rescue in sight. Being with Viola is so intense that it's easy to forget about everything. It's just me and her and it's all that matters. She's all that's *ever* mattered. And at this moment, I fucking need her as much as I need air.

VIOLA

The way Travis is slowly kissing me is almost too much for me to handle. I can feel him through his pajama pants and my panties, and it's so hard for me to restrain from pressing against him. My skin is on fire, while his mouth and hands encapsulate my body and soul. I remember dreaming about this when I was a stupid teenager with a crush that almost destroyed me.

Having Travis wrap his arms around me and steal my breath away doesn't seem real, and I keep wondering when I will wake up. But as he grabs my nipple between his teeth, I'm brought back to reality—to the here and now, and being together is more real than it will ever be.

I know where this will lead if we keep going. "You should be resting. No more gymnastics, remember?"

Travis threads his fingers through my hair and holds my face in the palm of his hand. "This isn't the time for logic, princess."

I allow a small smirk to cross my lips. "Why do you think these panties are still on?"

"You're playing with fire," he growls, adjusting himself.

"Well then, I hope I don't get burned," I say, trailing kisses down his body, as I inch his pajama pants down.

My eyes widen as I see how hard he is. He's wearing a shit-eating grin, one that quickly fades when I lick the tip.

"I want to make you feel good," I whisper, looking up at him. His mouth opens, then closes, and for the first time, I'm pretty sure he has no words. I'm taking control.

"Don't you dare move a muscle, or I'll end this," I warn, really wanting him to take his injuries seriously.

"But a good nurse wouldn't allow me to suffer." He smirks.

"What if I said I didn't want to be a good nurse today?" I place him in my mouth and swirl my tongue on his throbbing cock.

"As long as you're a really bad nurse, I'm good with that, too." He closes his eyes, and I focus on my movements while listening to his low groans. I try to take him all in my mouth while increasing my pace. Small moans escape him, and I'm pleased, knowing he's enjoying this as much as I am. I lick his shaft, not rushing, being the best damn nurse I know how to be. I grab him with my hand and place him in my mouth and move in a rhythmic motion, which causes him to tense beneath me.

"Princess," he whispers. "I need to feel you."

I know it's a bad idea because of his injuries, but I need him as much as he needs me. Instead of protesting, I stand. He smiles as he moves my panties to the side with one finger. I push the chair against the desk and straddle him, allowing him to know what he's done to me.

"You're so fucking wet," he says as I guide him in. The way he feels is indescribable, and I shudder as our ends meet. It's like lock and key finally together at once, both useless without the other.

We take it slow, not rushing, not wanting to put extra stress on his body. He nips the skin of my neck with his teeth, and I run my fingers through his hair as I take him—all of him—continuously. The chair squeaks out with angry squeals, and I'm afraid it will collapse if we continue, but it doesn't stop us. His mouth travels to my nipple, and his thumb moves to my clit. As he circles my hard bud, my body begs for relief. It's easy to lose control with him, especially when I'm on the brink of ecstasy.

Moments later, I'm traveling down a path of no return, losing myself in the sensation. Our lips crash together, and he tastes like strawberry jelly and toothpaste. I pant into his mouth, riding the never-ending wave as our bodies rock together. When I bite his bottom lip, Travis' body tenses. His fingers dig into my hips while he fights the impending orgasm that's building, but it's a losing battle. As he comes, Travis wraps his arms around my body and holds me tight, as if he never wants to let me go. We stay in that position for a while, slowly and passionately kissing one another, our eyes speaking words that our lips can't translate. We're frozen in time, and nothing else matters.

"You're beautiful. And I know what you're getting for your birthday, my birthday, and for Christmas."

"What?" I ask as I clean up.

"More lingerie."

"And I know what you're getting, too," I say sweetly.

Travis tilts his head and waits.

"Blow jobs."

Travis throws his arms in the air, like a referee confirming a touchdown. "I'm in! My birthday is every day of the week. I also like them for breakfast, lunch, and dinner. A good girlfriend would agree. And I'll be a wonderful, loving boyfriend and support it."

"Girlfriend?" I joke. I put on my clothes and try to smooth my hair back into a ponytail as the electricity of what we did streams through me.

"That's what you are. So, don't be a bad one, unless you're bad like you were a bad nurse." He winks, not even realizing his words catch me off guard. It's the first time he's said I was his *girlfriend* out loud. I know we agreed to be together, but the title makes it seem official, not a see-where-it-goes kind of thing that I worked up in my mind. Travis King is my *boyfriend*. It doesn't seem real.

Once we're presentable again, I spread my books out on the kitchen table and attempt to study, but I'm finding it hard to concentrate. A text dings on my phone, a notification from the university, saying afternoon classes are cancelled due to a flood warning. I literally do a fist pump.

"What's going on?" Travis asks as he hears my whoop of joy.

"Class is canceled. Saved by the rain! I love rain!"

He leans against the doorframe and gives me a look. "Thirty minutes ago, you said you hated it."

"Well, apparently, I love things that I sometimes hate," I say, not even realizing what I'd just said.

"I love you, too, princess." Travis smiles and takes a sip of his milk. My mouth falls open then I close it and open and close it again, but all he does is laugh.

"You're an asshole," I repeat the same words that he's heard me say a million times over the years. My eyes widen. "No more gymnastics for you!"

"But it's my favorite sport," he jokes, but his delivery is a little off, and I can tell he's not feeling well. It makes me feel guilty.

"Go rest. If you need something, just text me."

He nods and walks down the hallway. I sit at the table and have to force myself to stop thinking about him and us. Hours pass, and I get through my reading list. The rain is actually relaxing when I'm not fighting it. Once I'm finished, I feel great about what I accomplished. Just as I tell myself 'one more chapter,' the doorknob turns, and Drew walks in, smiling like he won the freaking lottery.

"Are you okay?" I stop reading and focus on him.

He's soaked from head to toe, but the goofy smile on his face isn't fading. He doesn't even notice that I'm here early. I guess it all just looks normal to him, but it's totally not.

"What's the matter, I can't be happy?"

I narrow my eyes. "Oh, you can, but you're usually not. You're scaring me."

He takes his boots off at the door then goes straight to his bedroom whistling—yes, whistling—and changes. When he comes back, he's wearing a zombie t-shirt and some basketball shorts. Cop by day, gamer by night, the dude is a chameleon.

"I'm ordering pizza. Cheat day to celebrate." Drew flicks open an app on his phone and seconds later the pizza is ordered.

I raise my eyebrows and shove my books into my bag. "What are we celebrating, exactly?"

"Mia called today. She wants to talk about us getting back together. I think this time it might really work out. Vi, she misses me."

I can't hold back the disappointed look that crosses my face. Drew deserves more than this. And she's played this game with him so many times over the past few years that it's almost sickening. Hearing her name makes my jaw clench because I know my brother is nothing more than her backup plan when she's bored. I just wish he could see it.

He stands and walks to the kitchen, coming back with a beer in hand. Yep, he's way too happy, and I want to be happy for him, but I can't find it within myself to do so.

Am I being hypocritical?

I force out a smile, not wanting to upset him. If this is what he truly wants, I'll find it within my heart to *accept* his decision, and I hope he would do the same thing for me. Accepting is not the same as liking, I remind myself.

He looks at me like I'm crazy. "You've got that strange look on your face again."

Drew isn't an idiot. He's a cop and has a sixth sense for this stuff. But every time someone mentions Mia, I just think, 'yeah, she's a Slytherin.' Hell, she might even be Voldemort, but that's yet to be determined. I close my eyes tight and open them, trying to get a grip.

"You're still here?" Travis says, plopping down in the chair beside me. "You were in such a hurry to leave after you fed me that shitty toast that I didn't think you'd stick around."

I turn and look at him, grateful for his saving grace. He looks more rested and not as exhausted as he did earlier, which makes me want to smile. The plate with the barely eaten toast is still on the table. Drew glances over at it and laughs before he sits on the couch next to me. I have to play this game, whether I want to or not. Just for now, I tell myself.

"Shut up, Travis. You should be glad I scraped the mold off for you."

"At least you're not eating kitty litter sandwiches," Drew says with a big smile. "I swear Vi fed me one when we were kids."

Now I genuinely am laughing. It was Pop Rocks and peanut butter—a secret recipe.

Travis notices how annoyingly happy Drew is, and questions it, just as I had. "What's up with you?"

Drew looks at me, and I know I'm interrupting their dude talk, so I take the cue and walk back to the table. I'm half-tempted to pull my books back out of my bag, but I don't. Instead, I get on my phone and pretend to be searching for something. I'm far enough to be away but close enough to still listen.

"Mia called again. We're going to talk about everything and figure out how to make it work because she said she couldn't get over us."

Glancing over, I notice Travis' reaction doesn't change. "That's great, dude."

At this very moment, I wish I could use *Legilimency* and read his mind, just like Voldemort did to Harry.

A million questions stream through my mind, and it takes everything for me to hold them back. Does Travis approve of this? What's his opinion about her and Drew? I make a mental note to ask him later. It can't only be me who thinks this is a bad idea. And she knows if she keeps running back to Drew, he will never have time to get over her. Ugh. Every day I dislike her a little bit more.

"I might drive up and see her on my next day off. She said she has a lot to discuss with me," Drew says, chugging his beer. "She mentioned a double date with her friend Kasey in a few weeks and asked if you'd like to join us."

I feel my cheeks go pink, and I try to pretend what Drew just said is irrelevant to me.

"No, dude. I'm good. No woman should have to deal with me looking like this."

My heart breaks a little because I know the cuts and bruises bother him. But I do an imaginary victory dance regardless. I clear my throat, letting them know this talk is over, and Drew sits back, still smiling. I shake my head and plop down next to him on the couch. I'm just a little pissed that Drew is trying to hook Travis up, or rather Mia is. I don't know what she's playing at, but she needs to back off, or she might find herself on the other side of the Avada Kedavra killing curse.

I try to ignore Travis, but he's smiling, because he knows Drew got to me.

"Panties still in a knot?" Travis asks nonchalantly.

"Aunt Flo, dude, I'm telling you," Drew says to Travis, pointing directly at me.

"I'm not about to start my period, idiots. Seriously!"

Travis laughs, and Drew joins in. I try to ignore them both.

The pizza comes, and we eat. The rain finally stops, and by 7:00 p.m. I'm yawning like an old lady. I give Drew a side hug before I leave. He was so sprawled out on cloud nine, he didn't even notice I didn't have or do my laundry. Maybe Mia will be the perfect distraction for him.

"Bye, *V*," Travis says with a smirk on his lips. I want to run to him and kiss him goodbye, but instead, I shake my head before I close the door. My heart is beating so fast as I drive home that I have to remind myself to breathe. Mia is trying to get Drew back. Travis is going to tell him about us. My life could easily transition into a soap opera.

When I arrive at my dorm, Ashley is making coffee cup cake in the microwave. Dorm life sucks sometimes. I couldn't help but make a face because it always smells so disgusting because she puts protein powder in there, too.

"I get by with what I can. Oh hey, there's some mail on the counter for you. I picked it up from the office this morning after class." She puts a spoonful of mush in her mouth and smiles.

I drop my books and laugh at how loud it is as the thud echoes from the high ceilings. Nonchalantly, I walk to the counter and start going through the piles of junk mail that are stacked up over break, until I come across a cream-colored envelope with a red seal. The front is addressed to Ms. Viola Fisher with a generic P.O. Box as the return address.

My heart begins to race as I peel the envelope open and read as fast as I can. When I read the words, "You've been selected for an internship with Union International," my heart stops. One of the largest corporations in the United States wants to give me, the book-loving Harry Potter nerd with little to no experience, a chance. Attached to the back of the letter is three pages of paperwork that must be submitted soon. The internship would start two weeks after graduation, and I would be required to move to Boston and live there for six months. I drop the letter on the counter, unsure of how to feel because I'm riding a rollercoaster of emotions. This is another thing to add to my list of worries, which seems to be getting longer by the minute.

Travis was right; opportunities do sometimes come when least expected. I never in a million years imagined that I'd be chosen out of the thousands who apply each year. I submitted an application on a whim, and now, as I stare down at the ivory paper with the precision-printed message, I realize I must make one the hardest decisions of my life. My entire future depends on it.

CHAPTER EIGHT

TRAVIS

Days when Viola is at school and tutoring in the evenings suck ass, and I wish even more I was able to occupy myself with going to the gym or even going into work. Since I'm not able to do either, all that's left are Drew's video games.

I'm not usually much of a gamer, but if I have nothing better to do, it fills the time. He has all the newest ones, including Call of Duty and Madden 17, so I've been switching back and forth between them. After Wednesday's close call with Drew asking about Viola, I knew we had to start being more careful if we were going to postpone telling him. My plan is to get us out of the house finally because God knows I'm going stir crazy being here all damn day, but also because I want to take Viola on our first lunch date.

At exactly 11:15, I hear the front door open and shut and Viola's footsteps against the hardwood floor. Her class ends at 11:00 a.m. and she's always consistent about being on time. It's one of the dorky little quirks I love about her.

"Are you limping?" I ask her as soon as I see her.

"Shut up." Her mouth twitches as she tries to hold her pout. "Leave all your comments to yourself, please."

She's feistier than usual today, and I fucking love it.

"Dammit. I had a really good one, too." I smile as she takes a spot next to me on the couch.

She looks at me and rolls her eyes.

"Rough morning?"

"No, I'm just not getting a lot of sleep these days." She gives me a pointed look.

"Me either, so maybe we should just suffer together and sleep in the same bed."

"Took you less than five minutes this time, huh?" She sighs, taking the game controller from my hand.

"Oh, it would've been less than a minute had you not been limping in here like you'd just ridden a horse." I grin, despite her side glare.

She finally cracks a smile, and my entire body lights up. "You suck at this game, by the way."

I focus my attention on the TV, where she's dominating, while I was just barely going to survive to the next level. "You are a true nerd, through and through."

"A nerd who could kick your ass," she fires back, and I'm tempted to throw that controller out of her hands and bury my face in her neck.

"Let's just see about that," I challenge, grabbing the other controller off the end table. She doesn't play much either, so I'm moderately optimistic that I can beat her.

"You want to wager?" The playful tone of her voice makes me smile. It's the first time all week I've seen her visibly relax without physically wearing her out first.

"Wouldn't it be easier to surrender, instead of going through the humiliation of losing to a cripple?"

She snorts and wiggles her ass to the edge of the sofa. "Don't you dare play the cripple card!" She laughs as I aim and fire at her on the screen. "You had my legs wrapped around your shoulders as you nearly split my body in half, so don't even try it."

The memories flood in and my dick gets hard just thinking about it. While I'm distracted by thoughts of her, she aims and shoots directly at me.

"Ha!" She pumps a fist in the air. "You're so easy."

I rub a hand over the stubble of my jawline and look intently at her. "So, that's how we're going to play, huh? You think a little dirty talk is going to distract me?"

"I think I just proved it, so...*yeah*." The smug expression on her face gives me life, but I won't admit that to her right now. I'll play by her rules if that's how she wants to play the game.

Tossing the remote down on the couch, I bring my fingers down to the bottom of my shirt and lift it over my head. She glances over at me, eyeing the tattoos on my chest and arms, opening her mouth, but doesn't say anything, and then quickly forces her lips into a firm line.

"I'm not the only easy one, princess." I wink, and she scoffs, turning away. I laugh at her denial because I know it's driving her insane.

I finally win a round, and instead of telling me off, she mimics my moves and sets her controller down before lifting her shirt over her head. She's wearing a tiny little camisole, and I can see her hard nipples at attention right under the fabric.

I stay silent, refusing to admit I'm much more interested in sucking on her tits than playing this game. Before starting her turn, she grabs the hair tie from her wrist and pulls her hair up, exposing her neck and chest. *Fucking hell.*

Except she doesn't stop there. Once her hair is tied up, she grabs her controller and drags it down with her to the floor as she lies on her stomach. She bends her knees and perks her ass up as she shuffles her legs back and forth in the air.

So, this is how she wants to play it...*game on, princess.*

However, before my trance is broken, she's managed to blow me up and begins giggling about how her plan to distract me is working. Before she can humiliate me again, I take matters into my hands and lower myself to the floor behind her, locking my knees around her thighs.

"What do you think you're doing?" she asks, looking over her shoulder.

"You didn't really think your evil little plan was going to work, did you?"

"I don't know. You tell me." She wiggles her ass against my thigh, which doesn't help ease the pulsating in my cock.

She's wearing shorts, which gives me an advantage, so I slide my palm up her shorts and cup her ass cheek over her cotton panties. She squeals and I squeeze it again.

"That's cheating!" She tries pushing my hand away, but I barely flinch at her movements. "No touching allowed!"

"I didn't agree to that, princess." I press the pad of my thumb against her pussy and circle the fabric of her panties. "You wanted to play, remember?"

A loud boom echoes from the screen, but I'm no longer interested in the war that's going on. I plan on engaging in a different game.

"Well, I'm not going to play by myself, so pick up your damn controller!" she demands, and I smile at her bossy side.

"I can play one-handed," I smirk, even though she can't see me. I give in and shoot a few rounds, pretending to give a shit about the game in front of us when I'd much rather play with what's inside her shorts instead.

"Stop it!" She swats my hand, laughing as she tries to keep her eyes on the TV. "If I'm going to kick your ass, I want to do it fair and square."

Tossing the controller back onto the sofa, I undo the top button of my jeans and then unzip just as fast. "When have you ever wanted to play fair and square?"

"What are you talking about? I always play fair." The tone in her voice does nothing to convince me, and I can see the corner of her lips tilt up when she glances back at me.

I slide a finger inside her panties and find her already wet and aroused. I know she wants it as badly as I do. The need to have her increases every time I see her, which isn't something I'm used to. I never wanted more with a girl before, but Viola makes me want all the days and nights with her, and even then, it wouldn't be enough.

"Travis…" she warns, but her body shivers against mine, giving her away.

Watching her, I can tell she's distracted and even more so, she likes the distractions. Her fingers are no longer moving along the controller, and her neck has gone weak, falling between her shoulders as I slide my finger inside her.

I can hear her arousal as I slide in and out, building her up until she's almost lost all control. Just before she clamps her pussy around my fingers, I grab my controller off the couch and fire right at her. The echoing of the gunshots whips her head back up as the screen fills with blood. She's dead.

"You asshole!" she screeches, picking the controller back up. "You totally did that on purpose." She looks over her shoulder and pinches her eyes tight.

I suck on my fingers that taste of her and smile. "And you fell for it, princess."

"All right, so it's going to be like that." She turns around, still on her knees. I watch as she drops her hands to my jeans that are already undone. "Looks like you were getting ready for me."

"I'm always ready for you." I flash a sly grin and place my hands on my hips.

"This is what happens when you tell a sex addict to rest and not have any physical activity for six weeks." She rolls her eyes at me as she palms my cock through my shorts.

"You get rebellious behavior?"

"Something like that." She laughs.

She slides her hand inside my shorts and begins stroking my cock. Her eyes stay focused on mine as she rubs the length of my shaft with one hand and circles her palm around the tip. She's working me into a frenzy, and I'm not sure how much longer I can hold back. I want to flip her over, pull her hips up until her perky ass is in the air, and fuck her until we're both stinging with carpet burn.

I lean down and cup her face, pulling her lips to mine as she continues stroking me. My other hand pulls down her camisole and bra until her breast is in my palm. She moans in my mouth, and I squeeze her breast, wanting every item of clothing between us gone.

She fidgets with the button of her jean shorts until she's able to unzip and pull them down to her knees. My hand slides down her back and cups her ass cheek, pulling her flesh against mine. She rubs the length of my cock in between her legs, against the panties that are becoming an annoyance. I need them gone.

My mouth lands on her neck, and I suck just under her ear, feathering kisses all the way down to her collarbone. She hums in response, and I can feel her body heating up.

She wraps a hand around my neck and pulls me down until her lips are pressed to my ear. "I've imagined you fucking me on this couch for years." Her words vibrate against the shell of my ear, and I'm about two seconds away from exploding in her hand.

"Goddammit, you can't say shit like that," I hiss, fighting every urge to bend her ass over the couch like she's begging for. I want more than anything to bury myself inside her, but I know she's still playing some twisted mind game with me.

"And why's that?" She looks up at me, her lips in a pout. "You don't want me anymore?"

"Don't be fucking crazy now," I say, knowing her angle.

"Then what is it?" she asks as she pulls her camisole over her head and tosses it. My dick rises higher to attention as I watch her wrap her arms around her back and unclasp her bra.

I swallow, deciding that I don't care what her angle is anymore; I fucking need her.

"Give me your controller," I say, reaching around her, but she stops me.

"No way." She blocks my hand again. "I'm not surrendering."

I tilt my head at her with a knowing smirk. "So, being a cock tease is your angle?"

"I work with my advantages." She grins, pushing her chest out.

Narrowing my eyes at her, I try to think through my next move. I don't give two shits about the damn video game, but I decide to play her little game. She wants to play hard to get; I'm the fucking champion at that sport.

Without giving her any indication beforehand, I grab her hips and flip her over before she has a chance to stop me. Her chest presses against the carpet, and I lay on top of her, keeping her under my control.

"Dammit, Travis!" She squirms, arching her hips off the ground, but I press my hard body into hers, and she barely budges. "You're such a damn cheater."

I place a kiss to her neck and smile. "You aren't the only one who works with their advantages."

"Muscles or not, I'm still going to kick your ass at this game." She grabs her controller, and I grab mine. She's not going to give up until the game is over.

I straddle her with my knees on both sides of her, carefully adjusting my weight, so I don't crush her, but just enough to make sure she doesn't try any more tricks.

Unable to pay attention, she's completely kicking my ass. Every time I aim fire at her, she sees me first and shoots. She's giggling, and wiggling her ass underneath me, tempting all the willpower I have left.

Knowing very well she's going to beat me before the game is even over, I decide I'd much rather win at our other little game. I set my controller aside and slide my shorts all the way down. Her cotton panties are next. Her curvy ass is perfection, and I slap it once before sliding a finger back inside her.

She stays completely silent, not giving anything away. I can tell she's trying to fight it, but in about ten seconds, she won't be able to fight anything.

As hard as it is, she's trying to focus on the video game, pretending she's not affected by me at all, but it's a lost cause. I'm about to make her forget her name. I press the tip of my cock against her ass. She arches her hips just enough so I can spread her cheeks and slide inside her.

I hear her breath hitch as she slows her movements on the game controller. She arches her hips again, letting me sink even deeper. Her pussy clamps around me, and I waste no time forming a rhythm. She finally drops that damn controller, so I take full advantage, grabbing mine just in time to fire shots at her while she's otherwise occupied.

With her cheek pressed against the carpet, she murmurs, "You dirty asshole."

I smile and toss the controller, wrapping a hand around her throat and whispering in her ear, "What did I say about playing games with the king, princess?" I drag the tip of my tongue along her ear and down her neck. "I'm about to teach you a royal lesson."

VIOLA

I forgot what it was like to be in a new relationship with the all-consuming, desperate to be near one another, sex 24/7 feeling.

In almost every romance novel I've read, the couple goes through a cycle of nonstop sex while waiting to get to know each other after the fact. I'm not opposed to the nonstop sex one bit, but I've known Travis for the last ten years. I already know him and trust him with every beat of my heart. I've had my doubts since this whole thing began, but every single day he proves me wrong, and I fall deeper and deeper.

And I never want that feeling to go away. Ever.

But what weighs on my mind is finally telling Drew about us, and what's going to happen after graduation. I'm a worrier by nature, so it's not easy to relax about things that bother me, but I get lost every time Travis and I are together. My mind blocks out the negative, and my body begs for his touch.

It never feels like enough.

Once my hands are blotchy and stinging from carpet burn, Travis and I lay tangled together on the floor. He kept me bent over, rocking back and forth inside me as I clenched my fingers underneath me. He wrapped an arm around my waist and rubbed my clit until I could no longer take it. His other hand grabbed my breast as I screamed out his name and he came inside me.

"I wonder if cum stains carpet."

He chuckles. "I was just about to ask what you were thinking about, but maybe I don't want to know."

I playfully pat a hand over his flawless abs. "It's a valid concern."

"Oh, definitely." I hear his condescending tone and know he thinks I'm being crazy.

"I'm going to Google it," I say, trying to sit up, but he pulls me back down.

"You are seriously the biggest nerd." He wraps his arm around me again and kisses the top of my nose. "I'll take care of it, okay? I think I have a little more experience in that area than you."

I roll my eyes at him and sigh. "Fine."

We lay in silence for a short moment, until my stomach begins growling and I realize I haven't eaten since before class this morning.

"That's it," he says, pulling us both up. "You need fuel."

"I can make something," I offer, reaching for my bra and shirt. "I can make a grilled cheese and soup if you want."

He grabs my hand and places a sweet kiss on it. "No. Not today, princess."

"Oh?" I raise my brows. "Are you going to cook for me then?"

"Even better." He places another quick kiss. "Today, I'm taking you out. Get dressed."

"Wait," I say, following his lead and standing up. "Like *out*, out?"

"Yeah. You're my girl, and I want to take you out for lunch. You okay with that?" His lips curve into a devilish grin, knowing exactly what his words do to me.

I pinch my lips, fighting the urge to plaster a big, cheesy grin over my face. Travis doesn't do dates—ever. Even in high school, his hookups never got the royal treatment that I know he's kept exclusively for me.

"Okay." I smile.

We both redress and clean ourselves back up. My hair looks like it went through the dryer and my makeup is smudged all the way down to my neck. I watch as Travis splashes water over his face and gargles with some mouthwash. We both stand in the bathroom, getting ready like we're some old couple that's been sharing a bathroom for fifty years. It's nice. Comforting.

He winces as he pulls his shirt back on, and that's when I notice the bruise on his chest is still dark.

"It looks pretty dark still," I say, facing him so I can analyze it better.

"It doesn't hurt, princess," he answers as if he's reading my mind. "Just a little sore when I raise my arms up, but other than that, it's manageable."

"Are you taking the pain meds?"

"Only at night, but I don't plan on refilling them either. I have a follow-up appointment next week, and they'll probably give me something that isn't so strong if I need it."

"You were lucky," I say, rubbing a hand over the fabric of the shirt. "Probably it was all those bulky muscles that protected you from further internal injuries."

"You say that like it's a bad thing."

I smile up at him. "It's not. Just that they could crush me in a second, so I'm sure they acted like a little extra padding during the accident."

"It's possible. I'm sure if I were some scrawny runt, I would've snapped in half."

"I know that feeling," I deadpan, hiding a knowing smirk.

He leans down and kisses me softly. "Sorry about that."

"I'm sure." I smile again, and I feel like my cheeks are going to swell from all the damn smiling I've been doing this week. "All right, King. Feed your woman."

"Lead the way, my lady," he says, following me down the hall. Since Travis' car was totaled, and he hasn't bothered to rent one since he's laid up, we have to take mine.

"Let me drive," he says as we walk out to my car, holding his hand out.

I give him a look, pulling the keys back out of his reach. "I don't know that I should trust you with Tatum."

"Tatum? You named your car *Tatum*?"

I put my hands on my hips and narrow my eyes at him. "Yes, Channing Tatum. Do you have a problem with that?"

"Depends. Do you have a name for all your favorite things?" he asks as we continue walking.

I roll my eyes, knowing where he's going with this. "Let me guess. You think all girls name their tits Mary-Kate and Ashley."

"I was going to say shoes, but if you name your tits, we have to talk about this."

I throw him my keys and walk to the passenger side. "Here you go, Justin Timberlake. Don't crash it." I flash a fake smile his way just to push his buttons even more.

As we drive to the restaurant, Travis' phone rings and I see Drew's name flash across it before he picks it up. He turns the music down and answers it after the second ring.

"Hey, man. What's up?"

They chat for a minute before he glances over and looks at me. I can't tell what they're talking about, but it gives me a funny feeling.

"Okay, sounds good. So, the both of you would go then?" he asks, glancing over at me again, and this time I furrow my brows in confusion. What the hell could he be talking about?

"Nah, I'll be fine. Feeling good as new already." They exchanged once again before he says goodbye and hangs up.

"Well?" I ask, anxious to know what Drew said.

"Apparently, you two are heading home this weekend."

"*What?* Why?" This is news to me.

"Your mom called Drew and said she wanted the both of you to come tomorrow and stay the night."

"What for?" I haven't slept in the same house as my mother in almost four years. I love her, but we don't have much in common anymore.

"I'm not really sure. He didn't know specifics." He looks over at me, concern written in his expression as he tries to read mine.

"Why don't you ask Drew if you can tag along? Tell him you'll be bored or something." I *really* don't want to go without him.

"You just want me as your secret sex toy, don't you?" He grins, and I want to smack that smile right off his cocky face.

"Now I remember why I hated you so much," I tease. I check my phone for any messages from my mom or Drew, and there are none. *Why the hell didn't she call me? Why didn't he?*

"Hate is really the sister of love," he retorts, flashing a mocking grin.

"Hate is also the cousin of murder," I fire back. His head falls back with laughter as he shakes his head at me. "Good to know sex doesn't filter your sense of humor."

"No, just my tolerance for assholes."

He presses a hand to his chest. "Ow. That one hurt."

I roll my eyes and smile.

We finally arrive at a charming little café for lunch. I'm so hungry that I warn Travis that I might order the entire menu. He grabs my hand as we walk inside, and for the first time, it feels like Travis and I are a real couple, outing ourselves to the world and going on a date. Although it's just lunch, it's a huge step for us.

Now all we have to do is tell the person closest to us both and hope he doesn't want to kill us together.

After lunch and dropping Travis off at the house, I drive back to school and call Drew on my way. I need to know what the hell is going on or it's going to eat at me the rest of the night.

"Hey, I was just going to call you," he answers.

"Oh? What about?" He can't know that Travis already told me, so I play dumb.

"Mom wants us to come this weekend and stay overnight. I told her we'd be there for lunch tomorrow, so pack a bag, and I'll come pick you up around ten."

"Don't I get a choice?" I add. "Did she say what the hell for?"

"No, nothing specific. And no, if I have to suffer, so do you."

I groan. Would it make me sound like a brat if I didn't want to go? But I don't want to disappoint my mom, so reluctantly I agree.

After hanging up, I head to class and immediately after, I head back to my dorm and pack an overnight bag. I make sure to bring a few extra books just in case and store them in my favorite Book Beau sleeves. I text Travis before crawling into bed, and tell him how much I'll miss him. I also make sure to remind him of the leftover Chinese food in the fridge that Drew brought home, so he doesn't go hungry.

And of course, being the cocky bastard that he is, responds with a smartass comment.

T: **Don't forget to talk shit about me all weekend, otherwise Drew might get suspicious.**

V: **Shouldn't be too hard. Been doing it for the past ten years :)**

T: **So, you have lots of practice then. But maybe just slip in a little mention about how big you think my dick is.**

V: **Not as big as your ego apparently!**

T: **You can't help but love both qualities about me though ;)**

I laugh to myself, knowing he's right about that.

I text him one last goodnight text before grabbing my Kindle and falling asleep.

I hear noises coming from outside my door, which means my roommates are up and have absolutely no consideration for anyone else in the house. Rolling over, I grab my phone and see a collection of text messages from Travis.

Top 5 reasons you have the best boyfriend in the world…

#1. You'll always look good on my arm (my very muscular arm, of course).

#2. I'll always let you eat the last French fry off my plate even if you dip them in mayo and it's the grossest thing ever.

I chuckle at the second one, remembering when we were kids that he always shared his fries with me because I always ran out before everyone else.

#3. I'll always let you be the first to count to 5 — you're welcome.

#4. Even though I'd never admit it publicly, I'll watch your cheesy chick flicks with you (mostly because I hope it ends with you underneath me).

I laugh at the memory of us watching *Bridget Jones' Diary*.

#5. I'll eat your pussy for breakfast, lunch, or dinner (actually all 3 because I'm a greedy bastard).

By his last text, I'm blushing like hell and giggling all at the same time. It still doesn't feel real. I decide to return the favor and text him back before I have to get ready and leave.

Top 5 reasons you have the best girlfriend in the world...

#1-5. She puts up with your shit.

Bonus reason: Mary-Kate and Ashley (you're welcome).

I smile proudly and finally get up to take a shower. Once I'm dressed and my hair is brushed, I head out to the kitchen where my roommates are all hovering over the coffeepot as if it's going to spew out million dollar bills at any moment.

"Who is this stranger?" Ashley asks with a smile.

"I think she lives here," Kate adds.

"We haven't seen you in years," Kayla exclaims in an overly-dramatic tone.

I roll my eyes as I drop my bag on top of the table.

"You're all drama queens," I fire back. "And for the record, I do live here, in between studying and trying to get some sleep."

"And getting laid," Kayla quips. Her light brown hair is twisted up into a messy bun, and her makeup is still on from the night before. We haven't hung out a lot this semester, but we've known each other for the past couple of years. She's usually the quiet one, too, so the fact that she's the one to mention that makes me suspicious of what they're all thinking.

I furrow my brows, acting confused. "I don't know what you're talking about." I pretend to look for something in my bag, but I know they can see right through me.

"You have it written all over you, girlfriend," Ashley speaks up. "You're gone for lunch almost every day; you're distracted when you actually are here, or rather, when you aren't locked up in your room, and you haven't been able to wipe that stupid giddy smile off your face for the past week."

"So, that automatically means I'm getting laid?"

"Yes," they all say in unison, and I blush, because dammit, I was trying so hard not to be *that* girl.

"Well, I'm pleading the fifth." I grab my bag and toss it over my shoulder. "I'm heading home for the weekend, though, so that means I won't be back until tomorrow."

"Did someone die?" Kate's question catches me off guard.

"No, why?"

"I can't remember the last time you went home for the weekend."

I shrug, knowing she's right, but not wanting to get into the details of it.

"Drew and I are just going for a short visit; that's all."

"Oh, you're going with your brother?" Kayla's voice suddenly increases an octave. Seriously? Why do all my friends want inside Drew's pants?

"Yes, and unfortunately, he's going to torture me with all the details of him and his lame girlfriend." I wish he wouldn't.

"He's still dating that same girl he met last summer?" she asks.

I shrug lightly, not sure what's going on between them at the moment. "On and off, so I'm not certain, but I know Drew's crazy about her." *God only knows why.*

"Well, tell him hi for me!"

"Uh, sure!" I slide my shoes on and head toward the door, waving to the rest of them. "Bye, guys!"

I see a text from Drew filter in and I quickly read it.

D: **Be there in 5. Your ass better be ready.**

I roll my eyes and scoff at his assumption that I wouldn't be.

V: **I've been waiting for over a half an hour. Your ass better have Starbucks and a blueberry muffin.**

I might've bent the truth a bit, but he doesn't have to know that. I see Travis messaged me back as well.

T: **To be fair to Mary-Kate and Ashley, I think they should be #1-5 on your list. They do work really hard on being firm, perky, and always make sure their nipples are at attention when I'm around. Not to mention, they have this**

superpower way of communicating to my dick anytime they're looking for some extra attention. I think that's a legit skill.

V: **You're ridiculous. P.S. Don't act so surprised at all my marvelous talents. My pussy has magical powers, too.**

T: **Wonderful. Now I'm hard.**

I laugh just thinking about how he probably really is hard.

V: **Told you. Magical powers.**

T: **Well if you want some REAL dick pics this weekend, just let me know :)**

Smiling, I respond.

V: **Why? You know a good porn site?**

T: **Don't tempt me, princess…**

V: **And what fun would that be?**

Drew pulls up in his jacked-up truck just as I hit send, so I stuff my phone into my pocket.

"About time!" I shout through the window. "I could've been kidnapped out here, I've been waiting so long."

"Shut up and come get your coffee, smartass."

"Someone's in a good mood this morning," I tease, throwing my bag in the back and hopping in the passenger seat.

"I'm always in a good mood; what are you talking about?"

I snort and snap my buckle in place. "Well, are you ready to get this over with?"

"I'd rather cut my right testicle off." He groans, pulling out of the parking lot.

"Well, I know a few friends of mine would be disappointed, so maybe leave them attached for now."

He finally breaks a smile and laughs. "Deal."

CHAPTER NINE

TRAVIS

I'm actually starting to enjoy waking up to no alarm. As hard as it is, I try not to text Viola while she's with Drew. The less distracted she is, the better, because her body gives her away, and we can't be having that. And the fact that Drew is around and Viola doesn't lock her phone ever makes it a little dangerous.

My cell vibrates in my pocket, and I pull it out and see my mother's picture flash across the screen. Quickly, I answer.

"I was thinking about driving over today to visit you. Want to go out for lunch?"

"Yeah, Mom, sure. I'd love to see you." I look around at the mini-disaster the house is in and can't help but glance at the spot where Viola and I christened the floor. It was a first for me, too.

An hour later, I decide to get dressed. I'm sure the whole Justin Bieber wife beater and baggy jogging pants look with messy ass hair wouldn't be acceptable. I at least have to try to look presentable for my mother.

When I hear a car door shut, I check the peephole. Before she can knock, I open the door and pull her into a hug.

"Oh, son! Your face."

I smile. "You should see the other guy."

"I was worried about you. I stopped by the hospital."

"I know, I know. I'm fine."

I lock up the house, and then we drive to a deli across town that she loves. Apparently, they serve the best chicken salad in all of California, or so she says. Once we order, I fill her in on everything that's been going on since the accident.

"So, your car?" She takes a sip of water.

"Totaled." I haven't thought about it too much. Next week I'll have to start taking care of business. That car was the first expensive thing I bought myself after I started working at Crawford Marketing.

"I know how long you saved for it," she says, looking a little sad.

"Full coverage is amazing. I'll get another one. But with heated seats and darker tint." I laugh, trying to lighten the mood.

"How's the job?" She's asking the usual questions to fill time.

After our food arrives, she takes a bite of her sandwich. I pick at my salad, but I'm not hungry, as usual.

"I'm waiting to be cleared to go back to work. I have a follow-up appointment next week."

"They still giving you a hard time?"

I give her a look that tells her everything she wants to know.

She shakes her head. "Remember when you talked about starting your own business? That was your dream for so long, Travis."

My mind temporarily wanders. "Yeah, I do."

"Have you given it any more thought?"

"Sometimes. But only when I'm having a super shitty day at work."

She gives me a look once the curse word leaves my mouth.

"Sorry, but you know what I mean, Mom. They can be so...*corporate*."

We sit in silence for a moment. "So, what's holding you back?"

I haven't thought about it in a while. It just doesn't seem feasible, considering I have a great job that pays me well. Most people in my class would have died to land the job I did so soon after graduation.

Over a thousand people applied for my position. I was the literal needle in the haystack. But I would be lying if I said I haven't thought about it. Sometimes I look at the people that have been there for over thirty years and pray that I'm not looking into the future. That thought is fucking frightening.

"The risk," I say after thinking about it a little longer.

Mom laughs. Her whole face lights up, and I realize how much I've missed her. "And we both know you're a risk taker. So, what's the real reason?"

"Start-up costs, I guess. I wouldn't know where to begin, and it seems like a lot of work. What if I fail?"

"And that's exactly how dreams die. Funding isn't an issue, okay? I've got some money put aside that I would be happy to loan you. And I know how much you save. Tell me this, have you ever failed at anything that you've really wanted in life?"

I'm not sure how we got on this subject. "Mom, I could never take your money. You're supposed to use that to get away."

The laugh lines along with the stress that she's endured over the years are on her face. My mother is my hero. She's stronger than anyone I've ever met, and my heart constantly breaks for her. But she won't leave. As much as I beg, she won't. I've offered to pay for an apartment for her. I've tried everything over the years. But she's just as stubborn as I am. Noticing my reaction and sadness, she gives me a sweet smile.

"Everything is okay. Since your dad's been sick, things have changed."

I take a drink of water. He's been sick for a while now. Lots of testing to try to figure out what the issue is, but I don't want to talk about him, and she knows that.

"He's not doing well, honey. Last week, we received his test results. He has a pretty aggressive form of cancer." Her voice drops low, almost to a whisper.

It's the first time I've heard this, and for a moment it catches me off guard. Cancer? I don't even have the words to explain how this makes me feel. This is why she wanted to have lunch because a conversation like this isn't one you have over the phone. All the pieces of the puzzle begin to fit together.

"I don't care." I know I'm being harsh and stubborn.

Knowing better, she gives me a look. Though he's not my favorite person in the world, I would never wish cancer on him.

"You're more compassionate than that. And whether you want to admit it or not, your father is a part of you. When he's gone, I don't want you to regret not seeing him."

"I left home for a reason." My body tenses and my responses are short. I just want to change the subject while I process it all.

"I know, I know. I'm sorry. I'm just worried about you and him, and it's a lot for me. I don't want you to regret anything in your life. There's a lot of things I wish I would have done differently and didn't. I don't want the same for you. Don't allow your internal anger to stop you from seeing your father while he's still alive. If any man on this earth has regrets, it's him. He knows what he's done." A single tear streams down her cheek. She wipes it with her napkin then recomposes herself. My mother is practically unbreakable.

I grab her hand across the table. "Mom."

She looks up at me, and I squeeze her hand just a little harder. "I'm sorry. I'm always here for you."

"You're my rock, Travis. Always so strong and brave. I love you."

"I love you too, mom."

We leave the restaurant and listen to oldies on the radio on the way back to the house. My phone dings and I smile when I see Viola's name.

V: **Please save me. Drew is singing Britney Spears. This is the longest, most torturous ride home ever.**

I smile as I type out a response.

T: **Well, I'm a SLAVE FOR YOU, baby, even though you're TOXIC, I was BORN TO MAKE YOU HAPPY.**

V: **YOU DRIVE ME CRAZY!**

T: **I'M NOT A GIRL, NOT YET A WOMAN!**

V: **That actually makes a lot more sense now.**

T: **Don't get cocky.**

I chuckle at our Britney Spears references and glance back up when Mom pulls into the driveway, and I reach over and give her a hug.

"Tell Drew and Viola I said hello."

"I will."

"Take care of that girl, Travis."

"Huh?" I'm confused.

"Viola. I know you two are seeing each other."

I give her a look. There's no way she could know this. Or could she?

"Mother's intuition. Mothers always know."

I smile, not denying it, and get out of the car. I stand in the driveway with my arms across my chest, and as she backs out of the driveway, I wave. Mom thinks she's sly, but someone she knows must have seen us together when we had lunch. I try to think back to that moment, but all I can remember is Viola's face.

I plop down on the couch, trying to focus. My father has *cancer*. It's a lot to take in, and so unexpected. Guilt sweeps over me for reacting the way I did, and I try not to get wrapped up in the thought of it. Next week, I'll call Mom and ask more questions. I'll be there for her. I have to.

Once the afternoon lag kicks in, I make some coffee and sit on the couch and mindlessly flip through channels. I lean back and prop up my feet. Before I fall asleep, my phone vibrates in my pocket. I pull it out and swipe it open.

It's a text message from...Mia.

M: **Travis? Is this still your number?**

I'm half tempted not to reply or say no. But a simple confirmation from Drew would ruin that.

T: **What's up?**

I'm not interested in what she has to say, and I'm a little pissed that she has the audacity to text me.

M: **Please don't tell Drew what happened.**

I read the text over and over again and don't realize I'm clenching my jaw until I hear my teeth grinding against each other.

T: **Nothing happened.**

M: **Good. I'm glad we're on the same page then.**

Her text catches me off guard. Same page? No, we're fucking not. We're not even reading out of the same book.

T: **What are you playing at? This isn't a fucking game, Mia.**

She instantly texts back.

M: **;)**

I'm half-tempted to throw my phone across the room, but the only person that would affect is me. My anger is seeping out, just like my father's had so many times over the years. Control. I need to find it—fast.

Instead of texting her back and saying exactly what I think about her, I take the higher road and ignore it. She's being a bitch. She's acting out. And as soon as I find the right time to speak to Drew, I'm going to tell him exactly what happened the night of the accident, whether he wants to hear it or not, because he deserves to know.

VIOLA

There was no legit reason for Drew and me to visit Mom this weekend. She just wanted to see her kids and mentioned the possibility of moving closer to the beach. There was no emergency, no death, no wedding, or birth announcement. It was Mom being quirky, like always. I swear if Phoebe on *Friends* were an actual person, she would be my mother. On the way over, Drew and I made up so many different scenarios that we began taking bets on why we were summoned. Needless to say, I won ten dollars that I will gladly be cashing in.

Sunday morning, I laid in bed for a long time before going into the living room. I could hear Larry and Drew talking about football, and I'd rather not. As soon as I woke, it's like Travis knew and texted me.

T: **I need you to hurry home.**

V: **Got an itch that needs scratching?**

I laugh, thinking about where we were and where we're at now.

T: **Something like that. And we need to talk.**

I don't type for a while. What does that mean, exactly?

V: **Well, mister, that sounds pretty serious.**

T: **By talk, I mean, balls deep inside you.**

I laugh.

V: **Well don't hold back AT ALL.**

T: **Did you expect anything less? ;)**

V: **Actually, no.**

Every day I'm awake, I feel like I'm living a dream. At breakfast on Sunday, I couldn't stop smiling.

"I love seeing my children so happy," Mom mentions after we eat. Once we help clean up, she hugs us both goodbye. "You both must be in love," she jokes.

My cheeks go pink, and I hurry to grab my bag before she notices, but I'm not quick enough. I make eye contact with her, and my deepest, darkest secrets are written across my face. She glances over at Drew, then back at me, before her smile widens. Being the man he is, he's completely oblivious to the fact that Mom just called me out.

"Let them leave," Larry says with a big smile. He reminds me of a big lumberjack, especially when he wears those plaid button-up shirts—his everyday wardrobe. Even he knows that if we don't rush out the door right at this moment, she'll keep us until after lunch. That's how she is; we have to escape while we can.

"Fine," she says, patting him on his stomach as he wraps his arm around her.

"I love you two. Be careful. Tell Travis I said hello," Mom says to Drew. I don't dare look at her, at the mention of his name.

"I'll tell him." Drew swings his bag over his shoulder, and we walk out to the truck.

"Mom's being weird, too," he says. "What's with you girls these days?"

She knows. Fuck. She knows too much.

"I didn't think she was being weird." I throw my bag in the backseat of his truck. It's so tall that I struggle to climb inside. This is why I wanted to take my car.

"All this talk about love. It kind of makes me sick. Oh, and the way she kisses Larry. Oh, my God! At least when I visit Dad, I don't have to watch him be with someone else."

Drew is rambling, and I'm okay with it. I feel kind of guilty that we didn't visit Dad while we were home, but Drew has to go into work today, and we need to get back.

Halfway through the middle of Drew's ridiculous playlist, a text rings out, and it's Courtney.

C: **WHERE ARE YOU? SERIOUSLY!**

I lean against the door and snap a picture of Drew driving. He's wearing a baseball cap and a shirt that's too small, which I teased him about this morning. His tattooed biceps are busting out from under the sleeve. She's going to like this too much.

OH. MY. FUCKING. GOD.

OVARIES EXPLODING!!!!!!!!!!!

I can't stop laughing. I interrupt him as he continues talking about work.

"Hey. Can you say hi to Courtney real quick?"

I hurry and press record on my phone to capture the whole thing. At first, Drew acts all shy and gives a sly little smile, but I know better. He's working the camera right now.

"Hey, Courtney." He winks at the end.

I turn the camera on myself and give her the evil eye before I stop recording and send it over. "She might actually die."

"Why?" He glances over at me completely confused. He really has no idea the affect he has on women, especially her.

"No reason. She mentioned something about you and handcuffs, and well it's gross and kind of makes me sick."

He bursts out laughing. "The cop fantasy? *Really*?"

"Oh, you're aware of it then?" I say, waiting for my phone to detonate with texts from her.

"Don't all women dream about that?"

"No. Definitely not. Gross. I think you ruined that one for me."

C: **Can you have him take his shirt off too?**

I scoff. Drew looks over at me as I type a message back to her quick.

V: **OMG! Give you an inch and then you want my brother naked.**

C: **I wish I had an inch of him. And hey, you started it!! Give him my address. I'll get him out of your hair.**

V: **YOU'RE RIDICULOUS!**

"So, what did she say?" Drew asks, and I think he genuinely wants to know.

"Trust me when I say you're better off *not* knowing." I leave it at that. Because ew.

"Come on; I want to know."

I shake my head, and he reaches over to grab my phone. I go into a panic as he reads Courtney's text message that is thankfully still on the screen and I rip it out of his hand. Note to self: Always lock cell phone.

"Holy shit! Your friend's a freak!"

"Who will seriously murder me if she ever finds out you read that."

On cue, I get another text message, and it's from Travis. I open it up and see a picture of a dick. His dick. Hard. Longing. Waiting. The words on the bottom say 'For Mary-Kate and Ashley.'

I instantly blush and fumble to password protect my phone, not even able to reply back to him. Courtney's text messages go off like crazy, and I sit there frozen, trying to ignore them both. Travis is a dead man the next time I see him. But it's Drew's words that pull me back to reality.

"Have you seen a woman at the house by any chance?"

My face scrunches and I try to process this odd question. "What?"

"I just have this suspicion that Travis is seeing someone. Wondering if you've seen her around between classes."

My heart is hammering, and my throat goes dry. "Nope."

"Hmm," he says, not paying attention to my anxiety. Thankfully.

"I'm going to find out who it is." Drew takes the exit toward the campus. He has that detective look on his face while he looks out toward the road. It's scaring the shit out of me.

"Probably some cum-drunk slut," I add.

"No. No. This seems different. I can't put my finger on it yet. Shit, what was that girl's name that he really liked?"

"I have no clue," I say, utterly unamused. I wish the conversation would end. Over the years, there were probably tons of girls he liked. And I don't want to talk about it.

"Yeah, the one he joked about marrying before she cheated on him. Do you remember her? It's the only one that lasted more than a few days."

Silence.

"He just seems happy, like he was when he was with her before she became a raging bitch. But that was years ago. It's going to bother me until I think of her name."

My cheeks heat, but I continue staring out the window. I don't know this story, and while I want to ask questions, I don't want it to seem out of place. It must have been before I moved closer or started hanging around them again. Because I have no recollection of this story. Instead of getting tied up in it, I snap into my Travis-King-is-an-asshole mode and allow the words to flow out.

"It's probably the pain meds that are making him seem so happy. And honestly, I don't give two shits about Travis King, okay?" It kind of hurts to say that. I've said those words so many times over the years, and it seemed natural, but right now it seems awkward and foreign.

"All right. Jesus Christ. You don't have to bite my head off. Sorry for bringing it up."

By the time we pull up to my dorm, my mind is running so fast that I'm at a loss for words. I didn't know Travis even joked about marriage with someone or that it was that serious. Or that he, of all people, had been cheated on. I thought his relationships were just wham-bam-thank-you-ma'am one-night stands, but maybe my perception over the years was distorted by jealousy.

"Drew." I turn to him before opening the door.

"Yes?"

I know he's in a rush, but I have to tell him about Boston today. "I..."

"Vi, I'm in a hurry. I can't be late to the station."

"I was offered an internship in Boston at Union International."

His face lights up, and I can tell he's excited for me. "Viola! That's amazing! I'm so happy for you, sis." He leans over and gives me a big hug. "So when are you leaving and all of that?"

"I have to accept it first, but two weeks after graduation."

"You have to accept it. There's no question about it. And that's SOON. Does Mom know?"

I shake my head. "You're the only person I've told so far."

"I'm proud of you. Now get out, Bill Gates. I've got a city to save."

"Is this where I cue in the Superman music?" I grab my bag from the back and hop down. "Thanks, Drew."

"Bye, Vi. I'm happy for you. Congratulations."

Sometimes Drew can be a douche, but to know that he's supportive of this makes it a little easier to handle. I've been going back and forth with it for the past forty-eight hours, and I have to tell Travis. I look up at the dark clouds rolling over the horizon, and I pray that I'm not making one of the biggest mistakes of my life.

CHAPTER TEN

TRAVIS

Drew comes home, changes into his uniform, and is out the door in all of ten minutes. The dude is like fucking Batman. One minute he's in regular clothes, the next he has a gun strapped to his side, ready to fight crime.

Just like clockwork, Viola texts me.

V: **You know what I could go for right about now?**

T: **A piece of King cake?**

V: **Ha! Some coffee. Want to join me?**

T: **Did you really have to ask?**

I'm smiling, which seems to happen a lot when I'm thinking about, talking to, or around her.

V: **I'll be there in 5.**

On time, Viola pulls into the driveway but doesn't get out. Instead, she honks. I can't help but laugh at the pathetic horn on the Prius. It's like a cartoon car with a cute little *meep-meep* sound.

"You need a Mustang or something. One that roars when you honk."

She gasps and rubs the steering wheel while I buckle. "Don't listen to him, Tatum. He's just jealous because you've got the Magic Mike moves and he doesn't."

"Magic Mike? Ha. I've got the Travis King moves, which trumps any of that lame shit."

She blushes as I run my hand up my shirt, revealing my stomach. Once she glances down, I lift an eyebrow and laugh. "You're too easy, princess."

"Ugh. Why do you keep doing that?"

While she drives, I place my hand on her thigh. "So, I had lunch with my mother yesterday."

"Really? That's great." She grabs my hand.

"She told me my father has cancer."

Once she pulls into the parking lot and puts it in park, she turns her whole body and searches my face, trying to read me. "Are you okay?"

Since I heard the news, I've been stuck in limbo about it. I'm not sure if I'm sad or not, and it's a strange feeling. I can't really explain it. "I'm okay."

Viola leans over and gives me a hug. With her arms wrapped around my neck, I can feel the love pouring out of her. "I'm sorry," she whispers.

"It's going to be okay. So how 'bout that coffee? They have venti mocha grande chocolate shit here?"

"It's a venti white chocolate mocha with an extra shot, occasionally made with soy. And if we go in there spouting off that lingo, they may kick us out and ban us for life. They are pretty much anti-establishment." She lifts both eyebrows and puckers her lips with a hard head nod.

"I'll take your word for it."

Before I open my door, she glances over at me. "Do you want to just get it to go?"

"Embarrassed to be out with me, princess?" I'm fucking with her, and she notices.

"I want to be alone with you while I can."

Dammit, she's so beautiful. I don't even argue with her about it.

"Only if I can drive." I shoot her a wink, and she doesn't protest. I'm not sure if I should be driving, but since I'm not on any pain medication, I don't see an issue with it. I know I haven't been cleared yet, but when have I ever followed the rules?

We order our coffees, and I drive past the college, turning down a few side streets until we arrive at this little park I found my senior year. Never being one for the library, I used to come out here and study. When she sees people walking their dogs and children playing, her eyes widen. It's a happening place.

"Talk about a diamond in the rough! This park is awesome."

We get out of the car, and I take her hand and lead her across the grass to a picnic table under a tree. The sun is high in the sky, but dark clouds tumble in. It looks like it could start raining at any moment, but we continue toward the low-hanging branches.

I sit next to her, with our backs pressed against the tabletop, and we watch the people in the park.

"I have something to tell you," I whisper into her neck. I love the way her skin smells like fresh spring flowers.

A soft moan escapes her. "Hmmm?"

I open my contacts list and hand her my phone. "I deleted all the hoes."

Viola bursts out laughing and looks at me like I've lost my mind. Maybe I have.

"Why?" She gasps.

"Because you're the only hoe I want." I reach over and tickle her.

"I'm not a hoe." She swats at me, fighting back her laughter. She tries to tickle me back but sucks at it.

"You're my hoe." I interlock my fingers with hers as she leans over and kisses me.

"You're so damn romantic."

"I try." I smile before I take a sip of my coffee.

"Oh, I owe you an ass kicking for that picture." She narrows her eyes at me. "Drew almost saw it, idiot!"

"Shit. I'll allow you to spank me if you want," I quip.

She glares at me. "He's onto us. Like for real onto us. He asked me if I had seen a girl around the house due to the way you're acting. So get your shit together, King!"

"What, seriously?" Now I'm confused. Drew has never cared about my sexcapades.

"Yeah, he mentioned you were acting the same way you did when you were dating some chick, the one you joked about marrying."

My body stiffens, and I swallow hard. She notices my reluctance and turns and looks at me, waiting for me to explain.

"Viola, that was a long time ago, when we first got the house. I was never going to marry anyone. I was nineteen and horny, and she was a cheater. That's ridiculous." And the truth.

"Good to know the only thing that's changed is your age." She smirks.

I offer a shrug.

"Anyway, he's going all Sherlock Holmes on us. He said he would find out who it was and you know how he gets. I'm hoping Mia derails him."

Mia. Funny how she keeps popping up in conversations.

"Not good." As soon as the words leave my mouth, a bolt of lightning strikes out. Viola jumps, nearly spilling her coffee on herself, which causes me to laugh. Without warning, rain pelts from the sky like speeding bullets and it hurts like hell. We stand, leaving our coffees behind and Viola runs across the grass with everyone else.

"I hate the fucking rain," she yells, ignoring the children around, trying to cover her body with her jacket.

It hurts to move quickly, so instead of jogging with her, I walk, taking my time. I'm already wet, might as well be soaked. By the time I climb inside, she's shivering even though the heater is blowing on high. Water is dripping from the tips of her hair, and when she looks over at me, it takes everything I have to hold back laughter. She really is a rain hater.

"What a day to wear white." A sly smile slides across my lips because her shirt is like tissue paper, sticking to her skin.

Viola smiles and opens the middle console. She pulls out an envelope with a red wax seal stamped on the back. It's been opened already. Before saying another word, Viola glances down at it, holding it a little too tightly. I'm not sure what's going on until she hands it to me. I open the envelope and pull out the letter that's addressed to her in a fancy writing. The words seem to leak off the page as I read because I realize what this means. Viola is *leaving,* and it crushes me. I glance up at her and can tell she's upset. She covers her face to hide the tears.

"Whoa. No need for that." I open my arms, and she falls into them. After a moment, she pulls away, and I grab her shoulders.

"Viola. This is a huge deal. Please tell me you're going."

She looks up at me, her eyes finally meeting mine, and I can see a small glimmer of relief. "You're okay with this?"

"Trust me when I say I want to be selfish, but this is something that you cannot pass up. Union International? They choose five people a year for their internship program. This is an opportunity of a lifetime, and if you don't go, I'll withhold sex from you for the rest of your life."

She snorts. "As if you could handle that. But what about *us*?"

I take her hand in mine. "We'll make it work, princess. And you thought I was bad now? I'm going to be a greedy bastard with you until you leave. So dry up those tears. I know you're going to miss the D, but it's only six months. And we can video chat." I wiggle my eyebrows at her. "Plus I'll fly up to visit once a month."

She finally cracks a smile. "But what if I'm offered a position at the end of my six-month term? That's usually what happens, you know."

Somehow I didn't think about that one, but it doesn't matter. "We'll cross that bridge when we get to it. Promise me, princess. Promise me you won't worry about us, and you'll take that internship. It's the Harvard of all opportunities."

I hand the letter back to her, and she returns it to the envelope.

"I promise."

"Good."

Leaning her head against the seat, she sighs. "I thought this would be easy."

"What's that?"

"Leaving. For years, I wished I could get away from it all. I wished something like this would happen. And now that it has…" Her words fade away.

"My mother told me that not taking risks is how dreams die. If you want this, go for it. Don't let your worries, insecurities, or fears stop you. I've already told you before; I'm not going anywhere. I would wait a lifetime for you, and I mean it."

"If you want to see other people–"

"FUCK NO!" I don't even let her finish. "Knowing you're mine, no matter how far away is enough for me. I'm not sure if you realize this or not, but I don't want anyone else, Viola. I want you. *Only you.*" I lean in and tuck wet, loose strands of her hair behind her ear, and kiss the fuck out of her. She pours herself into me, and I don't want her to leave. The distance will be hard. But over the years, I've learned patience, and I would selflessly wait as long as she needed.

But I can't help but think about how Viola has always been around. I'm not sure I know what life is like without her, as odd as that seems. Even when

Drew and I first moved closer to campus, she would still drive up on the weekends and pester us—mainly me—but she was here. Knowing that she's moving in a matter of weeks doesn't give us very much time to be together. We'll have to make every moment count as the time clock ticks down.

VIOLA

Though I'm sad to be leaving, I'm relieved to have told Travis. He deserved to know as much as Drew did. But him knowing doesn't make it any easier. I'm pretty sure it makes the decision even harder. All my life, I've been stuck in this loop of trying to make the best grades, and when it's finally paid off, I don't feel happy about it.

"Will you come inside?" Travis asks when we pull into the driveway.

"Do you really think that's a good idea? Drew is on the prowl."

"Fine. Let's go somewhere else then."

I'm confused, which seems to be happening a lot lately. "Uh, like where do you suggest?"

"Your dorm?"

I make a face. "Not quite. There would be three girls with cups on the door trying to listen."

"All righty. I've got an idea." Travis picks up his phone and begins texting someone. His phone buzzes a lot, and at the end, he's grinning.

"What have you done?" I question, warily.

"Let me drive. My surprise."

"Are you sure you can handle Tatum?" I open the door and step out; he slaps my butt hard before he climbs inside.

"Handle Tatum? I will destroy him."

Travis reverses out of the driveway, causing the wheels to squeal as he heads toward the stop sign. I'm pretty sure my car has never been driven like that.

"Oh, my God. Don't drive my car like you rented it."

"I'm driving it like I stole it, princess." He tilts his head at me as he accelerates toward the freeway. "But the good news is, we're getting fifty miles to the gallon."

We talk about everything and nothing all at the same time, not once bringing up the fact that our days together are numbered. As much as I try, I can't help but think about how much I'm going to miss this.

There are still so many firsts to be had, and Drew doesn't even know. At this rate, we could probably hold off telling him until after I leave, not allowing it to disrupt what we have going on. If it's not broken, maybe we shouldn't fix it, right now.

An hour passes, and I start to grow suspicious. Travis takes the exit off Highway 580 and loops under the bridge. I look past him and can see the choppy water of the bay. He slows, and then pulls into an empty driveway and a house with no lights on.

"Come on," he says, turning off the car and leading me up the sidewalk by the hand.

On the front—surrounded by seashells—is the address. A big bay window faces the water, and I can almost imagine people inside looking out. The view is breathtaking.

"What are we doing?" I reluctantly ask.

"We're walking."

"Smartass."

He types a code into the front door, and like magic, it clicks open. The inside is dark, and he runs his hand against the wall.

"*Lumos*," I say, and as soon as I do, the lights flick on. "And you think spells don't work," I scoff.

"I never said that. You've obviously put one on me." He leans his shoulder against the wall and watches me marvel. The house is beautiful. The ocean-themed décor, paired with the long wall of books, makes it feel cozy.

"Whose house is this?" I run my finger across so many classic books. It's like I'm saying hello to old friends.

"An old college friend who owes me big-time. His parents bought him this house when he received his acceptance letter and a full scholarship. Instead of dealing with the hassle of selling when he moved to New York, he just Airbnb's it. So..."

"You called in a favor?"

Travis nods. "And now I'm going to fulfill a fantasy and fuck you against that window."

The space between us vanishes and Travis' lips are pressed hard against mine.

"Do you trust me?" he asks, flipping off the light, allowing the setting sun to bleed in.

"I trust you with my heart."

He smiles against my lips, running his hand up my shirt, palming my breast. "*Good*."

A chill runs down my spine as he undresses me. Though his hands are careful, his mouth is dangerous, needy. Meeting his intensity, I undress him, until we are both standing naked in front of the large bay window. The street is quiet, and when I turn to look outside, the burnt sun sets over the horizon. Travis moves my hair from my shoulder and bites down, causing a mixture of pain and pleasure to soar through me. With his erection against my ass, he moves me forward until my breasts are pushed against the cold glass before he slides in. Just the thought of someone being able to see us makes me want to lose control, and he makes it too easy.

Travis gives absolutely no fucks, and takes me hard and rough, just like I want. He tugs at my hair and bites along my neck and shoulders. The intensity of him is almost too much to handle. We aren't quiet. We fuck loud and hard and don't give two shits if the world sees us as he slams into me against the window.

I beg for more.

I beg for it harder.

And he's relentless, one-upping my requests, and I want him to.

The king is using his royal cock in ways I've never experienced. And I love it.

The euphoria of him is so much I almost forget my own name, and I've resorted to gibberish. I'm pretty sure Travis is trying to break me or leave his imprint, but he already has. I won't be forgetting this any time soon.

He flips me around, grabbing my nipple between his teeth as he slams his cock in me. I lean my head against the cool glass, and I have no idea how he's doing this with broken ribs, but I don't even question him. He's in total control tonight. It's as if he's fucking away all of his emotions about me leaving and I'm happy for the release. I'm happy to forget about it all and be lost in nothing but the moment, for once. My body is a slave to him, and I ride the orgasmic waves over and over again, only to be selfish and want even more. My sexual appetite matches his, and I'm proud of that.

"You're a dirty girl, V." He smirks and spins me around, slapping my ass before he continues. He doesn't even rub it like the book boyfriends in my romance novels. But oddly enough, it turns me on even more. "Don't even say it," he warns. "V officially stands for vixen." He wraps my messy hair around his fist and forces me to look into his eyes. "*My V. My vixen.*"

"I'll always be yours, Travis." The words fall out of my mouth, and my warm breath creates a fog against the glass.

"Princess, when you say things like that…" He groans in my ear, and the emotions that swirl through me are indescribable. I feel him tense behind me, and I push harder against him until he loses himself. Warmth fills me, and he leans his head against my shoulder. We stay like that for a long moment, taking each other in, deep pants and heavy breaths.

Travis takes a step back with me in his arms and glances past me at the window. He rubs his hand across the stubble that graces his perfect jawline. I turn and see my breasts and ass imprinted on the glass and can't stop the laughter, but I'm not embarrassed. Hell no, I'm proud because somehow Travis has broken my sexual shell into pieces.

"The housekeeper will have fun with that one." His smile is perfect, and I can't help but admire his abs and how low his jeans sit on his hips when he zips them. I follow his happy trail all the way down to the lingering hard-on. Swallowing hard, I take a mental snapshot of this exact moment, not ever wanting to forget it.

After a moment, Travis sits on the couch and stretches out his legs. No words are spoken between us and I snuggle in next to him after putting on my bra and panties, compliments of Courtney and Victoria's Secret. With our naked skin pressed together, he wraps his arms around me and I focus on his heartbeat and the sound of his breathing.

The clock on the wall lets out a loud gong on the hour, scaring the shit out of me. Travis holds me a little tighter and lets out a loud bark of laughter. I glare at him, then at the clock, knowing that it's our cue to go. Saying goodbye is going to become harder with each passing day, but I try to push the nagging thought to the back of my mind.

"I don't want to go." I pout.

"Let's stay. I've got the house until the weekend."

My eyes widen. "Seriously? That must have been a helluva thing you did for this guy."

"He basically owes me his firstborn." He gives me a cute little side grin.

My eyes widen, and I'm intrigued. "I want to hear more of this story."

"He helped me with finals, and I helped him snag the girl. She fell in love with his computer programming ass and the rest is history."

I burst out into laughter. "Oh, my God."

"It was better than paying for tutoring."

I smack him on the chest, and he pulls me closer. "You are so wrong for that."

"So whatcha say princess, am I having you for breakfast?" Travis asks, with an eyebrow tilted up.

I need to be studying, but I *am* ahead at the moment...

Fuck it!

Moments like this will be few and far between, and I don't want to take another one for granted. I nod before kissing him.

"Bon appétite," I whisper across his lips.

Somehow we fall asleep on the couch, and hours later Travis is patting my arm for me to move. He grabs my hand and leads me to the master bedroom. I fold the blankets down from the king-sized bed, and we climb under the sheets. It's the first time we've slept in the same bed together without a care in the world. I roll over, and Travis holds me tight, as if I'm water that will slip between his fingers. But that won't happen because nothing in my life has ever felt so right.

Not caring about school or Boston or anything, I fall asleep with a smile on my face.

CHAPTER ELEVEN

TRAVIS

It's been three weeks since I snuck Viola up to the house on the bay, and even though we find every chance to be together, it was one of those moments I'll never forget.

I hate that we're keeping it a secret from Drew, but a part of me worries things will change between us once he knows. There's no saying how he'll react for sure, but I can't imagine it'll be good.

However, now that I have a rental car and I've returned to work, it's a little easier to avoid Drew and meet up with Viola on nights he's home. She still comes over on Wednesdays, and I still find ways to taste her when he's not looking.

My phone dings with an incoming text message as I walk into work, and I smile as I read Viola's name across the screen.

V: **My financial marketing professor just announced an additional extra-credit project to**

be added to our finals! OMG, he's trying to kill me because I'm a sucker for extra credit!!!!!!!!!

T: **But marketing is your thing, babe! You've got this!**

I answer her text, trying to encourage her and brighten up her mood. She's been an absolute mess the last couple weeks as graduation approaches. I know she's a genius, acing all her classes, and is already a shoo-in for the apprenticeship this summer, but I know freak-out mode is inevitable until she walks across that stage toward her diploma.

V: **Since when did you trade in your suit and tie for a pair of pom-poms?**

I smile at her smartass response—exhausted, stressed, and still able to run her filthy mouth.

T: **I'll role-play for you any day, princess. As long as you're the one with the pom-poms...and only the pom-poms.**

As soon as I walk into my office, she sends another message.

V: **Cheerleader fantasy? Really?**

T: **Does that really surprise you?**

I set my briefcase down and sit behind my desk. I've only been back a week, and I already have a huge project. Alyssa has been glued to Blake, so that's a relief.

V: **Actually, no. Just know that my fantasy consists of cloaks, wands, and nerdy glasses. Oh, and you must speak in an English accent.**

T: **Hmm, that's very descriptive...like you've been thinking on that for a while…**

V: **A Potterhead never tells…**

T: **I'm sure I could persuade you. You aren't the only one who can cast spells. Just wait until I Slytherin ;)**

I turn my computer on and start scrolling through my emails. I miss the days of being home with Viola and just being able to lay low with her, especially now knowing she'll be leaving in a month. I haven't allowed myself to think about it too much, considering I want to make the most of the time that we have left before then, but I know I'm going to be completely lost without her.

V: **Show me what you've got, wizard boy! P.S. Good luck on your presentation today! I packed an extra invisibility cloak in your bag just in case, but I doubt you'll even need it! Kill it!**

T: **Now who's sporting the pom-poms? ;)**

V: **I mean…don't fuck it up, muggle.**

A knock at the door directs my attention up to Blake who is standing in my doorway. He's been pretty edgy since my return, and I have a feeling he liked my absence.

"It's time." He nods his head to the hallway. "Everyone's meeting in the conference room in five."

"Right behind you," I say, grabbing a file folder with my notes and paperwork and double-checking that I have everything.

Standing up, I look around at the once-promising office that has now turned cold. My heart is no longer here, and the thought of starting my firm becomes more appealing each day. I used to live and breathe this job, but ever since Viola, she's been the one to breathe life back into me.

I fucking rock my presentation, and once the meeting is over, Blake walks back to my office and asks me to go to a lunch meeting with him. I'm hesitant, considering our history, but he sold me on the company picking up the tab, so why not?

Alyssa watches us both intently as we make our way out. She's barely said more than a sentence to me, so I know something's up. I just can't quite put my finger on it.

I text Viola before heading out.

T: **You'll be happy to know I kicked ass and am now heading out for a work lunch meeting. I expect a celebration tonight…in the form of your naked body on top of mine while you yell how much harder you want it.**

I slide into the company car with Blake; he takes the driver's side, and I sit in the passenger seat. He buckles up, and I check my phone once again for her response, but so far nothing. I know she's swamped right now, so I shrug it off. Talking with her always makes my days go by faster.

"So, I bet you're glad to be back finally. I hear bed rest can suck for a king." Blake's attempt at small talk is laughable, but I go along with it anyway.

"Yeah, it did. Good thing my roommate's little sister was around to help me some." The words flow out before I can stop them.

"Violet, right?"

"Viola," I correct. "She lives on campus nearby, so she wasn't too far if I needed anything."

"How convenient." I notice his condescending tone and pinch my lips to force back a smug smile. It was *very* fucking convenient, but of course, I won't say that to him. The less he knows about my personal life, the better.

Once the awkward lunch from hell is over, and Blake not-so-subtly threatens my position at the firm, I make a little detour before heading home. Since it's Wednesday, Viola will be over tonight, and I'm going to have to use all the willpower I don't have to keep my eyes and hands off her.

Knowing that Viola leaves for Boston in just a month, I want to give her a going-away gift that will ensure she comes back to me. I know that's selfish on my part, but I've been waiting ten years for the girl of my dreams, and I'll do whatever it takes to make sure I don't lose her again.

I've been thinking about it the last couple of weeks, and I found just the right one for her.

After picking up the gift, I arrive back home, fortunately before Drew, so he doesn't question me.

V: **I'm heading over soon. Is the coast clear?**

I read Viola's text and immediately send one back. I can't wait to see her.

T: **Yes. Get your ass over here. I have a surprise.**

V: **What kind of a surprise? Should I bring my wand?**

I smile at her response.

T: **I'll be the one with the wand, princess ;)**

V: **Let's hope you know how to use that thing before you break it :)**

I shake my head at her response, loving her filthy mouth.

T: **Was that really necessary? Low blow, princess.**

V: **Sorry, King. Sometimes you have to pay the price of being a smartass.**

I set my phone down and get her gift ready, so she sees it when she first walks in. I know she's going to lose her mind.

Hearing Viola's car pull into the driveway, I immediately greet her at the door. She smiles, and I press my lips to hers before she even has a chance to speak.

"Well, hi," she says, gasping for air.

"Hi." I smile in return. "I have something waiting for you."

I lead her into the house and down the hallway to my bedroom. "Are you ready?"

"Nothing's going to pop out at me, is it?" She pulls back slightly, and I wrap a hand around her neck and pull her lips to mine again.

"No, unless you're into that kind of thing." I wink at her, and she holds back a smile.

"You have no shame." She chuckles against my mouth.

I softly kiss her lips once more and pull back slightly as I open my bedroom door.

Stepping out of her way so she can walk in, she immediately gasps and runs to the bed, where an eight-week-old puppy is wiggling with excitement, anxiously waiting for her to pick him up.

"Oh, my God!" she screams—her excitement addicting as I follow behind her. "You got a puppy?" She picks him up and holds him close to her chest. "He's so sweet!" She rubs his fur against her cheek.

I wrap an arm around her waist and pull her into me. "I got *you* a puppy."

Her eyes widen as she looks up at me. "What? Why? I mean, I can't have a puppy in the dorms. What about when I leave?" Her bottom lip trembles, and I can tell she's not getting my whole point.

"He's going to live here with me until you come back."

"He is?"

"Yes." I smile confidently. "That way I know you'll come back. I know you can't resist puppies."

She chuckles, rubbing the length of her chin along his face. "So he's collateral? I don't come back, and you get to keep the puppy?"

"I don't want to keep the puppy, princess. I just want *you*."

She tilts her head and narrows her eyes. "You have me. Regardless of being gone for six months, I'm not going anywhere. We'll still text and Skype, and I'll call you every night. I'll be back before we know it." Her words are reassuring, but I can't help but notice the tone in her voice isn't as certain.

"Well then, think of him as a thank you gift."

She repositions him on her chest and soon his eyes are closing as he rests his head on her shoulder.

"A thank you gift for what?"

I brush my fingers through her hair and look her in the eyes. "For taking care of me and making sure I was fed and properly cleaned."

"Oh, yes. Those showers were a terrible inconvenience for me." She smiles and presses little kisses to the puppy's cheeks.

"So what do you want to name him?"

We sit down on the edge of the bed and take a good look at him. He has fluffy golden fur and dark, beady eyes.

"He looks like a Gryffindor to me. Gryff for short."

I throw my head back and laugh. Of course, she'd give him a Harry Potter name. I rub my hand along his back as he rests peacefully on Viola's lap. "Sorry, little guy. We didn't stand a chance on giving you a more manly name, but I'll be sure all the single ladies know you're macho and badass."

Viola chuckles and rests her head against my shoulder. "Now I'm going to have to say goodbye to two special men in my life."

"Don't worry. I'm sure we'll keep each other company."

"You're going to have to feed him while I'm gone. And take him for walks. And give him baths. He'll probably want to sleep with you, too. They usually miss their brothers and sisters for the first few weeks after being separated." She continues to ramble until I finally interrupt and shut her up.

"Viola!" I shout. "I think I can handle a harmless little puppy."

She tilts her face up, uncertainty written all over it. "What are you going to tell Drew?"

"Don't worry about Drew. I'll take care of it."

We lie on the bed, petting and playing with Gryff. He chews on our fingers, my comforter, and even Viola's hair. The way her face lights up when she looks at him makes me so damn happy, and I wish I could bottle up this moment and just keep it this way forever.

I remember Viola telling me how much she wanted a dog. She asked for one every Christmas, and like clockwork, it never came. I didn't grow up with pets, except one old cat that my mother cherished like a baby. I never got close enough to it to consider it a companion, but Viola would go nuts every time someone would walk a dog past their house. She talked about dogs like she did her books, and I knew she'd always wanted one. Some girls want a pony; Viola's always wanted a puppy.

Even though she lives in the dorms, and she'll be leaving for Boston soon, I wanted her to have Gryff. Another reason to come back, even if it ends up being for the wrong reasons.

VIOLA

No matter what I do, I can't wipe the stupid grin off my damn face right now. Gryff is smothering me in kisses, and Travis is looking at me like he wants to rip off all my clothes, which is probably accurate. This is Travis, after all.

"Thank you," I whisper as we both lie on the bed with Gryff sleeping in between us. "It's the sweetest thing anyone's ever given me."

"Yeah?" He raises a brow. "Feel free to show me just how thankful you are."

"Sorry, King. There's a new man in my life now." I pick up the puppy and set him on my chest.

"I can give you puppy dog eyes and lick your face if that's what it takes." He rolls to my side and faces me. "Or if you prefer, I can lick you somewhere else, too."

I smile at his attempt. "Drew's going to be home soon, and unless you want him to find me with a puppy in your bed, I have to get up."

"Well, it wouldn't be the weirdest thing he's ever found in my bed." He flashes a smug smile, and I'm tempted to smack that look right off his face.

"Perhaps it's a good thing Gryff will be here while I'm gone. He can keep an eye on you," I say, climbing off his bed. "He'll be my little spy."

"You don't trust me?" He places a hand over his chest and pouts with those sad, pathetic eyes of his.

"I do, it's the hoes I don't trust," I say matter-of-factly.

He sits on the edge of his bed and pulls me in between them. "You have nothing to worry about, princess. I promise you that. It's just going to be Gryff and me, waiting until the day you return to us."

My heart pounds in my chest as the words sit on the tip of my tongue, but I can't push them out just yet. I love him. I think I've always loved him, even when I hated him, but I can't help feeling scared to say those words aloud. I'm worried if I do, it'll jinx everything we have going for us so far.

Drew walks in the door thirty minutes later and immediately curses the second he sees the dog run toward him. "Travis?" he calls out, bending down and picking the puppy up. I'm watching him from the living room, but he hasn't yet seen me. "Did a new roommate move in that I'm unaware of?"

"He's mine," I say, bringing his attention to me. "Isn't he cute?" I smile, hoping he won't ask a million questions about him, but I know better.

"Yeah, adorable," he deadpans. "Why's he in my house?"

"Because he lives here," Travis chimes in, stalking from the hallway without a shirt on. *Dammit. Why is he shirtless?*

"Since when?" Drew asks, setting him down and watches as he runs back to me.

"Today," I answer, picking him up. "Travis gave him to me as a thank you gift for taking such good care of him. Is it okay that he stays here?" I give him my best pleading look, and pout out my lips.

He sighs, setting his gear down on the table. "You're okay with this?" He directs his question to

Travis. "I mean, you basically bought yourself a dog, man." He shakes his head a little, with an amused chuckle.

"Yeah, it's fine. But it's Viola's dog. She'll take care of him when she's around and then…" He slips his hands into his front pockets and shrugs carelessly. "I'll take care of him until she's back."

I watch as Drew furrows his brows at Travis, trying to read his intentions. "Something weird is going on."

"Drew, c'mon. You know I've wanted a dog forever." I keep my eyes locked on his, knowing he'll cave any second.

He inhales through his nose, and I watch as his chest rises and falls with a deep sigh. "Fine, whatever. But I'm not picking up any dog poop. I deal with enough shit at work; I don't need more of it when I come home."

I smile in victory but hide it behind Gryff's head. I know Travis and I dodged another bullet with Drew, but now isn't the right time to tell him.

"Are your clothes in the wash, Vi?" Drew asks from the kitchen. "I need to throw a load in."

"Just set it down by the washer, and I'll throw it in after I change mine over."

"Okay, thanks. I'm going to hit the gym for a couple of hours then."

I nod, and he disappears into his room for a few moments before he resurfaces in his workout clothes. "Fuck!"

I nearly jump from the couch and run down the hallway when I spot Drew standing in front of a pile of dog poop. "Oh, no." I pick Gryff up and hold him close to my chest. He's shaking. "He didn't mean to. He's just nervous."

Drew walks around me without saying another word, and I know he's already unhappy about the puppy. He heads down the hall, and I exhale as I hear the bathroom door click shut.

"I'll clean it up, princess. Don't worry. Drew's been an emotional mess the past couple weeks. It's not you."

It may not be me, but I can think of a certain someone who is probably the cause of all his pent-up aggression. *Mia.*

Once Travis cleans up the mess and sprays the carpet, he calls me to the kitchen. I hear him banging around pots and pans, and I can't help wonder what the hell he's getting into now.

"I know you said you didn't want anything of mine near your mouth, but I make a really kick ass pasta dish."

"A puppy *and* dinner?" I ask with a smug smile. "You sure know the way to a girl's heart, don't you?"

He cups my cheek and pulls me in, so our mouths are just barely touching. "Just yours, Viola." He presses his lips to mine for a deep, passionate kiss. "You were always the girl."

"And you were always the boy, Travis King."

He wraps his arms around my waist and attacks my mouth with his tongue and lips. I take everything he's offering and more.

"Let's skip dinner," he whispers against my mouth. "I'd *much* rather have dessert instead. What do you think?"

"Too much dessert in your diet isn't a healthy balance," I say.

"Since when have I cared about a healthy balance?"

I laugh and press my palms against his chest to push him away. "Drew's home," I remind him. "In fact, I should probably be cursing you out or something before he walks back in here."

"Or we could just tell him?" He arches a brow.

I drop my shoulders and frown. "You know how that would work out if we did it right now?"

"Oh, c'mon. He'll get one good punch in, and then—"

"Travis!" I scold, and he laughs. *Asshole.*

"He always takes long showers after work, so we have some time to kill." He brushes loose strands of hair behind my ear and smiles.

"Good. Then you can make that dinner," I say.

He groans, adjusting himself. "How the hell am I supposed to cook with this distracting me?"

"Hmm..." I pinch my lips together, pretending to ponder it. "How can we remedy this little situation?"

I kneel down and start undoing his belt. I can feel how hard he is underneath the fabric of his jeans. I stare up at him, still shirtless, and study the tattoos that cover his arms and chest. I want to lick my tongue all the way up his body and suck on every design, but I stay focused on getting his jeans undone instead—*for now anyway*.

Once I successfully strip him out of his jeans and boxer shorts, I palm his cock and begin stroking. He nearly stumbles at the first touch, and I know I'm the only one in charge right now.

"All right, chef. Get started."

"What? Right now?"

"Yes." I turn my back against the oven, and he turns to face me so I can suck the tip of him. "You cook. I'll get started on dessert."

"Fuck, Viola," he hisses when I slide my tongue along his shaft. "You really want me around sharp knives and a hot stove when you have my dick in your mouth?"

I nod, running my tongue along the edge of his tip as it twitches from the warm, teasing contact.

"You realize I'll end up cutting my damn hand off or something."

"Then I suggest you be *extra* careful."

"No way." He moans, leaning his hands on the stovetop and sliding his dick deeper into my mouth.

I pull him out and tease him once again, watching as he nearly crumbles over me. "C'mon, King. You don't want to play?"

"*Goddammit,* Viola," he hisses, knowing exactly what kind of game I'm talking about. "Fuck, princess. Your mouth is fucking perfection."

"Don't forget the rules," I say, reminding him of our little game. "You come before dinner's ready, you lose."

"Sounds more like a win to me," he says smugly, trying to control his breathing.

"And if you don't, you get to come somewhere else…" I drawl, lingering my words because he knows exactly what I mean. The only reason I agreed to those terms is because I know Travis King well enough to know he'll never be able to hold off that long.

"Game on, princess."

CHAPTER TWELVE

TRAVIS

Drew strides back into the dining room just as I'm setting the table. I can tell something's bothering him by the way his features tighten up and how he brushes his hand through his hair. I know he's been talking about Mia a lot lately, but he hasn't really said much about her since the last time he told me they spoke.

"What's going on?" Drew asks, nodding his head toward the table.

"I've got some food in the oven. You want some?"

"You made dinner?" He arches a brow in disbelief.

"Yeah, Viola said she was hungry, so I put something together."

He pulls a chair out and sits down. "Since when can you cook?"

"Since now," I fire back. "You going to eat or drill me all night?"

"Sorry, man. Mia is driving me nuts."

"I thought you two were going to talk or something?"

"Well, we were, but she won't tell me anything until we're face to face, and just by the tone of her voice, it doesn't sound good."

I pinch my lips together, knowing exactly what Mia *should* tell Drew, but knowing her, she'll twist it around somehow and play the victim.

"When is she coming, then?"

"My next day off isn't until next Wednesday, so she's going to drive up Tuesday night and spend the night."

I contemplate giving him a heads-up, but I'm not really in the position to be delivering bad news. "Well, hopefully, you guys can work it out." The words come out sincere, but not at all believable.

"It's just driving me insane. Is it that bad she can't just tell me over the phone and put me out of my misery? I've even contemplated taking a sick day and driving up there myself, but she's in the middle of studying for her upcoming finals, so I just have to fucking sit and wait."

Viola walks in before I can respond. "Maybe Gryff can cheer you up." She holds the puppy up with a wide smile.

"Doubtful."

"Geez. Now who's the one manstrating?" She cradles Gryff to her chest and takes a seat.

He sighs. "So, what's the deal here? Are you two like...*friends* now?"

I see Viola's body go stiff in her chair and know I'm going to have to be the one to smooth this one over. "I thought you'd appreciate no fighting for one night." I flash a small smile, shrugging nonchalantly. The oven timer goes off, and I walk back to the kitchen, leaving Viola alone with Drew.

I can hear her talking to him about the puppy and trying to get him to warm up to the idea of having him at the house. By the time I bring the food in, he's smiling and holding Gryff.

"Well if Mia and I don't work out, at least Gryff will be around to keep me company," he says as he gets licked by the dog.

I walk back out and bring in some drinks before sitting down. Viola grabs the spoon and starts scooping dinner onto her plate. After Drew sets Gryff down, he grabs the dish next.

"So, King, first a puppy and now dinner? You trying to get into my sister's pants?"

Before I can answer, Viola chokes on her drink and nearly spews it all over the table.

"You all right?" Drew turns and asks.

She coughs a few more times before rubbing a hand over her throat. "Yeah, uh, just went down the wrong pipe."

My heart is beating out of my chest at the tension in the air and a part of me just wants to tell him right now and get it over with, but I know Viola would kill me if I did. I promised we'd tell him when she was ready.

"So? Someone want to tell me what's going on?"

"I'm seeing a guy at school, Drew, so just calm down," she says before I can even get in a word. She says it so genuinely that I would almost believe her if I didn't know any better.

"Who?"

"You don't know him. Just some guy in my chem class." She stabs her fork into the pasta and takes a bite.

"I thought you took chem last year?" he asks, narrowing his eyes at her.

I see her throat move as she swallows and I can tell she's nervous. I feel like I should say something, but I don't want to make Drew more suspicious than he already is.

"I did. That's when I met him."

She's blushing, but thankfully Drew doesn't notice.

"Well, what's his name?"

"Whose?"

"The guy you're seeing?"

Without thinking, I blurt out the first name that comes to mind. "Toby." I squeeze my eyes closed and curse to myself. "He's kind of quiet."

She doesn't make eye contact with him as she picks at her food.

"You mean a dork?" I speak up, breaking the awkward tension.

She glares at me right on cue, and I wink in her direction. "If by dork, you mean has a higher IQ than you can count, then yes."

I release a cough to choke back the laugh that threatens to release. Fuck, she's good—always throwing shit right back at me.

"Isn't Courtney's boyfriend named Toby?" Drew asks, breaking the spell between us.

"Uh, yeah. Well, he was. They broke up a while ago." She grabs her phone, and her fingers begin flying over the screen. "Actually I was going to invite her over to meet Gryff, if you don't mind."

Drew shrugs, his mind suddenly occupied, and I want to high-five Viola for her quick, witty answers.

We finish eating in silence, and I watch as Viola feeds Gryff scraps off her plate. Her phone dings with messages from Courtney. Using her to sidetrack Drew was brilliant on Viola's part—another reason to reward her later.

Just as we're cleaning up the table, Courtney walks in and immediately squeals when she sees the puppy.

"Oh, my God!" She bends down and picks him up. "He's so cute!"

"I told you!" Viola beams.

"I just want to smother my face in his fur!"

"Quit making it weird, Court." Viola laughs and leads them both into the living room, leaving Drew and me alone in the kitchen.

"So, this thing with Mia is really bothering you, huh?" I try and make small talk because I'm not really sure if he wants to talk about her or not.

"Yeah, I have a feeling it's something bad. Did she say anything to you that night?"

"Well, actually, there's something I've been torn about telling you or not, but I figured it was best to let Mia tell you instead."

"Fuck, man. I don't know if I can wait that long. I can't focus on anything."

Before I can respond, Courtney lets out a loud laugh, directing us both toward the living room. I watch Drew's facial expression soften, and I know he could use a good distraction right now.

"I'm going to the pet store to pick out some toys and food for Gryff. He'll probably need something to do while you're at school," I say to Viola as I head toward the door, hoping she catches the hint.

I take a step behind Drew and nod my head toward him and then once again at Courtney. Viola picks it up right away and scrambles to stand up quickly.

"It's my dog, and I want to spoil him, too."

I lift an eyebrow at her and almost forget that we're not alone. "If you want to *come,* I'll allow it."

She smirks at my innuendo. "I do, and I'll drive."

VIOLA

C: **Did you seriously invite me over just to leave me alone with your brother?!**

"She sounds pissed," Travis says, laughing as he reads her messages on my phone. "What should I respond?"

"Tell her to take the opportunity and seduce him."

"I'm not writing that," he deadpans. "I'll tell her to send a tit pic."

Laughing, I reach over and grab my phone from his hand. "Shut up. She'll be fine."

Once we arrive at the pet store, Travis grabs Gryff's leash and leads us inside. We pick out a handful of chew toys, treats, dog food, and a little bed.

"You know he'll probably never sleep in that," I tell him as we check out.

"Why not?"

"He's a puppy! He's going to want to sleep next to a warm body."

"I'd prefer your warm body."

"I'm sure he'll let you spoon him when I'm gone."

"Okay, fine. But I'm calling dibs on being the big spoon."

We walk out of the store with a large bag of dog food and two bags filled with toys and treats. "Hand me your keys," Travis says, holding his hand out. I dangle them in front of him, and he grabs them before I can pull away. "Nice try, princess. Now I get to drive the Prissy Prius."

I scowl at his nickname for my precious car. "I'm going to teach Gryff to bite you anytime you make a snide comment."

"And then I'll just unteach him, and when you come back, I'll have taught him all kinds of good stuff like fetching beers from the fridge and taking out the trash."

"Geez, don't set your standards high or anything." I roll my eyes as I get into the passenger side with Gryff. "You think we should drive around before going back home?"

"Are you expecting Courtney to make her move finally?" he asks, turning the key and shifting into gear.

"So, it's that obvious, huh?"

"Not to Drew, apparently. He's kind of blinded by the fog of Mia."

I sigh. "So, Drew really never asked about that night with Mia?"

I see his throat tighten and I wonder if I hit a nerve. "No. I've offered to tell him everything, but she should really be the one to."

"Do you think she will?"

"Honestly? No." He shrugs. "If she tries to pull any of her usual shit, though, I'm telling him, whether he wants to hear it or not."

I pinch my lips, wanting to ask him, but not wanting to sound like I don't trust him. Mia has always been up to no good, but I trust Travis' judgment.

Instead of saying anything, I distract myself with my phone and see that Courtney has sent me multiple text messages.

He has the best laugh ever. *sigh*

OMG I want to have his babies.

Would it be weird to cut a piece of his hair off and sleep with it?

Our babies would be so pretty with my blue eyes and his wild dark hair, don't you think?

He winked at me.

I just died. DIED.

DEAD.

"Good lord," I murmur, shaking my head. "Courtney shouldn't be left alone with Drew. I almost feel bad. Perhaps I should've warned him before we left…"

"Nah, it's good for him."

"She's not usually this crazy, but she's crushed on him since the first day they met."

"Let me guess. Drew barely flinched."

"Pretty much. He wouldn't recognize flirting if it smacked him in the face, pulled his hair, and gave him a titty twister."

"Jesus. Remind me not to piss you off."

I shoot him a look, and he smirks at me.

I send Courtney a text.

V: **Code red: We're on our way back. If you're naked, warn us now.**

C: **Oh like you haven't seen me naked before?**

V: **Well, I didn't plan on making it a habit.**

C: **Fine...but if you must know, Drew and I are at least an arm's length apart, so I'd say the friend zone has been set in place. :(**

"He friend zoned her," I tell Travis, typing out my response. "If her signs were any brighter, he'd go blind."

"Should've seen him in college," he snorts. "Girls were nearly crawling at his feet, and he was just so oblivious to it."

I nod in agreement. "I imagine a lot of broken hearts followed."

"Yeah, that's why this whole thing with Mia pisses me off. I wish he'd just let her go and move on. She's bad news."

I swallow again, fidgeting with Gryff's collar as I think of a way to bring up that night. Figuring the best way is just to rip it off like a Band-Aid, I ask, "Has she cheated on him?" Cringing, waiting for his reaction, I watch as his fingers tighten around the steering wheel.

"She claims she didn't, but she was with a guy when I found her."

My blood boils, and I'm tempted to call her up myself and tell her to stay away from Drew, but knowing the conniving bitch she is, she wouldn't, just to piss me off even more. In a weird way, it's also comforting to hear she was with another guy, which solidifies my trust for Travis.

"Not surprised," I say on a shallow breath.

We pull into the driveway and Travis takes Gryff from me before getting out. "Let's take him for a walk." He flashes a knowing smile and winks.

We silently walk hand in hand as Travis holds onto his leash with his free hand. It's so peaceful and easy, and I almost forget Drew is in the house sulking.

"I'm really going to miss you when you leave," he says in a soft tone. He doesn't look at me, but I can see that his mind is going a thousand miles a minute.

"I'm going to miss you, too." I squeeze my hand in his, letting him know everything I don't know how to say. "Gryff will like taking all these walks with you when I'm gone."

"He'll be pretty big by the time you return."

"Maybe show him a picture of me every few days, so he doesn't forget," I say, smiling and finally getting a laugh out of him.

"I can do that, but just know they'll be the ones of your tits and ass." He smirks, and I playfully bump my hip into his.

We walk a few more steps before he stops and pulls me into his chest. "I hope you know I would wait for you, even if it was a year or six years. Every day you're gone is going to suck major ass, but I'll be thinking of you every second."

"You know you really suck at not making me feel guilty." I pout, sticking my lower lip out at him.

He leans in and pulls it in between his teeth before releasing it. "Good. I want the guilt to consume you." A smile plays at his lips, and I can't resist smiling back at him.

"It's just six months," I remind him. "That's easy peasy."

He sighs, brushing his thumb over my cheek. He presses a soft kiss to my lips, and I melt into him. Gryff starts whining, tangling his leash in between our legs.

Travis breaks the kiss and untangles the leash while muttering a few curse words.

"Maybe you can take him to a few of those puppy classes and get him all trained before I'm back." I smile at my brilliant idea.

"He might need more than just a few." He groans, adjusting the leash again and leading us back to the house.

Courtney is in heaven when we return, and she makes me promise to invite her over again soon to 'visit Gryff.' Travis and I avoid each other the rest of the night while I finish laundry. Drew's already suspicious, so the more distance between us right now, the better.

The weekend flies by, with studying for finals and coming over to play with Gryff. Fortunately, Drew works all weekend, so we don't have to pretend while we're together. He continues wallowing around when he's home, so I do my best to cheer him up and casually mention Courtney in conversation. As expected, he doesn't take the bait, so I'm left watching him mope on the couch instead.

By Tuesday night, Drew is so damn anxious; I can't take it anymore. Mia is to arrive any minute, and like usual, I sit on the couch, pretending to act indifferent. Travis has been bringing some of his work files home to look busy while Drew is home.

"Dude, drink this," I hear Travis say. I look up and see him handing Drew a shot. "You're wound up tighter than a G-string. You need to relax."

"I'm trying," he says through clenched teeth, taking the shot and finally pouring it down his throat. "But I haven't seen her in so long, and I have no idea what she's going to say, which is making me anxious as hell."

He pats him on the shoulder and pours more whiskey in his shot glass. "Whatever happens, man, I'll be here, okay?"

"Thanks." He pours it down and holds it back out for a refill.

Tires crunch in the driveway, and we all look toward the door. Goose bumps cover my skin, and I can't help feeling nervous for Drew.

"Do you guys mind staying out here while we talk in my room?"

"Whatever you need," Travis answers, walking toward Gryff and me on the couch. You can barely see the front door from the couch.

We both sit silently, waiting to hear the first exchange. Drew opens the door, and we wait. Finally, footsteps enter the house. Her heels click on the hardwood floor as Drew wraps his arms around her for an awkward hug.

"How was the drive over?" I hear him ask. She mumbles a quiet *not bad,* and soon Drew is leading her down the hall to his room and then a click of the door.

I glance over at Travis who looks like he's sweating and about to vomit. Even though I've told him—*and myself*—over and over that I trust him and that we're going to make it work when I'm gone, I can't deny the heavy feeling inside my chest that something isn't right. Part of me regrets not hearing the whole story of that night, but proving I trusted him was crucial for our relationship.

We sit in silence as we watch the TV on a low volume. Gryff is asleep in my lap and the sound of Drew swinging his bedroom door open startles him awake.

"King!"

I jump at the volume of his voice. He's not pissed; he's *enraged*.

Travis jumps up and starts walking toward them. As much as I want to follow, I stay put. I don't need to bring attention to the fact that I'm following Travis or that I'm eavesdropping on them.

"The fuck?" I hear Drew shout. "Are you fucking kidding me?"

Finally, I can't take it any longer and set Gryff aside as I stand up. I tiptoe out of the living room and down the hall where I can hear Mia crying and Drew yelling.

"That's not how it happened," I hear Travis say, defensive and short.

I take another few steps until I can peek through the door gap and look inside.

"Then please enlighten me." Drew crosses his arms over his chest, his feet planted firmly on the floor, ready for a fight. "Explain how your lips landed on my girlfriend's."

My eyes widen as I unintentionally release a loud gasp. All three of them turn their heads toward me, and before I can control it, tears start falling down my cheeks. Drew pushes the door open wider, so the four of us are now in an awkward circle.

"What the hell are you doing in here?" Mia asks with a scoff. Her face is red, and her cheeks are puffy, but I don't believe her fake performance one bit.

"I heard yelling. I was just making sure everything was okay."

"Everything's fine, Viola," Travis says, but I refuse to look him in the eyes.

Drew cocks his head and studies my face, and I know he can see right through me. "You've got to be *fucking* kidding me!" he roars, turning his head toward Travis. "Kissing my girlfriend wasn't enough, you had to nail my sister, too?"

Oh, my God.

Thud.

My heart is pounding so hard; I bet they can all feel it. too.

And as if that revelation wasn't enough, Mia speaks up once again. "Oh, he tried more than that. Why do you think I was stripped down to my panties?" The words leave her mouth, and I instantly want to pummel her into the ground.

"Good question, Travis." Drew looks at Travis again, and I can see the fire brewing in his eyes. His blood is boiling. "But what's even a better question is how the fuck could you betray me like that?"

Before Travis can answer, Drew grabs him by the collar and pushes him up against the door. "My fucking sister, man?"

"Drew, no!" I reach out, but Mia steps in and blocks me.

"What the hell were you thinking?" He pushes his body into the door once again before releasing him. "I would've forgiven you for touching Mia, but my sister?" He shakes his head. "You're dead to me."

Tears well on the brims of my eyes and I can't hold them back anymore. Visions of him and Mia instantly flood my mind, and I can't take it anymore. I rush down the hall, grabbing my purse and shoes on my way out the door.

Travis yells behind me as I near my car. I ignore him and throw my shit in the backseat as soon as I unlock it.

"Viola, wait! Please!" He grabs my elbow and spins me around. "Let me explain."

"I don't want to hear any more lies from you." I pull my arm out of his grip. "I *trusted* you," I hiss.

"You're going to believe Mia over me?"

"So are you saying you two didn't kiss?" I challenge.

He brushes a hand through his hair as his jaw ticks.

"That's what I thought." I turn and reach for the door handle, but he stops me once again.

"That's not how it happened, Viola."

I roll my eyes and let out an amused chuckle. "Classic, Travis. Seriously."

"Stop being so damn stubborn for once," he growls. "She kissed me, Viola. Not the other way around. I have zero interest in her."

I shake my head and narrow my eyes at him. "That doesn't even make sense. Either you kissed, or you didn't."

"Okay, yes, but I didn't kiss her back. She threw up on her dress and ripped it off, so I had her lay in the backseat. That's all that happened. I swear, Viola."

"So you're telling me you two didn't make out in your car? The same car we've been together in?"

His head falls back, and he groans out in frustration. "It wasn't like that."

"So, how could you not tell me? I said I didn't need to hear the whole story because I trusted you, but I asked if anything had happened between you two and you said no. Now it looks like you had something to hide after all."

"Because it was nothing! She gave me a kiss I didn't want and now she's all pissy because I rejected her. That's the only reason she's saying those things now."

"Even if she's the one that kissed you and you pushed her away, that's more than just *nothing*. Especially considering she's your best friend's girlfriend. That should've been something you told me. Now I stand here like an idiot, thinking you were being one hundred percent honest with me."

"Because it meant absolutely nothing to me! I didn't want you to worry for no reason because I don't want anything to do with her. I never have. I don't care about her. You're all I want, Viola."

"Well, then it's a shame you gambled away my trust on someone that meant nothing to you."

"Don't say that, Viola. Please. I would never hurt you." He grabs my hand and secures it between both of his over his chest.

"You already have, Travis."

"Viola, *please*."

Tears fall down my cheeks, and I don't even have enough strength to wipe them away. "How can a relationship work if there's no trust?" I ask, and he doesn't answer. "It can't." I pull my hand back, and he reluctantly releases it.

"I will do whatever it takes to gain your trust back, but I promise, you have nothing to worry about. The one-night stands, the girls, and guys' nights out—I'm done with all that."

I shake my head and close my eyes. "It's too late, Travis. I can't do this again. I've given you my heart, and have been in love with you for so long that I just can't let you throw me away again."

"That's the first time you've ever said that." His voice is low, and when I look back up at him, I can see he's crying, too.

"And it'll be the last."

"Viola..."

I reach for the door and slide inside, shutting it behind me. He's looking at me with his hands behind his head—his eyes red and swollen—and I can't fight back the tears. I shift the car into reverse, and once I'm able, I shift again and watch him in my rearview mirror. He's bent over, his knees supporting the weight of his hands as he shakes his head.

My heart is lying in that driveway, shattered into a million pieces, and I'm not sure it'll ever beat right again.

CHAPTER THIRTEEN

TRAVIS

Viola's graduation is tonight, and she hasn't responded to any of my messages, calls, or emails. It's been over a week. It's killing me. I need her so fucking bad. It feels like I can't breathe without her in my life. As much as it makes me sound like a pussy and an asshole, I don't think I've ever truly felt this way before.

After Viola had stormed out, Drew sent Mia home, and he's barely looked at me since. The fact that he's more pissed about me being with his sister than the situation with Mia says a lot about their relationship, but that doesn't matter because she's full of shit. She always has been. I'm pissed that I ever supported their toxic relationship because somehow it's bled into and affected my own.

On top of that, Alyssa has started coming around my office again, offering me her 'services,' and it's taken all of my willpower to calmly ask her to leave instead of kicking her ass out like I so badly want. I'm actually proud of myself for keeping my composure, considering my world is rocking on its axis.

This week fucking blows.

And fuck! I miss Viola.

She should be here with this fucking dog and me. Gryff whines all night long, wakes me up at least three times to go outside, and barks at every car or person that goes by. The little fucker sleeps all day and then wants to play all damn night. I can't even be mad at him for being so damn annoying because he reminds me of her. When I think about how much she loved him, it makes me smile. He even still smells like her, so when he climbs up on my bed and nuzzles his way under the covers, I wake up with her scent surrounding me, and it's fucking torture.

Not trying to be a crazy ex, but somehow seeming like one, I parked outside her dorm one night, hoping I'd catch her walking in or out, but she never did. I'm not sure what I would have said to her anyway, so it's probably best she didn't. I figure she's probably staying with Courtney, but I don't know where she lives, so I'm stuck begging over voicemail for her to return my calls. I've left so many messages that her voicemail eventually became too full to receive any more.

I need her to let me explain, to tell her the whole truth and not Mia's twisted version of the truth. She has every right to be mad at me, but I can't bear the thought of her flying across the country without seeing or speaking with her first. So even though Drew has made his feelings loud and clear to me coming to her ceremony tonight, he can't stop me. Their family is coming, too, so it's not like she'll be able to deny my existence.

I'm gone before he arrives home and find myself mindlessly driving around before I end up at the parking lot with a dozen red roses and a card. I scribble a note inside the card and will give it to her whether she wants it or not.

There's so many smiling faces walking into the auditorium, and I try really hard to play the part. A lump forms in my throat knowing I will see her for the first time in over a week. Over the years, I've given her a million reasons not to trust me; but this time, my innocence is so fucking tragic that Shakespeare could have written it.

Right before the ceremony starts, I find a place to sit. The venue is crowded, and lots of people are holding signs for their loved ones. After the commencement speech, the announcer begins calling names by departments. My body goes rigid when I hear *Viola Fisher* followed by Summa Cum Laude. Not that I ever doubted her, but she received the highest honors and I'm genuinely happy for her and so proud. The smile on her face grows, and the tears in her eyes form as she walks across that stage. She's wanted this for so long, and now the time has come. I wouldn't have missed this moment for the world.

Hooting and hollering and sounds from air horns come from an opposite corner of the room, and I instantly spot Viola's parents and Drew. And it fucking hurts not to be sitting with them. They've always been my second family, and now I'm the outcast.

Viola sees them, raises her diploma with a fist pump, and walks back to her chair. On top of her graduation cap, I'm pretty sure it says Mischief Managed in golden letters. I can't help but laugh at her Harry Potter nerdiness.

The next name that strikes my attention is Courtney Bishop, Magna Cum Laude. Holy shit, she's a little nerd, too. *Well, who would've guessed that?* Courtney walks across the stage with her long blonde hair in waves and big high heels, and she treats it like a catwalk. A bunch of high-pitched whistles ring out close to me, and I turn and see what must be her entire family. Most of the men are wearing cowboy hats, and the women's hair is heaven high. I can't help but chuckle.

Once the students exit, I watch Viola glance around the room, as if she's looking for someone. *Me, maybe?* I want to stand up and yell her name, but I stop myself. The time begins to pass quicker, knowing I will see her face-to-face in a matter of minutes. I watch Drew and his dad make their way down the stairs, followed by Viola's mom and stepdad. Though there are tons of people in the room, I keep my eyes on them, knowing Viola will be searching for them, too. I head outside where everyone is huddled, waiting for their loved ones, and when I turn the corner, I see her. Our eyes lock and the smile on her face fades. It's just the two of us in a sea of people, and all I want to do is kiss the fuck out of her. Instead, I tuck my lips inside my mouth and force my way through the crowd toward her. She gently shakes her head, giving me a silent warning, but I don't care.

Before I'm able to mutter a word, Drew steps up and hugs Viola, pretending I'm not there. Viola looks at him and looks at me, and it breaks my fucking heart that she's in this situation, which was exactly what she was worried about. Apparently, I'm a liar and betrayed my best friend. It was never supposed to end this way.

I hand her the roses and the card and give her a hug regardless of how stiff her body goes when I touch her. "Congrats, princess," I whisper in her ear, before releasing her and walking away. As much as I want to hang around, leaving was the best thing I could do because her parents would force me to stay once they saw me. The last thing I'd ever want is to ruin her special day.

By the time I get back to my car, and I'm out of the parking lot, I feel like a million pounds are sitting directly on my chest. If I had the ability to go back in time and tell her every detail from the night of the accident, I would, but we all know that only happens in the movies. Where's a damn time-turner when you need one?

I drive to the campus coffee shop and order one of those organic soy shit coffees and sit at a secluded table away from the dude reading poetry about broken hearts. Regardless of how lost I feel at the moment, I still find myself rolling my eyes. Each time the bell above the door rings out, I look up, hoping it's Viola. After an hour passes, I drive back to the house, go to my room, and shut the door.

Gryff is so happy to see me, and I feel bad for pushing him away. I lie on my bed, turn on the TV, and he tucks himself beside me.

"It's just you and me buddy," I say as I pet his little head. "But she'll be back."

VIOLA

I'm a big ball of emotions. Between all the changes in my life, graduation, moving, and the break up, I'm a mess. I've felt every emotion that exists in the last ten days as if I'm checking them off a master list. At first, I was hurt, distraught, and upset, which transformed into me being livid about the entire situation. Then, I wanted to pull a Courtney and go all crazy ex-girlfriend on his ass. His new Challenger almost got a dozen eggs cracked across its shiny black paint, but instead, I kept my distance. It was the best thing for me to do. I avoided Drew's house like the plague and even did laundry at Courtney's this week. But I miss my routine and poor little Gryff.

Drew hasn't been able to look me in the eye, and I'm just as pissed at him as he is at me. I want to strangle him. And I've already warned him that if he even mentions Mia's name around me, he better call for backup because his police buddies are the only ones that'll be able to save him. She's a liar and a cheater, and she's full of misery. I will no longer sit by and take it. He barely acknowledges my existence, and I won't accept Mia and him, so we're at an impasse.

After graduation, our parents take us to dinner, and it's awkward as hell. Afterward, I drive Drew back to his truck, and we exchange a few sentences with one another, but that's it. I hate that he's pissed at Travis and me, but what I hate even more is his stubbornness about the whole situation. As I pull up to his truck, he turns and looks at me, but I speak first.

"Are you going to keep acting like a big ol' baby until I leave?" I ask him directly.

He rolls his eyes at me. "My best friend, Viola. Why?" The hurt in his tone doesn't go unnoticed, and guilt washes over me again. It's a dirty sensation.

"Please don't be mad at me. It's killing me to know you're throwing away your relationship with me and your best friend."

"I don't hate you, Vi. I'm just agitated. I realize you're leaving. You're growing up, and I won't be around to protect you. All I've ever wanted is for you to be happy. That's all I've ever wanted for Travis, too. But you both felt the need to lie to me. Two people I trusted with my life both snuck around behind my back together and betrayed me. I should've realized it when you got that fucking puppy." He shakes his head with an aggravated sigh.

Low blow. Gryff was a thank you gift, but I won't correct him right now. It's the first time he's admitted any of that, and I hate that it's come to this—that he's hurting because of our actions. It's everything I wanted to avoid in the first place, but I know my actions have consequences.

"I'm not a little girl anymore, Drew," I say when he finally looks up at me. "Just so you know, Travis wanted to tell you right away, but I asked him not to because I wanted the timing to be right." I let out a sarcastic laugh as if the timing would ever be right.

He shrugs, unaffected. "He broke the bro code on so many levels, Vi. You don't mess around with your friend's sister behind their back—no exceptions," he states firmly.

"I know. But you won't have to worry about it again because I'm leaving anyway. Everything I love will be in Cali, and I'll be thousands of miles away. I'm sorry. With graduation and the internship, I was busy focusing on that." My eyes begin to water, and I'm allowing my emotions to slip again. I wipe a tear that streams down my face and try to compose myself.

"It was a lot for me to deal with. So, please, if you're going to be pissed at someone for not knowing, direct your anger toward me. As much as I want to blame him, it's not Travis' fault. I never wanted or intended to hurt you, Drew. You're my big brother. My hero. One of my best friends, and as much as you piss me off, I love you. I'm really sorry it happened this way, but I can't be sorry it happened, even if it was a big mistake."

Drew sits there for a second, looking straight out the window as if he's absorbing all of my words. He lets out a sigh and then a small chuckle. "You're still a nerdy little brat; you know that?"

"And you're going to miss me when I'm gone. Are we okay?"

"I forgive you this once but only because we're family and Mom says I have to like you." Drew jokes just like he used to when we were younger. I let out a sigh, knowing we're going to be okay. His phone vibrates in his pocket, and as he pulls it out, I glance down and see Mia's calling.

"I'll see you later, sis." He gets out and answers it immediately.

Even after all the trouble she's started, Mia still has this hold over him. I wish he could see through the bullshit, but perspective is everything, and I can't be a hypocrite.

Before I put the car in drive, I catch the sweet smell of the roses Travis gave me. Though he shouldn't have, I'm glad he was there to acknowledge the accomplishment. It meant a lot, but I don't have the words to tell him that yet. My heart still hurts, and I'm still learning to push all of the memories we spent together to the side. They say distance makes the heart grow fonder, but a part of me prays that distance will help me forget.

I reach in the backseat for the red envelope. The front has a couple kissing in color while the rest of the image is in black and white. Inside, the card is blank, but in all uppercase letters, he wrote:

CONGRATULATIONS, PRINCESS! I'M SO PROUD OF YOU! GRYFF & I LOVE YOU!

Below that is a note in his signature scribble handwriting. *I still plan on driving you to the airport so I can see you one last time before you leave. I miss you. I miss us.*

For a moment I close my eyes and can smell the hint of his cologne on the card.

I peel my eyes open and study it for a moment longer before shoving it back into the envelope and setting it in my middle console.

Thinking about his written message, I feel torn. We'd planned on him taking me so that we could spend those last moments together, but now I'm second-guessing that plan. I'm afraid I won't want to leave if I see him again. Maybe a clean break is what we both need.

As soon as I pull up to my dorm, I get a text from Courtney.

C: **Drinks tonight?**

V: **How about I watch you drink? I'm not in the mood. I have to start packing.**

C: **DEAL! Be there in an hour, after I ditch my family.**

I walk inside with the roses and card. I place the flowers in a vase and lean against the counter and look around at everything I'm leaving. After a few more minutes, I go to my room to make sure I didn't forget to pack anything. The few boxes stacked against the wall will be shipped to my new apartment on Monday.

Other than a few more books and clothes, everything is ready to go. But it's easy moving when most of the furniture is screwed to the wall and floor.

It's funny how time seems to crawl by, then in a blink of an eye, it's like years have passed. College has been my life for the last four years, and it's bittersweet to be leaving, to be opening a new chapter in my life.

A pound on the door lets me know Courtney has arrived, and I can't help but shake my head as I rush to the door. When I open it, she's still wearing the tight little black dress she had on under her graduation gown and high heels that make her tower over me.

"Well, come on, I need a stiff drink after dealing with the Beverly Hillbillies. Oh, you didn't know they came from Texas *to* California?"

I laugh. "I'm sure they're not that bad."

She playfully rolls her eyes and steps inside, noticing the flowers on the counter. "Oh, my God. You got roses? Seriously? From who?"

My eyes meet hers, and I don't even have to say. She immediately knows.

"Maybe you should talk to him?"

"No team Traviola talk tonight." My words come out harsher than I intend them to. Court gives me a small smile and nods her head. Ever since that night, I haven't been able to talk about him, but the whole out-of-sight, out-of-mind thing is total bullshit. Often, when I'm alone, I find myself wondering what he's doing and I'm so tempted to text him, but I don't. My heart is so ready to betray my mind, but I can't. I need to focus on my future while learning to be alone.

"Come on." Courtney loops her arms with mine and drags me to the Jeep. I'm going to miss this so damn much, and it makes me sad that she won't be able to capture me whenever she wants. As she starts it, she bends down and yanks off her heels, throwing them in the backseat. "Those fucking heels…"

The top is down, and the wind is blowing through my hair. Courtney is singing at the top of her lungs, driving way too fast, and all I can do is smile.

"Where are we going?" I ask.

"Cheesecake Factory?"

"You must want to make it to second base tonight." I joke with her because this is where all the college guys bring their girlfriends for date night when they want brownie points to redeem later at night.

She pulls into the parking lot and reaches in the back for her heels. "If we were in Texas, I'd just go barefoot."

"You're ridiculous." I laugh.

"It happens all the time. You have no idea."

We walk inside, and she leads me straight to the bar. Before she even sits down, she's ordering a Martini. I order water and a piece of Godiva chocolate cheesecake. Chocolate fixes all wounds.

"What are you going to do now?" I ask her when the waiter slides the slice of heaven in front of me. She grabs my fork and takes a bite. "Yup, died and went to heaven." She smiles, but then frowns. "Honestly?"

I nod.

"I have no idea. Just thought I'd kind of wing it. My lease doesn't end until the end of the year." She shrugs. "Not sure."

"You stress me out." I laugh. "Your grades were nearly perfect. You could get a job anywhere."

She nudges me. "*Your* grades were perfect. I'll just live life vicariously through you."

After she finishes my cheesecake and her drink, we both start yawning. Who would have thought graduation would be so tiring? We drive back to my dorm, and before I get out, I turn and look at her. This overwhelming sense of sadness takes control, and I lean over and give her a side hug. Courtney unbuckles and pulls me into a big hug and wraps both arms around me. I laugh, thinking about how much we look like lovers, but it's not even like that. She's the sister I always wished I had.

"I'm going to miss the fuck out of you, Lola."

"I'm going to miss you too, Court."

"Who's going to keep me sane when you're gone?" We break our hug.

"Maybe I'll get Drew to," I say with a smile.

Her eyes widen, and I get out of the Jeep. "Don't you dare tease me like that!"

"Who said I was teasing? Bye!"

She smiles and reverses the Jeep so hard the tires squeal. I hear Taylor Swift blaring in the distance, and I know that it might be the last time we get to hang out before I leave. I'm still questioning if leaving is the right choice, but I hope to God it is.

CHAPTER FOURTEEN

TRAVIS

Another dreadful day at the office has me second-guessing returning early in the first place. I feel fine, but the awkward tension between Blake and me is undeniable. Alyssa walks by my office, licks her lips, and pulls her skirt up just before walking off.

I know the two of them are still plotting something against me, especially now that Alyssa is officially the Director of Global Sales. I'm so tired of their shit that I've been thinking more and more about my mother's idea of starting my own small marketing firm. The thought scares the shit out of me, but I know it'd be a great investment for my future, and the more I think about Viola being my future, the more I want to make the best of it.

I call my mom on my way home from work, ready to talk about this business opportunity. It's been a good way to bond without talking about the elephant in the room—my father's cancer—and if I'm going to visit him anytime soon.

The verdict: undecided.

"If you need a loan for the start-up costs, my offer still stands," she tells me again.

"I know, Mom, and I appreciate that. I just think this is something I need to do myself. Grown-up stuff, you know?"

"You may be a twenty-four-year-old man, but you'll always be my little boy, Travis."

I smile and shake my head, even though she can't see me. "I know."

Once I pull into the driveway, we say our goodbyes, and I'm actually relieved to see that Drew is home already. It's been over a week since I've seen Viola after her graduation ceremony, and between work and Gryff, I've stayed plenty busy, but I still miss her like crazy. Things haven't exactly smoothed over between Drew and me either. I hate all the tension between us, but I'm hoping we can resolve that soon. I betrayed his trust, and I'm willing to do whatever it takes to fix that. On the other hand, I'm worried Viola and I will never be the same again.

As soon as I open the door, Gryff runs to me and starts licking my face immediately. I pet his head and back before setting him back down.

"Who's a good boy?" I say in an embarrassing, high-pitched tone that Viola convinced me he liked. He follows me as I walk farther inside.

"Hey, man," I say as I step into the kitchen, where he's steaming vegetables. "Ugh, man. Smells like ass in here."

"Fresh vegetables," he clarifies. "Meal prepping for the next week."

Drew is as obsessed about what he eats as much as he is about working out. I give him props for sticking to it, but I would die if I couldn't binge every once in awhile.

"Chicken and veggies. Sounds delicious," I say with a mocking tone. He knows I'm giving him shit, but he doesn't fire back.

"You get used to it."

"So, I was thinking with Viola leaving next weekend that we should sit down and talk. Get everything out in the open, because I hate this awkward tension between us. I want to tell you everything about that night and the actual truth of events. I know it won't change what's already happened, but I want us to move forward."

I watch as he digests my words. He sprinkles seasonings over the veggies and places the lid back on the pot. He turns around and finally looks at me, uncertainty etched all over his features, and I worry about what he's about to say.

"Viola already left." His words hit me like a ton of bricks, yet I can't comprehend them.

"Wait, *what*?"

"She left two days ago. Booked an earlier flight."

I blink, my mind racing and I can't think straight. She wasn't supposed to leave until next weekend.

"Why? You didn't tell me. She…" I lose my words as I fight back the anger that's brewing inside me.

"Sorry, man. She asked me not to say anything. She said she had to leave and start fresh." I can tell he knows this is hitting me hard as he rests a hand on my shoulder. "We had talked before she left, and I know that what you two had was real and that you both had strong feelings for each other, but she'll always make her future a priority over everyone in her life. She's always been that way."

"I was supportive of that, but we'd planned on me taking her to the airport, at least. I didn't even get to say goodbye."

"I don't think she knew how to say goodbye to you."

Gryff begins pawing at my slacks, directing my attention down to him. I knew she loved Gryff and would've wanted to see him one last time, so the fact that she just left both of us behind leaves me almost speechless.

"So, I guess that means she doesn't want to talk to me either?" I mutter, mostly to myself, but I know Drew heard me.

"Give her some time to adjust, and then try reaching out to her. She might come around. You never know," Drew offers.

I hope he's right.

I can't fathom not talking to her for six months. But what if she meets someone else and forgets about us completely?

The following day, Drew is off work, and I take the opportunity to sit down with him. I want the chance to explain that night, and why I kept the truth about Mia and Viola from him. I know what's done is done, but we have a history, and I can't let something like this burden our friendship.

"So, what do you know? Or rather, what all did Mia tell you?"

"We haven't spoken much since that night. She's called me, but there weren't many details. She still claims you made a move, stripped her down, and then climbed into the backseat with her and started messing around."

I cringe at his words. The mere thought of that happening sickens me.

"Fucking hell, Drew," I mutter, brushing my palms along the thighs of my jeans. "I never touched her."

"I can't say I'd be surprised if that's the truth. But Mia has no reason to lie."

"Mia doesn't need a damn reason to lie, Drew! She's a psycho! She wanted to hurt you, and for some reason wanted to throw me under the bus for her own personal amusement."

"I'm not saying I believed her. But considering your history, and then finding out you hooked up with Viola, it just made her story more believable."

"Look, I know I'm far from perfect, and I have my fair share of fuck ups when it comes to chicks, but I want to be with Viola and her *only*. When I ran into Mia, she was with another guy, and he was screaming in her face. He hit me, man. I'm pretty sure my ribs were broken before the accident. I got her out of there, and she started freaking out, so I pulled over into a gas station parking lot. I tried to calm her down, and the next thing I know, she's coming at me. I didn't kiss her back, and I guess she felt rejected because she came up with some bullshit lie that I touched her."

Drew's soaking up my words as his expression tightens. I know he doesn't want to hear about Mia being with another guy, any more than I'd want to hear that about Viola, but he needs to hear the truth.

"So, how'd she end up naked in your backseat?"

"Once I pushed her back and told her I was in love with someone else, she got all hysterical. She was already freaking out about the fight at the diner, and was feeling sick, and the next thing I know she pukes all over herself. I gave her my shirt to clean up, but it was all over her dress. I told her to lie down in the back and settle her stomach. I didn't have any blankets, so she just took the dress off."

He nods as I finish the story. "I don't remember anything after that, but I swear on my life that I would never touch Mia. Viola owns my heart, and I'm pretty sure she always has."

He looks up and smiles at me. "Well, you better be sure to win her back then."

"Trust me. I won't stop until I do."

Over the weekend, I drive up to my childhood home. I didn't call and give my mother a heads-up because I kept changing my mind. The closer I got, the more nervous I felt. I hadn't seen my dad in years, and I wasn't sure what to expect now that he was sick, but I felt it was something I needed to do. At least for my mom's sake.

"Travis!" she squeals the moment she opens the door and sees me. "I can't believe you're here!" She takes a step forward and wraps her arms around me.

I smile as she squeezes me a tad too tight. She notices I wince and quickly steps back. "Sorry, I'm just so excited you're here."

Shrugging with a guilty smile, I say, "Well, I figured it was finally time to come home."

She leads me inside, and I follow. Everything looks the same, and it feels like I'm walking through a time capsule from my childhood. My father is sitting in the living room in the same chair he's always sat in, usually with a six-pack and the remote, but this time he's with a magazine and a glass of ice water.

"Look who came for a visit," my mother says, grabbing his attention up to mine. His reaction is clear. He's completely shocked, but he doesn't make the first move to speak.

"Hi, Dad."

"Son." He nods. "You look good."

"Thanks." I follow my mother's lead and sit on the sofa across from him. "You do, too." The first thing I notice about my father is that he's sober. I think it's the first time in my life I've seen him sober.

"Wish I could say I feel as good as I look, but..."

"Yeah, Mom told me." I brush a hand over my jawline. "What's the diagnosis?"

"Stage four cancer." He says it as casually as if I were asking him about the weather. He looks like he's accepted the terms of his destiny, but when I glance over at my mother and see her frown, it's obvious she hasn't. I know she loves my father and will go through this with him until the end, but I wish he had treated her better to merit such loyalty.

We spend the afternoon talking over lunch. It's been years since I've felt like I've had a family, and even though I still have a lot of resentment toward him, I'm glad I came. I know my mom is going to need a lot of support, whether she wants to admit it or not.

VIOLA

It's been a week since I've arrived in Boston, which is beautiful in the summer, but I'm still suffering from the jet lag. The three-hour time difference has messed with my sleeping schedule, and I'm so exhausted. I've been struggling to wake up to my alarm every morning. I've also been suffering from these annoying headaches and nausea. I looked it up, and I guess it's pretty common if you experience jet lag, so I'm hoping my body gets used to it soon. Either that or the nerves are wreaking havoc on my entire body.

Even texting Drew or Courtney is becoming a challenge. When I'm up and ready for work at eight, they're still in bed and barely functioning. I've learned not to expect a response from Courtney until my lunch break.

I only brought the essentials with me, so unpacking was a breeze. I managed to find a furnished studio apartment, and with the company's payment plan, it's actually affordable. It's only four hundred square feet, but it's cute and works for me. The day after I arrived, I FaceTimed Courtney and showed her around. She nearly gasped when I showed her the tiny bathroom.

"Can you even pee in there?" She asked as I gave her the tour. The answer is yes, but it's not easy. The door has to be left open. Otherwise, my knees hit the paneling.

The kitchen isn't a kitchen at all, but rather a kitchenette with a tiny sink, a mini fridge, and a one-burner stove. It doubles as my bedroom, which is fine by me since I'm only home to sleep or shower anyway. But the one bonus is the rooftop deck and community garden I get to use.

I've been at the firm five days now, which is terrifying and exciting all at once. My boss, Henry O'Connor, is extremely intimidating. I do most of the bitch work, but I know once I prove myself, I'll be able to handle some group projects.

By the time my day ends and I make it back to my little hole of an apartment, it's after seven. I'm exhausted and hungry, and the only thing that keeps me sane is talking to Courtney throughout the day. Drew checks in on me every couple of days, and I know he's worried about me, but I need to prove to him and myself that I'm capable of doing this. I left home at eighteen, graduated college with honors, and now I'm ready for whatever the real world throws at me.

C: **It's been years since I've gotten laid. My vagina is starting to prune.**

The first thing I see when I wake up is a text message from Courtney, from the night before. I laugh and send her a text back.

V: **It has not been years, and unless you've been soaking it in hot water for months, I doubt it's pruney.**

Surprisingly, she messages me back before I even roll out of bed.

C: **Well, it sure feels like years. At this point, I'd be lucky to even remember how to do it.**

I snort at her dramatics.

V: **I don't know...I bet it's just like riding a bike. Your vagina's instincts will kick in and you'll be dry humping in no time.**

C: **No one says dry humping anymore, Lola. Plus, don't tease me with that shit... you either put out or GTFO.**

Burying my head into my pillow, I laugh, and it feels good.

V: **I need to get ready for work. Buy yourself a dildo and get some practice in. Talk later!**

Once I'm half-ready and out the door, I hail a cab and finish my makeup as we swerve around the traffic. Union International is right in the heart of the city, so there are a lot of places within walking distance for lunch or coffee, which is nice.

There are four other interns I work with, but only two of us work for Mr. O'Connor. His name is Liam, and he's from Miami. He's been super sweet and helpful as I've adjusted to everything around the firm.

"So, any big plans for your first official weekend here?" he asks as we step into the elevator.

"No, not really. Unless you consider FaceTiming my best friend and reading big plans?" I say with an easy laugh.

"Well if your big plans fall through, I'm meeting up with some friends for a drink downtown if you feel like joining. Here, I'll give you my number." He holds his hand out, waiting for my phone.

Instinctively, I unlock it and hand it over. I figure it can't hurt to have a friend around here, especially if I'm going to be here for six months or longer.

"Awesome, thanks," I say as he hands it back.

"I texted myself from your phone, so I have yours too, just in case."

I nod, unsure of what to say. I don't want to assume he's hitting on me because I have no intentions of hooking up with anyone while I'm here, especially someone from the office. I've been thinking about Travis nonstop since I left. I feel guilty for leaving without saying goodbye, but I knew I had to. I knew if I saw him, I would run into his arms and never get on that plane regardless of how hurt I was. I couldn't let a guy get in the way of my future, not after all the hard work I've put in and all the goals I've set for myself. Travis will always have my heart, but for now, I need to stay focused on me. If we have anything worth saving, it will be there in six months.

The weeks fly by, the hours blurring into days, the days into weeks. Liam becomes a good friend and introduces me to some of his local buddies. He shows me around the bars and best seafood restaurants. It feels like another world out here, but I'm soaking up everything this experience has to offer.

Travis texts me every few days. When I first arrived, we didn't talk for two weeks, probably because he was hurt I left without saying anything.

Then one night he sent me a picture of Gryff, with the caption *We miss you*. I cried the moment I saw his sweet little face. Before I could respond, he sent a second picture of the two of them lying in his bed, and Travis sticking his lower lip out in a sad pout. I about lost it. I missed him so damn much, but I knew I had to stay strong. This was good for me, and I had to remember that. Travis and I were in a complicated situation, and all I wanted was to get to a neutral place again where it stopped hurting.

So, now he sends me picture updates of how big Gryff is getting and he asks how things are here. We don't say much other than that, which right now, is enough for us. I know we'll have a lot to talk about when I visit for the holidays.

About halfway through my apprenticeship, I catch some kind of summer flu. It's awful, but I work through it until I'm off on the weekend. It doesn't ease up, so Liam surprises me with soup and crackers.

"You look pale, honey," he says, placing a cold, wet washcloth on my forehead. "Are you hungry?"

I press a hand to the cloth and shake my head. "Not really. I just feel really queasy."

"I'll bring your trash can by you just in case." I watch as he stands up and walks the few feet to my kitchen and grabs it. He's tall and built. He has shaggy blonde hair, which totally adds to the surfer vibe he gives out when he's not in his suit and tie attire. He overdresses for work and claims it's going to help him climb the corporate ladder before he's thirty.

"Thanks," I say, watching as he sets it down next to me. "I think I'm just going to try and sleep it off."

"Yeah, good idea, hon. I'll lay on your couch and wait for you to wake up so you can eat."

"No," I argue. "You don't have to sit around and wait on me. I'll be okay."

"Nonsense. You need to get better so I have someone to go salsa dancing with."

I let out a small laugh. "I never agreed to that in the first place."

He tilts his head and frowns.

I groan. "We'll see."

He smiles and flashes me a wink. "Get some rest. I'm going to binge on your Netflix."

I sleep for the next three hours, and when I wake up, it's dark outside, and Liam is still watching TV on my sofa. He pauses it the moment he hears me rustling under the covers.

"Hey." He smiles. "How do you feel?"

"Better, I think. I need to pee."

He laughs and goes back to his show. I grab my phone as I walk to the bathroom and see that Courtney has messaged me three times.

V: **Sorry, I was sleeping. I think I caught the flu.**

I send back to her urgent messages.

C: **The flu? What are your symptoms?**

I respond with everything I've been feeling this past week.

V: **Vomiting, nausea, queasiness, headaches, hot flashes and sweats. Liam brought me some soup, so I'm going to try eating some of that and see if it helps.**

C: **How long have you been sick?**

V: **Off and on about a week or so. I think it's going around work.**

I reply back, heading back out to my bed.

C: **Well unless it's homesickness, I'd say it's pregnancy that's going around your office!**

V: **OMG! I am not pregnant! I haven't had sex in months!**

The last time was with Travis, of course.

C: **Have you missed your period?**

It takes me a while to think about it because I can't remember. Which I realize is not a good sign. I've been so busy that I haven't paid attention. I open the calendar on my phone and count back the days from when Travis and I were together, to the last time I remember having my period.

Three months ago.

V: **I can't remember the last time I had it...I've been stressed and busy. But I'm on the pill, so it's probably just the flu.**

C: **Yeah...the flu that makes you skip your period for three months and doesn't go away, but comes and goes...sounds LEGIT.**

Dammit, Courtney! She's totally making me freak out right now. There's just no way. I would've been able to tell by now.

V: **My body always gets weird when I'm stressed out. Stop jinxing me!**

C: **LOL! Too late for that... go buy a test and FaceTime me!**

V: **I feel way too shitty to leave my apartment right now and I'm not asking Liam to go on a pregnancy test run.**

I told her about Liam when we first met, and at first, she thought we were hooking up, but once I told her I thought he was gay, she backed off. However, I'm still not totally sure about that.

C: **You better find out quick then. There's a long list of stuff you'll need to be doing if you are…**

I sigh, taking in a deep breath. I can't even fathom that right now.

V: **I'll call you tomorrow.**

"Are you okay?" Liam's voice directs my attention back up to him.

I blink away the tears and set my phone down, needing to clear my head from the revelation I just had. "I don't know."

CHAPTER FIFTEEN

TRAVIS

Six Months Later…

"You can set the computers and printer over there," I say, directing the delivery drivers as they wheel a big hunk of plastic and boxes into the building. At random moments, like right now, I think about Viola. Though it's been six months since she left for Boston, it seems like yesterday and each day she's not here is heartbreaking torture. Randomly we text back and forth, but it's not the same. Honestly, it hasn't been since she left without allowing me to explain myself fully. She took my heart with her, and I'm waiting for her to personally deliver it back to me. To this day, the only woman I want is the one who stole my heart—Viola Fisher.

Somehow I've managed to stay busy and put my focus on getting my business off the ground. The sign for King Marketing will arrive in the next thirty minutes and is being installed on the outside of the modest building I leased. The sign in the office that hangs on the wall behind the reception desk has the logo on it, *King Marketing: Where you're treated like royalty.* I laugh at the memory of Drew giving me so much shit over it too, but now he says I should have the logo printed on t-shirts so he can proudly wear it.

As I stand back and look at the reception desk and the open office space, I think about how proud Viola is that I really did it; I started my own business. I don't burden her with all the details, knowing she's staying plenty busy right now, but I know Drew is keeping her up-to-date. With the holidays approaching, the grand opening and scissor cutting ceremony isn't until after the new year. I've invited community leaders, potential clients, and even the mayor, but the only person I want to be there is *her*.

As I look around, I remember how empowering it was to leave Crawford Marketing five months ago. The accident and Viola leaving was the wake-up call I needed. Going after my dreams is scary as fuck, but the reward is so much greater than the risk, and so far I haven't regretted my decision. I now laugh at the day I took control of my career and gave Crawford Marketing the hypothetical middle finger. Blake was reaming my ass, as usual, something about not using time stamps on printed documents, and it all just clicked. There was no way I could stay there any longer—not with the tension, the lies, and the whole corporate vibe.

As Blake continued to shout at me, I stood up and started grabbing small items off my desk and tossing them into my briefcase. He was so far up his own ass; he didn't even realize what I was doing. After asking him if he was done, I told him 'I quit.' Hilariously, he told me I couldn't quit and demanded I get my ass back to my desk. I laughed in his face and walked out of my office without looking back. All the stress that miserable job caused instantly disappeared when I took my final step out the door. I wished I would have done it sooner.

The following day I wrote out my business plan and continued to push forward on opening my own marketing firm. As ready as I am, and knowing I've given it my all, I'm still nervous as fuck because failing is not an option.

Once the computers and printer are set up, I realize I should've hired an IT person to make sure the networking is installed correctly. Remembering Viola mentioning Courtney being a computer genius, which still shocks the shit out of me, I decide to ask Drew for her number.

T: **Hey, do you have Courtney's number by chance?**

D: **Who?**

T: **Courtney. Has the hots for you. Viola's crazy blonde friend. Usually parading around in cowgirl boots and red lipstick.**

D: **Thanks for such a vivid picture. No, I don't, but I'll ask Viola for it.**

He sends it back to me in under a minute. I'm sure Viola was more than willing to give it to him, probably because she thinks Drew wants to ask Courtney on a date or something. It actually makes me laugh. I would've texted Viola and asked myself, but our conversations haven't been anything more than small talk or pictures of Gryff. She texts me about her job duties and her friend, Liam. She posts pictures of them together on Instagram, and it drives me insane that she's spending so much time with him, even though she swears they're only friends.

I don't tell her how much it hurts to have her gone or not to know where we stand. I don't tell her it feels as if we're in limbo, and I have no idea if she'll ever move back or if we'll ever be an *us* again. I don't tell her any of those things because I fear it'll scare her away forever.

Although I've given her the space she's clearly asked for, it's killing me inside. I want to beg her to come back to me, tell her I need her, and that every day since she's been gone has been the worst day of my life. But I know that isn't fair to her. She's worked so hard for this opportunity, and I can't be the one to get in the way of it. I know she's making a life in Boston, and although it still pains me to know she doesn't trust me, I'm not giving up on us. I'll never give up on us and will do whatever it takes to gain her trust back. I know she'll be home soon for the holidays, and that'll be my chance to lay it all out for her. She won't leave again without knowing exactly where I stand.

Union International will more than likely offer her a full-time position; they would be idiots not to, but it'll be her decision to accept or decline.

The selfish part of me hopes she hates the snow as much as she hates the rain and will come back to sunny California without a second thought.

The loud sound of a truck entering the parking lot directs my attention out the window, and I see the sign installers have arrived. I stand outside as they use a lift to attach the sign to the outside of the building, and I'm so damn excited about it. I snap a picture and send it to Viola with the message: ***It's really happening***.

V: **That's amazing! I'm so proud of you :)**

Her words mean the world to me.

T: **Thank you, princess. I hope you'll still be in town for the scissor-cutting ceremony. I'd love to have you there.**

She doesn't respond, and I know I've pushed too far. If we weren't three thousand miles apart, I know our relationship—or whatever the hell you want to call it— would be in a completely different place. I try to be cautious when telling her how much I miss her, but sometimes I slip up, which throws a wrecking ball into the conversation. My feelings haven't changed, regardless of the time that's passed, and I'm pretty sure I've made that clear.

Once the sign is installed, I decide to lock up for the night and head home. It's been a long-ass day, and the next two weeks are going to be even more hectic with interviews and pre-booking appointments with potential clients.

As soon as I walk into the house, Gryff is at my feet, barking and jumping all over me. He's so fucking happy to see me every day that it puts a huge smile on my face. I open the front door and allow him to run outside. We have a daily routine now. Every night after I come home, I let him out, and he runs around the yard. Then he chases the neighbor's cat, and I hope he never catches it. Once he's done, he rushes inside, and I feed him his treats and stock his water and food dishes. He's a spoiled little shit, and I'm pretty sure I'm the trained one instead of him.

After taking a shower, I relax on the couch, and Gryff lies down next to me. He places his head on my lap as I watch the news and suddenly remember I forgot to text Courtney.

T: Hey. It's Travis King.

How original. I roll my eyes at myself. I don't know why I'm nervous.

C: THE Travis King? To what do I owe this honor?

She doesn't even ask how I got her number or she doesn't care. Either way, I'm ready to make a deal with her.

T: **I have a business proposition for you.**

C: **Depends what it is. I might be too busy getting my nails and hair done.**

T: **Way to live up to the cliché.**

C: **Way to be an asshole.**

T: Well, it is my specialty.

C: All right, King. Get to the point.

T: **I heard you're good at tech shit, and I need help with setting up the new computers at my office with our network and installing the firewall and all of that stuff. I pay well.**

It takes her a long time to respond, and I start wondering if asking her was a bad idea.

C: **That depends. Can you get me a date with your stud best friend?**

T: **I'd try but I have a feeling he's against prostitution.**

C: **You don't know until you ask!**

I'm not even sure what to say back. Whoring out Drew would be the cheapest way to get this done, but maybe not the most ethical. I laugh because she doesn't seem to have any filters about this. Before I can respond, she sends another text.

C: **Geez. I'm just kidding! You're no fun to mess with if you don't take the bait. So what time and where?**

T: **Tomorrow around 11? I'll text you the address.**

C: **You got it, boss!**

I groan.

T: **Don't make me regret this.**

C: **I already do.**

I laugh and shake my head. I really hope she knows what she's doing. If I didn't witness her graduating with honors, I'm not sure I would've ever believed she was a little genius because she doesn't put off that nerdy, smart girl vibe. Her accent, blonde hair, and blue eyes give her a Southern belle vibe but mixed with sorority girl gone wild. She's completely opposite from Viola in almost every way, but maybe that's why they get along so well.

At least now, I'm able to relax a little, knowing that part of the business will be taken care of—*hopefully*.

Hours later, Drew comes home in his gym clothes with his uniform thrown over his shoulder. He looks like he's had a day from hell and when he cracks open a beer before he does anything else, it's confirmed.

"Wanna talk about it?" I ask him as he sits down on the couch and starts mindlessly flipping through the channels.

"I'm pretty sure I'm never going to get over Mia."

I hate hearing her name on his lips, and I hate seeing him so distraught. It's been months since the big blowout, and she still manages to string him along like a plaything. He's addicted to her, and regardless of what we all tell him, he can't let her go.

I think back to Courtney's text message, and an evil grin spreads across my face.

"How would you like to do me a huge favor?"

He chugs his beer until it's empty.

"What's that?"

"Bring lunch for Courtney tomorrow, at the firm, around elevenish?"

He gives me a pointed look. "Your favors are dangerous, King."

I throw my head back and laugh because it's true. All of Viola's and my rekindling started with a single favor—a lunch favor, actually.

"You're being weird," he says.

"If you wear your cop uniform, I might be able to get her to install the software on all of the computers I had delivered today for free."

Now he's the one laughing. "I'm not going to be your stripper!"

"Why not? I'm sure she'll keep her hands to herself." I smirk because we both know that's a lie. He gives me a look.

"It will be good for you. I don't know what she likes to eat, but I'm sure Viola knows. Please?"

"Maybe," he says, and I feel pretty good about my open attempt to play matchmaker.

In the morning, I work out, then go straight to the office and try to read through diagrams for these damn computers. I can't comprehend the nonsense. Right before eleven, Courtney pulls up in her Jeep, music blaring. She's wearing this crazy dress with big polka dots, and her hair is pulled up into a tight, high ponytail. I watch her reach over and grab a bright pink tool kit with her name embroidered on the outside. It takes everything inside me not to burst out laughing. She sees me inside, gives me a big wave, and then swings open the door like she owns the place.

"Whoa! Apple products. Nice work, King." Her eyes widen when she sees the large iMacs lined against the desks along the wall. She drops the heavy bag down on the front counter where my secretary will sit—as soon as I hire one. Shit, I have so much to do.

"Yeah. Only the best." I smile proudly.

"Agreed. So, whatcha got?"

I hand her a box of cords and CDs with a smile. "Can you help me install all of this and get the router and network set up, so it's protected?"

She puckers her lips and gives a playful eye roll. "Duh."

Immediately she starts wiring everything together, inserting discs and clicking through things quickly, like she's got all the steps memorized. Before finishing, she neatly zip-ties all the cords, so they look nice.

"You're good to go." She slaps her hands together with a smile.

I sit down at one of the computers and see the wireless network in the top right-hand corner.

"Oh, I set up a shared drive for everyone, too. You know, just in case you wanted that." She winks.

I didn't even ask for that, but it will be helpful during start-up to stay on the same page with my employees. My eyes widen. Shit, she really is a genius. Before I can even tell her thank you, a squad car pulls up in front of the building. Courtney sees me staring behind her with a smile, and she turns and catches sight of Drew. Now her eyes are the ones that are wide. She tucks loose strands of hair behind her ears and sits on the desk with her long legs crossed.

Drew walks in with a bag from the local deli and a bottle of fancy looking water. I'm pretty sure I saw drool drip down her chin, but I don't dare say a word.

"Ms. Bishop?"

Courtney's mouth falls open. Drew is fucking working this. I'm so proud of him for stepping out of his comfort zone because I know how hard this is for him. He ignores every girl that bats a lash his way, especially Courtney. But she deserves a trophy for trying.

She stands and puts her hand over her heart.

"Those damn handcuffs," she says under her breath and then realizes I heard her. She glares at my snicker, and I shrug.

"I was told your favorite lunch is a chicken wrap and pure coconut water," Drew says.

"Wait, what?" She's just as shocked as I am that he brought her lunch.

He hands her the bag, and she takes it with a huge smile on her face. This might be the most attention he's given her—ever. His radio goes off, and he answers back quickly.

"Hope you enjoy it," he tells her and then turns around and leaves.

Courtney leans against the wall and sighs. She's so damn dramatic.

"Oh, my God, Travis! Are you trying to kill me?"

I can no longer hold back my laughter. "No, I need your help!"

"I'll do it. I accept your offer."

"What?" I'm confused.

"Just tell me when we open, and I'll be here. Especially if you can pay me in glimpses of Drew in that uniform."

VIOLA

Union International offered me a great salary, a decent-sized office, and a position I only dreamed of having six months ago. Considering my current situation, my only option was to decline, as hard as it was to say no. They even counter offered, giving me a twenty percent pay increase, but it wasn't enough to keep me grounded in Boston. I packed my stuff and shipped it to Courtney since I'll be staying with her until I find a place of my own. The last few months have been...well...*interesting*.

Drew and Courtney both know I'm not returning to Boston once I leave, but I haven't found the courage to tell Travis yet. He'll find out soon enough and when I don't leave after the holidays are over it'll be a dead giveaway. I begged them not to say a word because I want to be the one to tell him. I have to be. We have a lot to talk about, but the truth is, I'm not sure what to say to him or where to even begin. Just thinking about it gives me an anxiety attack.

I shove my carry-on in the overhead compartment of the plane and slide the window cover open, peering out into the distance. Soon we take off over a blanket of white fog, and as nervous as I am to be returning back to Cali, I'm happy to be leaving Boston and all the damn snow.

As the plane lands in California, I feel a little ridiculous wearing a baggy sweater and so many layers. I roll my sleeves up to my elbows and patiently wait while we deplane. I was cold, but now I'm sweating. Freaking hormones. A lump forms in my throat when I open my text messages and see Courtney is already waiting for me. This is happening. I'm really home.

After I pee, I wheel my suitcase through the airport, trying to find just a sliver of courage. I walk through the double doors, and Courtney is leaning against her Jeep with a big, goofy smile on her face. She takes off running in high heels and gives me a big hug.

"Oh, my God, Mama! Look at you!" She squeals and pats my tummy. I'm so happy she's excited about this pregnancy, because I'm still not sure how to feel, but I've felt like that since the day I found out.

Though I felt like death, I Ubered to the nearest pharmacy. The guy who drove me across town looked at me like I had the plague and I'm sure when I stepped out of his car he sprayed disinfectant all over the seats. I walked inside, and stared at the pregnancy tests, picking up a two-pack, which claims to be 99.9% accurate. I've never had to take one, and I almost find it hilarious that it's come to this point. Courtney is three thousand miles away but has me so worked up I have to know for sure. I'm pretty confident it's a virus. I've had the flu before. I know the symptoms, and I feel like death—totally the flu.

When I grab the cardboard box, I feel ridiculous. All the way to the counter, I keep repeating how I can't be pregnant. Birth control. I didn't miss a pill. Not one. I take a cab back to my studio apartment and somehow find the strength to climb the stairs. I read the instructions at least ten times before I take the stick out and pee on it, and then I wait. Almost immediately two pink lines appear.

No, no, no.

I take the other pregnancy test out of the wrapper and pee on it, too.

The first one had to be wrong. This could not be happening, not now, not when I'm at the beginning of my career and so far away from everyone I love. Just as fast as the other one, two pink lines.

I sit on the toilet and stare at it in shock. I'm not even sure what to do or say. Immediately I call Courtney, crying.

"Oh, my God, Lola. What's wrong? Is everything okay?"

"Court." I sit there a long time in silence as tears stream down my face.

"Lola? You're freaking me out."

"I'm…" I couldn't even say the words.

She pats my belly and brings me back to reality. I gulp thinking about how lost I felt when I told her, but she was there for me. I don't believe there was a time when she wasn't.

"So, I guess this sweater didn't cover up this bump?" I look down and laugh.

"I mean for the most part, but it's still totally obvious."

"Couldn't you have just lied?" I smile, but I thought I'd be able to face Drew without him instantly knowing. It's so hard to recognize the change in myself, but I thought it wasn't that noticeable with oversized clothes. Who the hell am I trying to fool? *Everyone.*

"I cannot wait to go shopping. Cute little clothes and hats and shoes. I LOVE BABIES!" She's talking so loud, her voice echoes through the parking garage. She grabs my suitcase and throws it into the back of the Jeep and slams her foot on the gas as usual. I shoot her a look, and she slows down. "Sorry, I forgot there was a baby on board."

I grin at her. "So, how was your wrap and coconut water?"

Drew texted me and told me what was going on, that Travis asked for a favor, and I'm happy he considered Courtney and looped Drew in on it. She's the best of the best and can help him with anything he needs.

"I'm so happy you're home and that you're finally going to be my roommate," she says as she parks outside of her place. We had talked about living together so many different times in college, but after being accepted into the common dorms, it was a lot easier to move my stuff across campus and not have to worry about paying rent.

"So, I got a job," Courtney says, wheeling my suitcase across the pavement to her apartment.

"Really?"

"Well, I kind of told Travis I was going to work for him." She bursts out laughing, and I can't help but laugh, too.

"Seriously? What did he say?" God, I miss him.

"He looked at me like I had lost my damn mind."

I know that look well.

"Have you?" We walk inside, and I see my boxes waiting for me in the living room.

"Yeah, probably a little bit. But my dad said no more freeloading. Either I get a job or move back to Texas and work on the ranch. How cliché is that?" She wrinkles her nose and makes a face. "And we both know I wouldn't survive one day of having dirt under my fingernails or sweating." She cringes.

"Oh, sweet baby Jesus."

"I know, right? I'm not going back to Texas. No way. Not with your hot brother showing up and bringing me lunch. And with me becoming an aunt and all."

I shake my head at her. "Well, if Travis goes for it, you totally should. He's dealt with enough shit from the corporate world, that I'm sure he'll treat his employees like gold. But honestly Court, it's marketing. You hated marketing."

She laughs. "Because it was boring! You have to admit it was boring."

"You have a point." I sit on the couch and prop up my swollen feet. "Oh, my God!"

She stands up and walks toward me. "What, are you okay?"

I look up at her, shocked. "Yeah. I just felt the baby kick for the first time."

"Baby Traviola loves me!" She sits next to me and places her hand on my stomach, and the baby kicks again. It's one of the weirdest sensations and makes this impending motherhood thing feel very real all of a sudden.

"Have you told anyone else yet?" She searches my face.

I shake my head. "Not yet. I'm not even sure what to say."

"Honestly, I'm sure you won't have to say anything." She gives me a smile then glances down at my tummy.

"Oh, shut it. I'm so nervous, Court. I'm really scared to tell Drew. I'm worried to tell Travis and my parents. I feel lost. What if Drew hates me? What if Travis writes me off? What if my parents make me feel guilty?"

She gives me a hug. "What-ifs don't mean shit. And no matter what, it's going to be okay. No one's reactions will change the fact that you're going to have a sweet little baby. Everyone will have to accept it. You're going to be the best mom on the planet, and I'm going to be the world's number one aunt. And you know if you need anything, I'm here. Okay? Always."

I nod, and she gives me a tight hug. Sometimes Courtney is completely ridiculous, but I love the fact that she's always on my team, rooting for me, no matter what.

On a whim, I pick up my phone and text Drew because the time for him to know is now. I can't hide this any longer.

V: **I'm home. Still up for ice cream?**

D: **Yeah, give me an hour?**

V: **Yep!**

My nerves kick into overdrive.

I glance at Courtney. "Want to drive me to Sugars, so I can tell Drew the big news?"

She lifts both of her eyebrows. "Are you sure? At an ice cream shop?"

"He won't make a scene in a public place." I laugh, but it's true.

"You're evil."

Time passes quickly. Courtney reluctantly drops me off, and while I wait, I order two scoops of strawberry ice cream and sit in a secluded booth in the corner of the room. I get lost in my phone, and only look up when I see Drew walking toward me with a scoop of chocolate. I was so into this new book that I didn't even see him come in or even order. As soon as he sees me, he smiles.

"Vi, you look good! The extra winter weight suits you," he says, grabbing my spoon and helping himself to my ice cream that I've barely touched.

I furrow my brows.

"You too, ass." I glare at him. He stops shoving the ice cream in his mouth, and I laugh. For the next thirty minutes, Drew catches me up on work and our parents. He talks about Travis and the business and even mentions Gryff. One person he doesn't dare talk about is Mia, because he knows better, and considering my hormones, I might lose my shit over strawberry ice cream. It seems as if all of their lives have gone on without me, and I feel like I've missed so much. My heart is racing, and I try to find the right place to tell him the news. After he complains about the cold, I just blurt it out.

"I'm pregnant."

At first, he doesn't stop talking, and I think he doesn't hear me, so I repeat myself.

"I'm pregnant, Drew."

His mouth drops open, and he sits there and stares at me like I slapped him across the face. I'm thankful there's no one else in the restaurant.

"You're going to be an uncle."

The fact that he's not saying anything is stressing me out. I know it's a lot to take in, so I sit there and wait for him to speak. Time slips through my fingers, and I cover my face with my hands because I feel the tears welling on the brims of my eyes. Gently he pulls my hands away so he can search my face.

"I'm going to be an uncle?" He sounds and looks shocked.

I nod.

"Who is the..."

"Oh, my God, Drew. Who do you think? I don't sleep around."

His eyes widen as he connects the dots, and I want to know what he's thinking. We sit there, staring at each other, and I wish Courtney would just walk in and say something that makes me laugh. My heart is beating so fast I can feel the pulse rock through my body.

Drew finally gives me a smile, and it allows me to relax just a bit. "Does Travis know?"

I shake my head. "Not yet, but I'm going to tell him as soon as possible."

"Yeah, he needs to know he's going to be a dad."

I swallow hard. "Remember that favor you owe me?"

"How could I forget?" Drew says.

"Can you help me tell Mom and Dad?"

CHAPTER SIXTEEN

TRAVIS

As I'm leaving the house to head to the office, I see a package from FedEx sitting against the door. Confused, I pick it up and realize it's the surprise birthday gift I mailed to Boston for Viola. Since her birthday is only a few days away, I thought I'd send her something nice—a pair of diamond earrings to match the heart necklace I gave her when we were kids. It really fucking hurts my heart to see the box sitting at my feet.

I pick it up and walk back inside as I send her a text.

T: **Refusing my packages now?**

Her text bubble instantly pops up.

V: **Huh?**

T: **I mailed you a package for your birthday and it's been returned.**

She doesn't reply as quickly, but once she finally does, I'm floored.

V: **It's because I'm back home.**

I read the text again, and it confuses me. *What the hell?* She wasn't coming home until closer to Christmas last I heard.

T: **What? You're here right now? You're early.**

I wish she would've told me as soon as she landed, and I know I'm probably not at the top of her list, but fuck, I'll fight my way back to the top. Still, for some reason, I thought I'd be the first to know.

V: **Yeah, I'm here permanently. Can we talk soon?**

Permanently?

T: **You tell me the time and place, and I'll be there, princess.**

I pick up the FedEx package and set it on the counter, wondering if it's too early to start drinking. I hadn't expected Viola to be home already, and now to hear she's not going back is a sweet surprise. Honestly, I'm unsure of how I should feel right now. A part of me is thrilled to fucking death that Viola is here, but another part of me is anxious. What does this mean exactly? I wish it meant that we'd have another chance to be together, but that's a dangerous game to be playing. On the other hand, just the thought of her being here puts a huge smile on my face. Every day since she left, I've wished she'd come back to Cali—come back to me—and now she has.

Drew wakes up and drags his ass into the kitchen and furrows his brows at the smile I'm wearing. I can't help it.

"Did you win the lottery or something?" he asks.

"Viola is home! Did you know?"

He gives me a nervous smile, but I try to ignore it. "Yeah, she asked me not to say anything."

I don't even comment, because it was the same words I'd said to him whenever we talked about Viola and me. She had asked me not to say anything until she was ready, and I didn't.

Drew takes the carton of milk out of the fridge and drinks it straight from the jug.

"Please tell me you don't do that all the time," I say, disapproving.

"Have been for about six years." Drew chuckles and rubs his face. "I didn't sleep very well last night."

"Sorry, that sucks." Work must be stressing him out again. He goes through these cycles where everything is great, then some days he's so stressed, I know to stay out of his way.

"If you only knew." He pauses. "Well, you might eventually," he mutters under his breath, but I don't give it a second thought. After he yawns, he heads back to his room. I brush off his weirdness and rip open the FedEx box to pull out the gift box wrapped in silver paper and take it with me to the office. I have my first interview with a prospective employee today, which makes me realize this is really happening. I've always heard that when a person finds a job they truly love, it will never feel like work. Each day I see my name on the sign, I understand that saying more. My name, my reputation, my money is all on the line, and the closer we get to opening, the more nervous I become, but I love the anticipation.

Before I unlock the door to the firm, I receive another text from Viola.

V: **Can you meet me at Courtney's?**

She attaches the address.

T: **I'll be there as soon as I can.**

After an hour of an interview from hell, I lock up. I'm anxious and nervous as fuck to see her again. It's been so long since I've seen her, I just want to wrap her in my arms and kiss the shit out of her. I want to forget everything that happened in our past and beg her to give us a second chance. Not knowing what to expect or what she'll say makes me the most anxious. There are so many different things she could say. The unknown suffocates me all the way to Courtney's place.

There's slow-moving traffic on the bridge, and I wait at least half an hour for them to clean up an accident. At least it gives me time to run through everything I want to say to her. There's so much I need to say; it's just finding the right words that make it nerve-wracking. I know I've fucked up so many times over the years, and I have to take her being back in California as if I've been given another chance. I refuse to fuck this up again. Truth be known, she might have to put a restraining order on me to keep me away.

Once I pull up next to Courtney's Jeep, my nerves take over. I rub my hand over my face and take in a deep breath before I grab the gift and get out. It will be the first time I've seen her since her graduation. As soon as I head down the sidewalk, I see Courtney getting ready to lock the door. Walking a little faster, she sees me and waits.

"She's asleep," she whispers.

"Should I come back later?" I ask.

"No, the time change has messed with her. I'm sure she'll be up soon." She opens the door, and when I step in, she waves goodbye and closes it behind her.

I stand there for a moment, watching Viola sleep on the couch, snuggled with a blanket around her body. She looks so peaceful and beautiful, and it's hard for me to not immediately go to her, pull her in my arms, and tell her I'm never letting her go again.

I sit in the chair next to the couch and wait for her. She looks way too comfortable for me to interrupt her sleep. Ten minutes later, she stirs, and her eyes flutter open.

"Travis?" She looks confused.

"Yeah, princess."

"Why didn't you wake me up? How long have you been here?"

"Long enough to know you're exhausted. I can come back later, if you want."

"No, that's okay." She sits up and pulls the blanket over her arms and crosses her legs. After putting on her glasses, she tucks hair behind her ears and nervously smiles. Her cheeks are rosy, and she looks as if she's glowing. Fuck, I've missed her so damn much, and I hope what she has to say to me isn't bad news.

"So..." she says. And it's immediately awkward, but I don't want it to be.

"So," I echo her words. I hate that there's a big elephant in the room, and I just want to get it all out so we can get over it and move on.

She tucks her bottom lip into her mouth and takes in a deep breath. "I'm really sorry for leaving without saying goodbye. I'm so sorry. You have no idea how much it hurt me to know that I hurt you. I don't think I would've ever left, even though I was pissed at you if I didn't leave right then. I know I wouldn't have been able to go."

Fuck, her words are like music to my ears, and I feel all the tension from my body begin to melt away. "You were hurt, too, princess. I understand why you did it. You're here now, so who cares? Okay? We've both made mistakes, and I'm sorry for ever hurting you."

After finding out she left, I was upset with her for days, and the emptiness never subsided. Heartbreak feels like grieving, and knowing I put her through that countless times over the years made me feel like I deserved it. But I forgave her months ago.

Viola gives me a small smile, and I can't bare the gap between us any longer. I stand and move to the couch, closer to her.

"I've missed you so damn much," I whisper. The closeness of her body causes my heart rate to increase. We're not even close enough to touch, but it's the closest we've been in half a year.

"I've missed you, too. And Gryff. He's still so cute. He's growing up too fast."

"He's our baby," I say with a laugh, but she doesn't smile like I hoped she would.

I can tell she's upset about something, and all I want to do is pull her into my arms, but I won't cross that line until she's ready. I won't rush this. "Is everything okay?"

She shakes her head, and the smile fades from my face. This meeting is beginning to feel all wrong. "You can tell me anything, Viola. You know that, right? I'm not upset with you, princess."

She nods.

My heart races, and I feel like I'm losing her all over again. Instead of waiting for her to tell me what's going on, I just start rambling, hoping she will open up to me.

"Are you seeing someone else?" I ask. That'd be the worst possible thing that could happen, but I'd still sit on the sidelines and wait for her. No, fuck that, I'd fight for her.

She shakes her head, and I can see she's becoming more emotional with each passing second. I move closer to her, wrap my arms around her, hoping to God she doesn't push me away. Sinking into me, she leans her head against my chest, and I hold her.

"I'm so scared, Travis."

I pull away and stare into her eyes. Now she's really beginning to worry me.

VIOLA

I don't know what to say. As he holds me in his arms, I feel like nothing else in this world matters, but I'm scared shitless. As I let out a ragged breath, Travis grabs my chin between his fingers and stares into my eyes. Before I get lost with him, I move the blanket from my stomach and stand up. At first, he doesn't notice, but when he does, his eyes widen, and he sits there, completely silent. Silence like this is what nightmares are made of, and it scares me.

"Please say something." I'm trying to stay strong, but know I'm losing it when I begin to choke up.

"Viola," he finally says, swallowing hard. "Is it..."

"Yours?" I arch a brow.

He searches my face and nods.

"Yes." I flash a confident smile, wanting him to know that I'd never do that to him. I hate that he even had to question it, but I can't blame him either. Travis King isn't the kind of guy you just move on from. I should know. I hadn't been able to in over ten years.

Immediately, Travis stands up and cups my face and covers my mouth with his. It sends shivers down my spine to feel his lips against mine again. It's been months since I've tasted him and it feels so good and so right to be in his arms again. He slows the kiss, and after he breaks apart, he presses his lips against my forehead before falling to his knees.

I watch as he places his palms against my swollen belly. I lift my shirt for him so he can feel my skin against his. He places a kiss right above my belly button before pressing his ear against my stomach.

His reaction makes me light up inside, and as I run my fingers through his hair, I think about how this will forever change us. I know deep in my heart that everything will be okay now that he finally knows and better yet that he's not upset about it.

He tilts his head up, and we lock eyes. "I want you and me and our baby to be a family, princess. I will go to every single baby appointment. You don't have to do this alone. I don't want you to do this alone."

I swallow, nerves brewing through me. "I know you're busy with the firm, so you really don't have to go to any trouble. I don't want to be a burden to you with all of this."

He stands up and wraps his arms around me and holds me. "Are you kidding me? Burden? Fuck that. I'll be there for everything. I *want* to be there for everything. Appointments, shopping, baby classes—all of it. Even changing the shitty diapers."

I let out a laugh, and it's the first time I've really smiled since telling Drew. "The baby has to be our priority. No sex, no..."

"*More* rules?" He gives me a sly grin.

I flash a guilty smile. "I just think we should stay focused on the baby, is all. It's been a long time since we've been together, and I don't want you to think I expect anything from you."

Travis tilts my chin until our eyes are locked. "I would never want you to go through this alone—no matter what. I want to be with you, and I want to raise this baby together. I've been waiting for you. I've never stopped loving you, and I never will. I don't know how to make it any clearer, princess. You're *it* for me."

I choke back a sob because his words are pure perfection. I feel like the worst person in the world right now, and all I want to do is give him everything.

"I just wish you'd told me sooner." I can hear the change in his voice now, and it's coated with sadness. "Were you even going to tell me if you didn't plan on coming back?"

Guilt washes over me, and I can't look at his sad eyes. "I didn't think you'd want anything to do with me after the way I left, and I couldn't bear it. I wanted to tell you as soon as I found out, but I was scared."

"Princess…that *really* hurts to hear you'd ever think that. I've wanted you since before I even knew what it meant to need someone that much. It would ruin me to lose you for good."

I can't hold back the tears anymore, and he catches them with his thumb over my cheeks. "I'm so sorry," I whisper.

"I would've been there for you every minute you needed me. I would've flown to Boston in a heartbeat. You aren't alone, Viola."

"Travis, I'm really sorry. I'm an idiot. I know I should've told you sooner, but I was so scared how you'd react, and it didn't really hit me at first. I know that's not a valid excuse, but I'm so sorry for hurting you. I don't ever want to do that again," I tell him, and I mean every word.

"Princess," he says, brushing a strand of hair off my face. "I understand you were scared and it's okay now. It's all going to be okay. I'll always be here for you. I'm not going anywhere."

He kisses me again, and it feels so natural and right. I didn't expect him to be this understanding. I played every scenario over in my head, and worst case, I'd be alone. I'd be a single mom, and he'd never want to see me again.

"Does Drew know?" he asks with a pointed look.

"Yeah, he does. I told him yesterday."

"Oh, okay; good. I wasn't sure if I should expect him to punch me in the face sometime soon."

"Well, maybe. But it wouldn't be for this," I say with a smirk.

"So, then he took it well?"

I shrug and purse my lips. "Minus a few choice words, yeah I'd say he did."

"And your parents?"

"Not yet. Soon, though."

"We can do it together," he says confidently.

I wrap my arms around him and pull his face to mine, so I can kiss him once more. I tell him I'll be right back and walk toward the kitchen because I'm in desperate need of some water.

As I glance over my shoulder at him, I see him watching me and admiring my new waddle. I study him and no longer see the boy I fell in love with all those years ago, but a man who will be the father of our baby. An *amazing* father.

"Damn, your ass looks great."

I glare at him. "I feel huge and disgusting."

"Are you kidding me? You're beautiful, princess."

Once I reach the kitchen, I grab a bottle of water and walk right back to where he's waiting for me on the couch.

"So, do you know if it's a girl or a boy yet?"

"No, I didn't want to find out until you knew."

He smiles and brushes his hand over the stubble on his chin. "Okay, good. So what is your due date? Do you know when you have your next appointment? Oh, my God. I just realized I'll need to tell my mother."

I let out a chuckle at all of his questions, but I understand, it's all a little overwhelming.

"Well...I'm due in late February. I made an appointment for Wednesday at three, and then the ultrasound will be right after that, but if you can't make it, it's totally fine."

"February," he repeats, nodding. "I'll pick you up, and we'll go together. I will never be too busy for you." He reaches for my hand and pulls me closer until I'm against his chest. He closes the gap between us with his lips, and when he kisses me, it's so easy to close my eyes and be transported back to six months ago—before our blowout, before Boston, and before the pregnancy. Travis and I have never had a 'normal' relationship, and now with a baby in the picture, it could get even more complicated, but as I feel his body pressed against mine, I feel nothing but happiness. Complicated or not, I know he'll keep his promise to me. He'll be there for the baby and me and won't allow me to do this by myself, even if I begged him because he's stubborn like that. Travis King is going to be a wonderful dad, and I'm going to be an awesome mom, and we're going to have a beautiful baby together. It still feels surreal. Even with him here with me—elated—it doesn't seem real.

"I've missed your lips," he says, pulling my lower lip into his mouth and releasing it.

"Oh, yeah?"

He presses another kiss on them. "Oh, yeah. Even these lips, too," he teases and smiles as I finally get what he was implying.

"I should've known you'd already be trying to break the rules."

"Fuck the rules. Your rules never stood a chance anyway." He grins, and I know he's right, even if I won't admit it.

"So, you'll need to tell Gryff he's getting a sibling."

"Why don't you come over and tell him yourself?" He arches a brow, and I know where this is going.

"Fine, I will."

"Maybe stay and have a sleepover."

I give him a pointed look.

"What? It's not like you can get pregnant *again*..."

"Are you seriously talking about getting me back into your bed already?" I frown and look down at my huge belly. "Like this?"

"Are you really that surprised?" He chuckles.

I sigh, knowing I really shouldn't be. "Some things never change, King."

I look down and take notice of the impressive tent in his pants. "Oh, God. You're serious."

He shrugs. "They say the heart doesn't forget, but I think what they meant was the dick..."

The door opens, and Courtney walks in with her purse that's the size of a small suitcase swung over her shoulder.

"Hey, boss," she says to Travis, drops the bag with a loud thud, and walks to the kitchen. He quickly adjusts himself when she's out of sight.

"Did you really hire her?" I whisper.

He laughs. "She kind of hired herself."

"I can hear you two," she yells from the other room, and we both crack up laughing. It feels good to be with him again. I might actually be able to get some sleep now without the anxiety of telling Travis weighing on me.

Courtney changes into a pair of leggings and a t-shirt. "Congrats on the bun in the oven, boss."

"Court!"

"What? We can start talking about it now that Travis knows, right?" She winks at me, but I glare at her. I made her promise me she wouldn't say a word until Travis knew, so I guess it's fair game now.

"I think that's my cue to get going," Travis says with a smile and stands up. "Oh, I almost forgot." He stops before making it to the door. Travis picks up a package and hands it to me. I glance down at it, and then back up at him before I tear the silver paper from the small box. I lift the lid and see a black velvet jewelry box inside.

"What's this?" I'm confused and kind of nervous to open it.

"Go on," Courtney says, her face all lit up. She's on the edge of the couch waiting. When I open the box, I immediately gasp. It's a set of heart-shaped diamond earrings, similar to the necklace he gave me for my thirteenth birthday.

"Oh, my God, Travis. They're beautiful," I gush. "But it's too much." I watch them glimmer in the light.

"I'd buy you the world if I could, princess," he says, dismissing my reluctance to accept them. "Go ahead, put them on."

After I put them in, I tightly wrap my arms around his neck and bury my face in his neck. "Thank you so much."

He wraps his arms around my waist and presses a kiss under my ear. "Happy Birthday, princess. I love you." He then presses his palm to my stomach. "I love you too, little one."

Travis flashes me an overjoyed smile, but before he can walk away, I grab his hand and pull him back to me. "I love you, too, Travis."

Saying it feels so right, and when the words finally leave my mouth, I mean them. I love him. I've always loved him, and it's time he knows. Travis leans in and gives me the sweetest, softest kiss on the lips.

He tells me he'll call me later before walking out, and I'm left reeling. The only thing that brings me back to reality is Courtney's big, long high-pitched aww. I forgot she was still here, because when his lips touched mine, the only two people that existed at the moment were us.

CHAPTER SEVENTEEN

TRAVIS

It's hard not to doubt my ability to be a dad. Considering I didn't have a positive male role model in my life, I question it, but each day I remind myself that I am not my father. No matter what, I'll be there for my son or daughter, and make sure to give all the love I missed out on. I'll try every day to set the example, to show love while being a parent. This kid isn't here yet, but my life is already drastically changing. I don't want to fail.

Even if I'm scared shitless that I will mess this whole dad thing up, I feel like I'm the luckiest man on the planet. At least that's what I keep thinking when I glance over at Viola as I drive to our appointment. It's no longer *her* appointments. I've made sure to take ownership of each and every one of them from now until the delivery date. *Our appointments, our baby, our future.*

I'm going to be a dad. It's a scary thought, but knowing that Viola is *the one,* and she's carrying our baby, brings such a sense of joy to me that it's almost unexplainable. Since she's been home, we've quickly fallen back into our old routine, but without all the wild sex. It feels great knowing there are no more secrets, and we can be as open as we wish.

The last few days, she's stopped by to visit Gryff and me, and I stop by Courtney's every day before I head home. Each time I leave her, it sucks. I want her to move in with me or for us to get our own place, but I'm trying to keep her stress free.

We pull into the parking lot of the doctor's office, and once we're parked, I grab her hand and kiss her knuckles. "Are you ready for this?"

She gives me a small smirk. "Somehow I don't think you're referring to the doctor's visit."

Arching an eyebrow up at her, I reply, "Definitely not."

"Then take me, Travis King. Give me your babies," she says with a laugh.

"Consider it done."

We get out of the car and walk inside. It's the first time I've stepped foot inside a gynecologist's office, and it feels like all the heads turn and stare at me. Viola smiles at all the women in the waiting area, but her body tenses with nerves.

Once she's checked in and they call her back, she steps on the scale and tells me to turn around so I can't see. As much as I want to remind her that I don't care what the number on that scale says, I want to respect her privacy as well. After that, they take her blood pressure and ask her if anything has changed since the last time she's been there. Considering she's pregnant now, she had a lot to update.

When the doctor arrives, they talk about a little of everything. It's overwhelming at first, but I try to keep up. I want to know all our options and birth plans and whatever the hell an epidural is. I want to be here for Viola as much as possible.

The doctor motions for Viola to lie down and lift her shirt. She measures her belly from underneath her breasts all the way down to her pelvis. She tells us she measures right on time for a late February due date.

She then presses her hands into her belly, and I watch as Viola cringes. I'm not sure if that's normal, so I'm tempted to say something, but it doesn't last but a moment. Soon the doctor is pulling her upright, and reminding her to take her prenatal vitamins.

Once the doctor leaves, I stand in between Viola's legs and cup her chin. "You are beautiful," I remind her.

She gives me a forced smile, but it's not believable.

"You are carrying my baby, and if that's not the sexiest and most beautiful thing in the world, then I don't know what is."

She finally smiles wide and kisses me.

The nurse startles us as she knocks on the door and pushes it open. "I believe you scheduled your ultrasound for after the checkup? Wendy is expecting you in the radiology department whenever you two are ready to head down."

We take the elevators down to the lower level and follow the signs to another receptionist's desk. The woman's name tag reads Wendy, and I know we're in the right place.

Once Viola's registered, we only have to wait a few moments before they call us back. An ultrasound tech, who later tells us her name is Kelly, greets us at the door and leads us down a hallway to a vacant room with a large flat screen TV hung on the wall and an ultrasound machine. Everything looks so foreign to me and I'm not sure what to expect, but I'm excited to be here with her.

Kelly instructs Viola to sit on the table and lean all the way back. Once she does, she looks over at me and smiles.

"What?" I ask.

"Are you ready to see our baby?"

I grab her hand and squeeze. "Yes, I can't wait."

Once Viola is settled on the table with her jeans unbuttoned and her shirt pulled up, Kelly turns down the lights and settles into the chair next to us.

"I saw in your chart that you don't know the sex of the baby yet. Do you want to find out today?"

Viola looks over at me, and she's beaming. "Do you want to know?"

"It's up to you, princess." Not knowing is somewhat killing me, but it wouldn't matter if it was a little girl or boy. I'd love him or her just the same.

"Can we wait? Make it a big surprise?" she asks, and I can't deny her excitement.

The tech smiles, and I nod.

Viola turns to the tech and smiles with an idea. "Could you write it down and seal it in an envelope for us?" Viola asks, and I want to know what she's up to. Of course, she notices.

"I thought we could open it on New Year's." She's enjoying torturing me way too much. "As soon as the clock strikes midnight."

I laugh at her sweet idea. "Let's do it."

"This is going to be a little cold," the tech warns Viola as she spreads the gel on her stomach so the wand will move easily across her skin and there's no air in between. I feel my heart begin to race as the tech places it on her stomach and moves it around until she lands on a pulsing beat. The room fills with a sound that reminds me of a washing machine. It's our baby's heartbeat.

"So, you've had no issues since your last appointment?" the tech asks.

"Nope. Everything's been great." She glances over at me and smiles genuinely.

"So, have you two picked out any names?"

"Not yet," we both say at the same time. It's something we haven't discussed yet.

I'm in awe that I can see our baby's face in a 3D image. I glance over at Viola, smiling as tears of happiness stream down her face. I stand up and grab her hand in amazement. "I can see the baby's mouth and nose."

"Everything looks perfect," the tech says with a satisfied smile. "Now I'm just going to take some measurements for the doctor, and then when I get to the lower half of the baby, I'll let you know so you can look away."

I'm half-tempted to sneak a glance, but I don't. I want to share that moment with Viola. It'll be something just for us.

"I'll print some images out for you to take home," she says, clicking some buttons on her machine. Once she's finished, she sets everything down. "Here are some tissues to wipe the gel off." Viola takes them and cleans her belly. It suddenly feels so real.

The tech hands us the 3D images, and we're both in awe.

"I can't believe we can see so much detail already."

"I think it's going to look a lot like you," I say, examining the images.

"Yeah?" she asks with hopefulness in her tone.

"Yup. Just add some glasses, a tiny wand in their hand, and *voila!* Miniature Viola."

"Very funny!" She wrinkles her nose and pulls her shirt back down. "Well, he or she will clearly have good taste in books."

"Clearly," I mock.

She stands up, and I hold her in my arms and kiss her hair and tell her how much I love her. "We're having a baby," I whisper. "We're really having a baby."

VIOLA

"I've got a surprise for you," Travis says as we head down the highway in the opposite direction of the hospital. The streets and houses are decorated with Christmas lights, and I think about how this will be our first Christmas together as a couple. He interlocks his fingers with mine and squeezes. When we pull up to the mall, I laugh at his choice of location.

"You're bringing me to the mall?"

"Thought you'd want to see Santa." He chuckles. "Actually, I'd like to spoil the shit out of you and my little prince."

"Prince? So you think it's a boy?" I grab the envelope out of my purse and wave it around. Inside on a piece of paper is the sex of our baby, and while I'm so tempted to rip it open, I don't.

His eyes widen. "New Year's. It's not too far away. Just a couple of weeks."

I lean over and kiss him, and he places his hand on the back of my head and pulls me even closer. We get out of the car and walk into the mall. Twinkling Christmas lights are strung from the trees, and it's so damn crowded that I almost second-guess this decision. Travis grabs my hand, and we walk through different stores, and he asks me questions about things I like. The next store we walk into is a baby store. He finds a onesie that has a crown on it and buys it immediately.

"But it's blue," I state.

"It's because we're having a boy. But if we have a little girl, I'll still dress her in it," he chuckles.

"If we have a little girl, you're going to be that scary dad with tattoos that doesn't let her date, ever."

"Damn straight. And she'll have a big strong uncle that carries a gun and handcuffs. No dating until she's thirty. I'm serious."

I shrug with a grin. "She'll just sneak around. Seriously, look who her parents are."

"We don't have to worry about it because we're having a boy."

"Okay, whatever you say."

As we walk past Victoria's Secret, he turns and gives me a smirk.

"Don't even think about it. I'm a house. The last thing I feel is sexy."

"Trust me, princess. You're sexy." He glances down to his crotch where I see an impressive growth under his jeans.

I'm laughing so hard I can barely catch my breath. The giggles take over and my stomach is bouncing so much that it makes me laugh to the point that Travis joins in. We look ridiculous, walking through the mall, losing our shit laughing.

He grabs my hand and leads me across the way where Santa is sitting.

"You're not serious."

"Come on; it will be our first family photo."

His smile is convincing, so I follow him down the decorated lane with plastic candy canes. Travis pays the teenager dressed as an elf and soon we're walking up the stairs on the stage. Santa pats his lap, and I laugh and sit.

"Have you been a good girl?" The old guy looks at me. He's such a great Santa; I don't even have the urge to pull his beard like I did when I was a kid.

Travis speaks up. "No, Santa. She's been a *very* bad girl."

My mouth falls open with a gasp. "King!"

"And what would you like for Christmas?" I look at Santa for a long while and then look to Travis.

"I have everything I want, actually." I mean every word. Instinctively, I touch my tummy. Travis is smiling so big; I wish they could take the picture right at this very moment so I can treasure it forever.

"There's bound to be something," Travis asks as if he was waiting for me to spill my guts to Santa and his elves.

"I'd like world peace," I say with a smile.

"A typical princess answer," Travis laughs.

Santa gives us a big *ho, ho, ho,* and I turn to look at the camera with a smile and the elf snaps the photo. Once it's printed and put into one of those cardboard frames with snowflakes along the side, she hands it to me. Immediately I open it to see. I'm looking at the camera, so happy, with my little baby bump, and Travis is looking at me with so much love and adoration that I can't help but turn to him and kiss him in the middle of the mall, regardless of all the people trying to walk past us.

From behind, I hear someone scoff, and I turn around to see Mia *Fucking* Montgomery standing there, with a smug-ass look on her face, and some dude next to her. Travis grabs my arm because I'm ready to kill her. She glances down at my stomach and then looks at Travis and bursts into an evil laughter. "I wonder how many other King babies are wandering around."

"Nowhere near the amount of sex tapes you have floating around the internet. Or the number of random dicks you've had in your mouth," Travis spits back at her.

Mia gasps then turns and looks at the bag of bones standing beside her—unamused—but he doesn't jump to defend her. Either it's because Travis could rip him in half or because he knows it's true.

I've not seen Travis this angry in years.

"Can't believe you settled for this. Look at her. You could have done so much better. Pity, really." She looks me up and down.

"You're a bitch! I'm *so* happy Drew finally moved on from your skanky ass," I say between gritted teeth, taking a few steps forward. People turn and look at us, and in any other circumstance I'd be embarrassed, but all I can see is red. My heartbeat rings out in my ears, and I want to punch her in the face, pregnant or not. She hurt my brother; she hurt Travis and me, and the damage she caused was almost irreparable.

Travis grabs my hand and pulls me away from her, but I'm seething to the point that I start crying. I'm pissed I can't gain control of my emotions, and I hate that people are staring at us. Once the adrenaline courses through me, exhaustion follows, with an extra-large dose of doubt.

"Come on. Let's get out of here," Travis says, rubbing my back.

After we're in the car, we sit in silence.

"I'm sorry, princess. You didn't deserve any of that."

"Did you hear what she said?"

He looks at me with sad eyes and nods. "You know what? Fuck her."

"She wanted you to," I add. All those old fears start flooding back in full force, and it puts me on edge.

"I can guarantee you the only King baby is the one you're carrying." He grabs my hand.

"No one else I've ever been with has made me feel the way you do. *Ever*. It's always been you, Viola. I've always reserved that part of myself for you."

I let out a ragged breath. "But what if you wake up one day and decide I'm not what you want? What if she's right?"

"And what if I counter that with another scenario? *What if* I wake up every day, knowing I love you more than I've ever loved anyone in my life? And *what if* I honestly believe I'm the luckiest man on earth because I've somehow snagged the girl of my dreams—the girl I crushed on as a kid, that forbidden fruit—and she's going to have my baby? Because that's the reality we live in, that we will always live in." He brushes his thumb against my cheek.

"You always do that," I say.

"What's that?" he asks as he cranks the car, the low rumble calming me.

"Say exactly the right thing at the right time." I smile.

On the way home, we share side-glances and the realization of how happy Travis makes me sets in. After being away from him for six months, I don't dare take moments like this for granted. I cherish each and every one of them, but I know there will be thousands more. No one will ever be able to take this away from us, because what we have is more than a stupid crush or a one-night stand.

It's real.

It's love in the rawest form.

CHAPTER EIGHTEEN

TRAVIS

It's finally the night I've been waiting for, and even though Viola's only been back for a few weeks, it feels like nothing's changed at all. Well, except that she's carrying my baby, we've been apartment hunting together, and she tells me she loves me every day.

Six months ago, I was at a dead-end job that I no longer felt passionate about. The girl of my dreams had just moved across the country, and my best friend would barely speak to me. I'd screwed up, and I'll live with that for the rest of my life, but I can't say I'm not happy about where that has all lead me. Drew and I worked out our differences; King Marketing is becoming a reality, Gryff finally stopped chewing on all my damn expensive shoes, and most importantly, Viola is finally mine. I couldn't be any fucking happier right now.

New Year's Eve used to mean going out with friends, getting drunk, and bringing back a random girl for a meaningless night together. I'm not proud of that tradition, but this year I plan to make a new one.

Viola has held onto her promise of finding out the baby's gender until midnight. We're going to open it together in the park, under the lights. I have a couple more gifts to surprise her with tonight as well, and she has no clue. Tonight's a night we'll both remember for the rest of our lives.

Viola sleeps over most nights now, and since she's restless the majority of the time, I let her sleep in while Gryff and I go for our morning walk and I brew the coffee. She's been snoring in her sleep, which keeps me up. Gryff sleeps at our feet, and when she's not kicking him off in the middle of the night, he's nuzzling his way under the covers and stealing them from me. The first thing we're getting once we move is a king-sized bed. And a bigger dog bed.

After our chilly walk, I grab the newspaper and pour myself a hot cup of coffee. Gryff sleeps at my feet as I scan the paper. Once I finish the world news section, I flip to the business overview where I see CRAWFORD MARKETING in bold letters.

Enron was one of the biggest scandals in 2001, and more than a decade later, another company is facing similar charges. *Crawford Marketing*, founded in 1970, has fallen under the same scrutiny of the Security and Exchange Commission. A formal investigation concerning the $400 million loss reported by the company in the fourth quarter will begin soon. Reliable sources have stated earnings have been misrepresented for an undisclosed time period, and embezzlement charges have been filed against Alyssa Crawford, daughter of the Chief Executive Officer.

I shake my head with a sly smirk on my face. I'm so glad I left when I did. Blake and Alyssa deserve each other after that stunt, and they'll be together forever—behind bars.

Drew slowly walks down the hall in just his pajama bottoms, his wild hair in a bun, and bags under his eyes.

"Rough night?" I ask, nodding my head to the coffeemaker. "There's some left."

"You could say that," he mumbles, grabbing himself a cup. "No offense, man, but when the hell are you two moving out? I can't take another night of her snoring."

"Soon, I promise."

"I don't know how you sleep next to that." He shakes his head, walking back over to the table and sitting down next to me. "It's like a train's coming right through the house."

"I don't." I sigh. "God, I hope after the baby comes, it stops; otherwise, none of us will ever get sleep again."

Drew laughs in agreement.

"What are you two laughing about?" Viola asks, waddling into the dining room.

"Oh, nothing," I say, reaching a hand out and bringing her to my lap. Drew brings his cup up to his lips and hides a smile behind it.

"How'd you sleep?" I ask her.

"As good as one can with an extra fifty pounds on top of them."

"Well, hopefully, you'll lose it all after the baby is here and we can *all* sleep again," Drew comments, and I wince, knowing immediately that Viola is going to chew his ass out.

"I meant the dog, asshole! Gryff kept nudging his way in between us."

"Oh, sorry!" He puts his hands up in an apologetic surrender, and I laugh at his expense.

"And I have not gained fifty pounds, thank you very much," she says with a scowl. "I've gained twenty-one, and the doctor said that was in the perfect range."

"You're beautiful no matter how many pounds you put on," I tell her, but she doesn't smile.

"You two suck." She gets up and walks into the kitchen. She's only two months away from her due date now, and I can tell she's getting anxious. "Come on, Gryff. Let's go stuff our faces in private where we won't be judged."

Drew and I sit in silence for a moment, and when I'm sure Viola is out of hearing distance, I lean toward him. "So, I have something to show you."

I reach into my pocket, and Drew speaks up, "Dude if you whip your dick out, I'm punching you in the throat."

"Hey, I did that *one time!* And I was drunk," I say in my defense.

Once I'm done showing off Viola's surprise, I stuff it back into my pocket before she and Gryff walk back in. "I'm going to take a shower."

"Want some help?" I grin, knowing she'll probably smack me for that one.

"I could use some help shaving. I haven't seen my vagina in a couple of weeks."

Drew makes a gagging noise, and Viola laughs at his expense.

"You did that on purpose," Drew complains.

"That's what you get for the weight comment!" she fires back. Gryff follows her down the hallway as I stand up and set my cup inside the sink.

"I hope you know what you've gotten yourself into," Drew says behind me. "She's feisty as hell on a good day. I don't even want to imagine when she gives birth."

"I plan to wear a cup that day. And maybe even a helmet."

"I heard that, Travis King!" she shouts from the bathroom.

"Oh yeah, forgot to mention her super-enhanced hearing. Some weird pregnancy hormone thing," Drew explains. "Our mom had it too when she was in her third trimester."

"Any chance she had an overactive sex drive after birth, too?" I chuckle as he rolls his eyes at me, looking horrified. "Hey, you go six months without sex and see what's on your mind twenty-four seven!"

"Six months, huh?" he asks with an impressed tone. "And your hand hasn't gone numb yet?"

"Surprisingly not."

He pats me on the shoulder. "Hang in there, man. You'll have sex again in eighteen years or so."

"Comforting. Thank you."

"I always save my best advice for you."

Once Viola and I are both ready for the day, we take Gryff for a walk in the park, where families are all set up to enjoy the fireworks when the clock strikes midnight. It's one of the dog parks around here, and even though it can sometimes be overwhelming, Gryff loves the interaction.

"So, are you getting excited about the reveal?" I ask her. We're walking side by side, holding hands, and I can't help thinking about how this night is going to change everything.

"I am!" She smiles. "You?"

"Oh, yeah. I'm already thinking of names for the little man."

She rolls her eyes at me, once again, for commenting about it being a boy. "I hope you aren't going to be disappointed if it's a girl."

"Of course not. I'm not sure I could handle another princess in my life, but I'm sure I could make room." I smirk, bringing her hand up and kissing her knuckles. "Have you thought of any names?"

"Yes, but I'm pretty sure you're going to veto them all."

"Do they have anything in common with a certain book series?" I arch a brow, knowing damn well she's thought of names based on her favorite books.

"Possibly," she says with a glare. "No movie characters, though."

"So, I guess Bridget Jones is off the table?"

She snorts and shakes her head at me. "Definitely."

"Damn. I was hoping one day to be able to tell that story as the night we christened the living room floor."

"Travis!" she scolds, slapping my arm. "I'm starting to think you get no votes now."

"Aw, you don't mean that." I push out my lower lip, and she lets out a dreamy sigh.

We walk out of the park and head back home. She's been doing pretty well, taking regular walks to keep up her momentum and strength. I know as the days get closer, she's going to feel worn down and tired, but she's been doing great so far. I'm super impressed with how well she's adjusted to everything.

"I can't wait until we can take the baby on our walks with us in the stroller," she says as we make our way inside the house.

"Well, when I'm at work, you guys will have plenty of time to go for walks. As long as you take Gryff, though. He's your bodyguard when I'm away."

"Well, until the baby is old enough to go to a sitter."

"Wait, what?" I ask, unhooking Gryff's leash. "Why would the baby need a sitter?"

"For when I go to work," she states, leaving me speechless. "I don't want to waste my degree."

"It's not wasting your degree, Viola. You'll always have it, but don't you want to be the one to raise the baby? I just figured—"

"That I'd be one of those stay-at-home moms that live in yoga pants, dirty t-shirts, and unwashed hair?"

"Well, I wasn't necessarily talking about the uniform..."

"Whatever. I don't want to be left alone all day long while you're at work."

"But I want to be the one to provide for you, for *us*. I left my corporate job with you in mind, Viola. I wanted to make sure our future was planned out."

"So, we're just going to make a dozen babies, and I'll stay home and cook and clean and then we'll be the next TLC spotlight family?"

I swallow, watching her steam into overdrive, and wondering how the hell I'm supposed to handle this situation when her hormones get the best of her. We probably should've discussed this before I made assumptions, but now I don't know how to get myself out of it without pissing her off even more.

"Okay, we can do whatever makes you happy." I take a step toward her, watching her chest rise and fall as she takes deep breaths. "Calm down, princess. We'll make this work; I promise you. We don't have to make any definite plans right now. Nothing is set in stone."

"Except for the fact that I have to pop this baby out of my vag."

"Well, yeah. Unfortunately, I can't fix that little detail." I watch as she fidgets. "Deep breaths, princess. Everything is going to be fine."

"I don't know why I get like this. One second I'm fine, and the next, I'm freaking out, overthinking everything and questioning if we're ready for this, and what if something goes wrong or what if I'm not strong enough to go through labor or—"

"Viola," I say firmly, grabbing her attention. "You are going to drive yourself insane, overanalyzing every little thing that might or might not go wrong. I'm here for you, okay? I'm not going anywhere, and whatever happens, we'll figure it out together. Got it?"

"Okay," she says softly. I bring her lips to mine and kiss her, reminding her exactly how much I love her. "Are you sure you still love this train wreck?"

"More and more every single day."

After Viola takes a shower, she ends up falling asleep on the couch with Gryff. I don't dare disturb her because I know how tired she gets. My parents are driving down to meet us for dinner tonight, which will be Viola's first time seeing them in years. I told my mom over the phone that Viola was pregnant, and she's been ecstatic over the news.

My father is sicker than before, and my mom is still doing everything she can to keep him alive. I know she loves him, and I admire her strength. I don't openly talk about it unless she gives me the impression she wants to, but tonight will be about new beginnings and the next chapter in our lives. As much as I look forward to this next year of our lives, I'm also enjoying every step of the journey along the way.

I peek at Viola once more before I step outside, needing to make sure she's still asleep. I dial Courtney and make sure to keep my voice low just in case her enhanced hearing takes effect again.

"What's up, boss?" She answers on the first ring.

"Viola's asleep, so I wanted to go through the events for tonight one more time," I say, pacing on the driveway.

"We've been over it five times!"

"Just humor me, Courtney!"

She laughs and lets out a loud sigh. "Fine. If that's what will get me a raise..."

"A *raise?* We haven't even opened the doors yet!"

"What can I say? My daddy taught me how to play hardball at a young age."

I brush a nervous hand through my hair and mutter a few curse words. "*Fine,*" I agree through gritted teeth. "I'll have Drew come twice a week to deliver lunch. Happy now?"

I can tell she's smiling on the other end just by the high-pitched tone in her voice. "Yes, very. Now was that so hard?"

"I knew I'd regret calling you that day," I mutter, knowing damn well she'll hear me.

"And now you're stuck with me forever. Get used to it, King."

"Can we *please* just go through the plan one more time now?" I'm losing my patience, and she knows it, too.

"Of course. Whatever you say, boss."

CHAPTER NINETEEN

VIOLA

I wake up to Gryff licking my face. He's pressing on my bladder, and I'm two seconds away from peeing myself.

"Get down, buddy." I push him slightly, and he jumps down, giving me the opportunity to roll off the couch. "Where's Daddy?" I ask him as we walk down the too quiet hallway. "Travis?" I call out, but no one answers. "Hmm, weird."

I use the bathroom and get myself something to drink. We should be leaving within the hour to meet up with his family, so I know he can't be too far away. I dig into the fridge and grab an apple to hold me over until dinner. I glance around and see the newspaper lying on top of the kitchen table. I shuffle through it until the words Crawford Marketing grabs my attention.

Well, well, well. Wouldn't ya know? Little Miss Blondie got herself into a little bit of legal trouble. I can't even feel sorry for someone like that. *Karma's a bitch, after all.*

"Viola?" I hear Travis' voice call out. I look behind me and see him all dressed up in a black suit and tie. I swallow, needing to control my breathing. He's always looked amazing in suits, but tonight, something is different. He looks incredible. And happy.

"Where'd you go?" I ask.

"I had to run a couple of errands. What are you doing?"

"I just woke up, and the baby was hungry, so we found a snack," I say as he wraps his arms around me, the baby bump putting more space between us than usual.

"I see that." He dips his head and takes a bite of the apple. "We have to leave soon," he reminds me.

"I know. I was just looking at a very interesting article in the paper." I purse my lips.

"Yeah, nothing like bad press for one of the largest firms in the state."

"Maybe that means Royalty Marketing will be the next best thing." I grin, knowing he's about to scold me.

"It's King Marketing, stop trying to make Royalty Marketing happen!"

I burst out laughing at his Mean Girls reference. "Oh, my God! Don't make me laugh! I might pee!"

"So, then I shouldn't do this?" He brings his hands down and tickles my sides. He laughs harder the more I squirm and as much as I try to back out of his trap, he doesn't let up.

"I see those chick flicks have really benefited you."

He finally stops torturing me and pulls me in close. "It was the only way to feel close to you for those six months. But after Drew caught me crying alone in my room to *The Notebook*, he basically stripped me of my man card."

"So, then is this the part where you ask me to slow dance in the rain and gaze into my eyes and say sweet nothings in my ear all night long?"

He chuckles, presses his lips to the shell of my ear, and whispers, "I told you I'm not like those guys in your romance books. I'll say exactly what I want, and what I want is to bend you over this kitchen table and fuck you until you count to ten. Or until the table breaks, whichever happens first." I feel his cocky smirk against my neck, but I know he's dead serious.

"If our baby comes out swearing filthy words, I know who's to blame."

"I'll plead the fifth." He leans down and kisses my mouth.

I wrap my arms around him and pull him closer. "How did this happen?" I ask, breaking the kiss but staying pressed against him. "How could I leave you for six months? Why did you wait for me?"

The emotions I feel for Travis are becoming too much for me to handle. They're overflowing, and I have been feeling more and more guilty for what I've put him through. Everything that happened between us, from being kids to teenagers, to where we are now. Some days I wake up and can't understand how we made it here.

"Why are you crying, princess?" He rubs his thumb over my cheek and catches the tears.

I shrug because I know the words won't come out right.

"Everything that happened needed to happen so we could make it to where we are right now. Happy, in love, about to have a baby…" He smiles so wide that it makes me start tearing up all over again. "I can't even be mad how it went down because look how things ended up, princess. You, me, our baby. It's all I've ever wanted, and I couldn't ask for anything more."

"You truly are perfect, Travis King. Do you know that?" I wipe away the rest of my tears and smile up at him, admiring how good he looks tonight.

"Only when I have my other half does it feel like my life is perfect, and that's only thanks to you." He tilts up my chin and presses his lips to mine once again. Damn him. I could stay here with him all day, and never tire of the way he kisses me.

"I have to finish getting ready," I groan against his lips. "I don't want to show up looking like a bloated, fat whale." I make a face as I step away and he pats me on the ass to hurry it up.

Once I'm dressed, my hair is curled, and my makeup is done, I'm nearly out of breath. That took more energy than I anticipated, and now I'm ready for another nap.

"This baby is sucking every ounce of life out of me, and it's not even born yet," I whine, grabbing my purse off the table and slipping into my flats. No heels for me.

"He's just preparing you for when he's here, and you'll need to function on only a couple hours of sleep a night."

"I'm telling you...it's a girl," I say as he opens the door and he follows me out.

"I guess we'll find out soon."

It's been years since I've seen Travis' mom and dad. I was expecting it to be awkward as hell, but surprisingly it felt like old times. Just like everything with Travis, it felt as if no time had passed at all.

His mother is ecstatic about the baby, and I know she's going to make every effort to come and visit us once he or she is born. His father has lost weight, and he's pale and noticeably weaker. I feel for Travis, and although their relationship has been anything but a solid one, I hope they can mend it enough for the sake of our baby. I'd love for his father to form some kind of relationship with our child since his days are going to be numbered.

Once we finish dinner, we order dessert and start talking about baby names. His mom gives us a list of family names, in case we needed any inspiration. I wish I could say that we plan to take the list into consideration, but I can't fathom naming our baby after Travis' great uncle, Seaman Gaylord King.

After dinner, we part ways. It's almost 9:00 p.m. and I'm not sure I'll even be able to make it to midnight to open the gender reveal envelope together. Drew is working, and Courtney is partying with a few other friends, so we have the house to ourselves, but I just want to lounge on the couch and read until I fall asleep. However, Travis, as usual, has other plans.

"Please tell me where we're going!" I beg from the passenger seat. He keeps his eyes on the road and his lips in a taunting smirk.

"We'll be there soon, just be patient."

"I hate surprises," I groan, getting a smile out of him.

Travis pulls into a suburban neighborhood and parks on the side of the road in front of a large Victorian house on a small hill. The streetlights glow over the sidewalk, and I can't place exactly where we are.

"What are we doing?"

He slides out of the car, and I watch as he walks around and opens my door for me. "Come on."

Confused and a little skeptical, I step out and let him take my hand. As he pulls me up, he shuts the door behind me and weaves his fingers through mine.

"Travis," I say as he leads me up the sidewalk. "What is going on?"

We start walking up the steps that lead up the hill to the stunning house. The house is pitch black, and it looks like no one is home.

Travis stops us about midway up the porch stairs and positions us toward the house. "So, what do you think?"

"About what?"

"The house."

"Um...it's gorgeous. Who lives here?"

He digs into his pocket and pulls out a small box. My heart begins racing, thumping hard in my chest as I watch him. He opens it slowly, and I swallow down the anxiety of what is happening right now. I study the little box in his palm and wonder if it's what I'm thinking.

"As of this morning, we do." He opens the box and pulls out a key with a red ribbon tied through it.

"Wait, *what*?" I gasp, my head spinning at his words because they make no sense. We've been looking at apartment ads, but nothing seemed to work out. "I don't understand."

"I made an offer on this house about a month ago, and it just closed this morning."

"But...I thought we were apartment hunting?" I'm thoroughly confused, and I don't know if it's pregnancy brain, but my mind is a clusterfuck of emotions.

"That was just to put you off of my surprise." He smiles. "I saw a sign for an open house and on a whim decided to go check it out. As soon as I saw it, I knew it was meant for you and me. There's a large dining room, a fireplace in the living room so you can read next to it, a large bathtub so you can relax once the baby's asleep, and even a little nook with built-in book shelves for your Harry Potter collection. Plus, there are four bedrooms, which means we can decorate one to be the nursery. The neighborhood is perfect. It's close to my job, has good schools, and there's a nice big backyard for Gryff and even room for a swing set. I didn't know if you'd come back to me, but I just knew I couldn't let it go. I put an offer in the next day, and they accepted."

"You bought it before I was even back home?" I ask, shocked and completely amazed by this man standing in front of me.

"I did."

"I can't believe you did that." I can't believe I ever doubted this man's love for me.

"I want to give you the world, Viola. You deserve everything and more, and now with a baby on the way,

I want to make sure you're both taken care of. No more games, no secrets or lies. I want us to be a family."

"I don't know what to say…" My eyes are watering, and I can't get a handle on my emotions.

"Say you'll move in with me," he says, placing the key in my hand and wrapping his fingers around my fist. "I can't imagine living here without you."

"Are you kidding me?" I squeal, wrapping my arms around his neck and digging my face into his neck. "I couldn't imagine anything better."

He cups my face and covers my mouth with his. We share a heated kiss, passionate and sweet. I love this man, and without any doubt in my mind, Travis King was always meant to be mine.

"Are you ready to come look inside?"

I nod my head furiously. "Yes! Oh, my God, I can't wait!"

He leads me to the door and gives me the honor of unlocking the door. I hold my breath as I push it open and look inside. He flicks the lights on, and I gasp.

"It's so beautiful," I murmur, trying to look at everything at once. "I can't believe this."

"Come on, let me show you the rest." He leads me into the living room and flicks on the lights, and once again surprises me. There's a white-lit Christmas tree and white lights hanging from the ceiling.

"What have you done?" I spin around with the biggest grin on my face; I can hardly contain myself. "It's gorgeous in here!"

He grabs my hand and leads me to the center of the room. When I look up, I see mistletoe hanging from one of the light fixtures and giggle. "You know you didn't need mistletoe to get a kiss."

He doesn't respond, so I assume he doesn't hear me. I spin around, ready to repeat myself, but when I do, he's down on one knee holding out a ring.

"What—"

"Viola, my *princess*."

"Travis, what are you doing?" I cover my mouth and squeal.

He grabs my other hand and smiles. "Remember earlier when I said that I couldn't ask for anything more because I was just so happy to be with you?"

I nod, holding back more tears.

"Well, I lied. There is one more thing that would make me the happiest man. One more question I need to ask you..."

I gasp.

"I know our relationship may seem unconventional to some, but it's our story, and it'll always be my favorite one, no matter how many other chick flicks you make me watch or how many romance novels you read."

I release a sob, laughing in between.

"Will you marry me, Viola Fisher?"

I nod because I'm too overcome with emotion to speak actual words.

"Yes? Is that a yes?" he clarifies, smiling up at me.

"Yes!" I shout. As he slides the ring up my finger, he places a kiss over my knuckles.

"You just made me the happiest guy in the world. Do you know that?" He stands up and cups my face. "The fucking happiest."

"And you say you aren't like the guys in my romance books?"

He leans in and kisses me, softly at first, and then opens my mouth wider with his tongue and presses deeper. I groan against his lips, and he grips my waist tighter.

"Dammit, I want to fuck you right now," he whispers against my lips, and I chuckle. "How's that for romance?"

"I'd say you nailed it."

"So, you ready to find out if we're having a little prince or princess?"

"Yes!"

CHAPTER TWENTY

TRAVIS

Nine months later…

"Courtney!" I bellow from my office. "Get in here, please!"

"Yeah, boss?" she asks, peeking her head inside. She's dressed up more than usual, which is really no surprise since it's Friday. Drew always stops in and brings everyone lunch at the end of the week. It's one of the arrangements I've had to make to get Courtney on my permanent staff. She's proved to be an asset, and after she had started getting offers from other companies, I knew I had to up my game to keep her even if that meant offering Drew as bait.

"I have a one o'clock interview, so any lunch shenanigans need to be done before then."

She steps in and rolls her eyes at me. "Please, Travis. Drew has made it very clear that we're just friends."

"But that hasn't stopped you from trying." I curl my lips up in a mocking smirk. She hates it when I give her shit for crushing on Drew.

"Well, I'm not a quitter," she says, shrugging. "Those cuffs might come out to play one of these days."

I snort and shake my head at her. "You'd have more luck devirginizing a monk."

"Hey, don't tempt me."

"Trust me. I'm not." Drew is an idiot for not taking Courtney up on her offers. She's gorgeous and smart and looks at him like he's the best thing since Nutella. But Drew isn't over Mia yet, which is a damn shame, so he keeps Courtney at friend-zone distance. As far as I know, they only talk and text each other about Viola, the wedding, or the baby. Courtney is the maid of honor, and Drew is my best man, which gives Courtney more excuses to be around him. I only hope he gets over Mia before it's too late and Courtney has moved on.

"So, where are you taking Viola this weekend?" It's our first weekend away since the baby was born six months ago in February. We haven't had a date night since, and we're ready to have some alone time without having to schedule it between feedings, diaper changes, and afternoon naps.

"That's a surprise," I retort.

"C'mon, I won't tell!" she pleads, but I know better. Those two tell each other everything. And I do mean *everything*.

"Fine!" She folds her arms over her chest and frowns. "But when you can't find the network IP address to the printer again, don't ask me!" She starts walking back out of my office.

Laughing, I yell for her to come back, and I tell her. "I'm taking her up to a cabin at Lake Tahoe. No TV, no Internet, no cell reception. Completely off the grid," I say with an anxious smile. "There's a landline for emergencies, though. I know Viola will worry if there's no way to call home."

"Good, you two need it."

"Trust me, I know. I plan to make Viola exhausted for an entirely different reason this weekend."

"Yeah, yeah. You're going to hump like rabbits. Spare me the details."

"Who's humping like rabbits all weekend?" Drew asks from the doorway, and Courtney spins around so fast, I swear she's going to fall on her ass.

"Your sister and Travis. They're going up to the cabin to bang all weekend."

Drew sighs. "That's an image I'll never get out of my head, thank you."

"Until you've walked in on them, you have nothing to complain about," Courtney says with a visible shiver.

"Well, that's what you get for walking into my office without knocking," I fire back, remembering that day very well.

"Sex on the clock, huh? How come when I suggest personal time on the clock, I get told to get out of your office?" Courtney quips.

"Get out of my office," I say without a beat.

Drew laughs and shakes a bag of food at her. "I have your weekly bonus."

"Perfect, I'll be taking my lunch break *on* the clock." She turns and glares at me.

An hour later, Courtney lets me know my interviewee has arrived and said to prepare myself. Rolling my eyes at her comment, I tell her to send her in. A moment later, the door swings open, and the moment I catch sight of her blonde hair and designer purse, I can barely hide the gasp that releases from my mouth.

VIOLA

I look at the clock and realize Travis will be home any moment. I haven't started packing yet, and I know he's going to want to leave as soon as his mother arrives.

Grabbing a suitcase from the closet, I glance at my reflection in the mirror and frown. I look like a hot mess; I haven't showered in three days, and my hair contains dry shampoo and baby spit up. It's piled on top of my head with a rubber band I found on the bathroom floor. Sweatpants and a holey t-shirt complete my less-than-glamorous look. I haven't worn makeup in months, and I can't even remember the last time I wore clothes that didn't come with a stain or an elastic waistband. But the truth is, I'd rather be at home with the baby than pushing papers in a corporate setting. I get paid in snuggles and coos, and I wouldn't give up those moments for a winning lottery ticket.

"Viola!" I hear Travis yell from the staircase. I quickly rush down the hallway and shush him. "Oops, sorry."

"You know it's naptime!" I whisper-hiss as he walks up the stairs.

"I know, I'm sorry." He wraps his arms around my waist and pulls me into his chest, pressing his lips against my forehead. "I'm just so excited to get some alone time with you this weekend."

"I am too, but I'm nervous to leave the baby."

"Don't be nervous. Everything will be fine. The baby will be fine. We'll be fine. I promise." He tilts my chin up and presses a soft kiss on my lips. "Are you going to be okay?"

"Yes, I'm just not feeling well."

"It's nerves, princess. We need this, okay?"

I shake my head, knowing he's absolutely right. It's been so long since we've had a night to ourselves. "I look like a disaster."

"You're gorgeous no matter what." He kisses me again, and for a moment, I lose myself in him. Breaking the kiss, he says, "Now go shower. I'll finish packing."

"How'd you know I didn't finish?"

"Just had a feeling," he answers with a mischievous grin.

"Am I that obvious?"

"Go," he pushes. "I'll check on the baby."

I walk down the hall to the linen closet and grab a couple of towels. Before shutting the door, I also grab a new razor, because Lord only knows how long it's been since I've shaved. As I'm walking back toward our bedroom, I stop just outside of the nursery and listen to Travis' soft voice.

"Well, hello princess." I peek inside, and he lifts her out of the crib. "Hey, my beautiful girl." He kisses her forehead and she coos.

Watching as he lays her on the changing table, I lean up against the doorframe and admire my amazing man and how wonderful he is with our daughter. He's a complete natural, just like I knew he'd be, but I know he had his own concerns, considering his relationship with his father. However, the love that pours out of him is infectious. Sometimes I can't even believe after all this time that we're together, engaged with a new baby, and in our own home. It feels too good to be true at times.

"You're going to spend the weekend with grandma, aren't you? Yes, you two are going to have so much fun, but you better be good for Nana. No pulling all-nighters again and refusing to eat your cereal."

She kicks her legs and stuffs a hand in her mouth as he changes her. I love watching them, even when it's everyday, normal stuff. He turns around and catches me staring.

"Viola," he says in a warning tone. "Go take a shower. We'll be fine."

I scoff and wrinkle my nose. "Fine. I'm going."

Once I've showered, shaved, put on a layer of makeup, and find clean clothes to wear, I head downstairs, where Travis has set our suitcases. He's in the living room with his mother, going through the list of things we wrote down for her. I trust his mother; I do, but I don't trust anyone alone with her just yet.

"You look beautiful," Travis says as I sit down next to him and reach for the baby. He hands her over, and I kiss her chubby little cheek.

"I feel like a changed woman," I say with a laugh. "Who knew a shower could feel so good?"

"You two are going to have a great time. No worries here, okay?" His mother tries to reassure me, but I still feel the nerves fluttering in my stomach.

"You sure you'll be okay all weekend?" I ask his mother.

"Of course. Go and enjoy yourselves. You two deserve it."

"Thank you, Mom," Travis says as he leads us to the front door. "I'll call you as soon as we arrive." He grabs our luggage as I squeeze the baby one more time.

Reluctantly, I hand her over to his mother, but I don't release her tiny little hand. "Don't forget she needs to be rocked before bed. And you'll need to burp her for at least ten minutes after she eats. Oh, and when she takes a bath, she needs the soap for sensitive skin."

His mother nods and smiles, knowing that I'm repeating myself once again.

"Viola," Travis warns in a deep voice. "They're going to be just fine."

"Okay, just one more kiss."

I press my lips to her cheek and then her forehead and then her other cheek. I inhale her scent because I just can't get enough. "See you in a couple of days, Ginny. I love you."

CHAPTER TWENTY-ONE

TRAVIS

"So where are we going?" Viola asks, fidgeting in her seat as we hit the highway.

"Someplace quiet, with no distractions or other people around."

"Where's that?"

I shake my head.

"C'mon," she whines. "Just a little hint."

"Let's just say...we shouldn't have bothered packing clothes, because—"

"Because you plan to fuck me six ways to Sunday?" she finishes for me with a hopeful smile.

"I plan to have you counting higher than six, princess." I smirk over at her, grabbing her hand in mine and placing a kiss over her knuckles. "Loudly, too."

"Okay, but I hope you plan to let me nap in between this time," she quips, referring to the first time we had sex after Ginny was born. She'd only been two months old and wasn't sleeping longer than three hours at a time. We'd taken advantage of an early bedtime and made love all night long. Before we even realized it, Ginny had slept six hours straight that night. Viola was so tired; she could barely keep her eyes open, much less walk.

"No promises."

"Do you really think she'll be okay? She's going to wonder why we're gone so long."

"She's going to be just fine, Viola." I know Viola's going to be worried all weekend, so I'll need to keep distracting her. "Oh, you'll never guess who walked into my office today for an interview." I'd forgotten all about it until now.

"Who?" She furrows her brows, and I hope I didn't make a mistake on mentioning it.

"Alyssa Crawford."

"No fucking way!" Her jaw drops.

"Yup. Stilettos and all."

She laughs, and the sweet sound makes me smile. "What'd you say to her?"

"I asked her what the hell she was doing there, and once she said she was looking for a job, I told her to get the fuck out, that there was no way in hell I would ever hire her. Then, of course, she offered me some special incentives, and that's when Courtney gladly kicked her ass out."

"Jesus." She sighs. "Girl has no class."

"She has no dignity."

"Maybe she's just one of those rich girls that's misunderstood. You know, like Paris Hilton."

"You can't be serious right now." I narrow my eyes at her, wondering if sleep deprivation has made her lose her mind.

"I'm sure she grew up in a weird environment, and it's tainted her. In fact, I feel sorry for her."

"Yeah?" I arch a brow. "And what about Mia? Is she misunderstood too?" I ask with a sly grin.

She cocks her head at me and scowls. "Fuck Mia. She's just a psycho that needs her teeth rearranged."

I laugh, and it feels good to be alone with her again after all this time. I love our little family and Ginny more than anything, but sometimes I need Viola and me just to be Viola and me again.

Thinking back to when Viola went into labor makes me smile. We had gone over possible baby girl names for weeks, but nothing was set in stone just yet. I knew she wanted something meaningful and special. Thinking it over, I knew that any name she picked, whether it be from Harry Potter or another one of her favorite books, would be perfect for us. Growing up, Viola was glued to her books, and that's what made me fall for her in the first place. She was a book nerd and proud of it, and I loved that about her. They made her who she is and the fact that she still quotes it every chance she gets lets me know we made the right choice.

Two hours later, we finally pull up to the cabin I rented. It's a cozy two-bedroom log house in Lake Tahoe with a stone fireplace, small kitchenette, and complimentary hot tub on the back porch.

"Oh, my God! It's so cute!" Viola squeals as soon as we're inside. I set our luggage down and grab her hand.

"Let's take a quick tour." I lead her around, recognizing most of it from the pictures I saw online.

"Travis," she says, tilting her head up at me, "I love it. It's perfect."

I smile back and cup her face. "It is. And so are you." I press my mouth to hers and part her lips with my tongue. She presses her body into mine, and I know I'm not going to be able to stop if we go any further.

"Are you hungry?" I ask against her lips, but she ignores me and wraps her arms around my neck, pulling me deeper against her. *I'll take that as a no then.*

She shuffles her hands down to my shirt and starts lifting it up. I take the hint and separate us just enough to throw it off. She releases a moan against my lips, driving me wilder than ever. God, it feels like it's been so long since we've been able to be alone. The passion has never cooled down between us, no matter how many miles apart we were.

"I've missed this," she whispers.

"Me too, princess. Fuck, I want you so bad." I wrap a hand around her neck, claiming her body as mine.

She brings her hands down and lifts her shirt up and over her head. Sneaking a glance at her, I smile when I see her breasts on display. Too impatient to wait for her to remove her bra, I pull it down and cup her luscious breasts. Her head falls back on a whimper, and I know she loves it as much as I do.

I'm hard and throbbing under my jeans. I don't think I'll be able to be gentle with her, or even take my time like I wanted to. The desire is too strong to control.

I cover her taut nipples with my mouth and suck on them until she digs her nails into my arm. I know she likes it rough, but ever since the baby, they've been extra sensitive.

"I can't wait, princess. I want to kiss and touch you everywhere, but I don't know that I can hold back." I place kisses along her neck and inhale her sweet scent.

"I don't want you to hold back. I need it," she whispers, almost as if she's begging me for it. "I need *you*."

"You have me, Viola. Always."

Reaching down, she tugs at my zipper. I can barely take it anymore. As I undo my jeans, pull them down with my boxer shorts, and free my cock into her palm, she wraps her hands around her back and unclasps her bra. As soon as I'm stripped down to nothing, she begins stroking me, and I squeeze her breasts once again. After a few torturous moments, I spin her around and bend her over the arm of the couch.

She squeals, but quickly regains her footing. Kneeling behind her, I pull her jeans and panties down until she's able to kick them off. I spread her legs apart and slide my hands up her thighs. Cupping her ass, I bend her over further until I see those pretty pink lips of hers.

When she arches her back, which pushes her ass out farther for me, I take that as an invite and slide my tongue up her slit. She shivers and I do it over and over until she begs for more.

I love the taste of her and can't get enough. I push one finger inside her, and then another. Sucking on her clit, her hips start going wild as she searches for her release.

"It's not going to be that easy, princess," I say, slowing my rhythm. I pull her cheeks further apart and dive back in, wanting to feel her release on my tongue.

"*Yesyesyes…*" she mutters against the cushions. I know she's about to lose her mind. I push two fingers inside again and work her until she's ready to collapse. "*Ohmygod*...fuck, yes."

"I want to hear you, Viola. *Loud*."

She grinds her sweet ass against my face until I feel her body tense. "*One*!"

I smile, knowing it's the first of many tonight. She tastes so fucking sweet as she comes on my tongue. My fingers slow down, but I'm not remotely close to being finished with her. I stand up and reposition her, so we're angled just right. Gripping her hips, I palm my cock and stroke it a few times before sliding inside her. At first, slow and deep. Her moans escalate louder and louder with each thrust. Then I lean over her body and cup her breasts with both hands as I speed up my pace and feel every inch push inside her—fast and deep, with no apologies. She's mine, and I'm claiming all of her.

She pants and moans and begs. This is the Viola I've missed. I love watching her be a mother to our daughter, and she's become an amazing partner, but if there's one thing that's never fizzled between us, it's the chemistry we share. The all-encompassing, must-have-you-now, love-you-more-than-ever-before kind of chemistry. A decade's worth of built-up tension, an explosive heat that's undeniable.

I place a hand on her back and slide it up her spine. Fisting her hair, I pull until her head falls back and I can see the outline of her throat. She moans louder, which only encourages my deep thrusts. I love the way her body looks right now, her skin soft and warm, her arms sprawled out in front of her as she tries to regulate her breathing, but it's no use. I don't plan to be finished with her anytime soon.

"Do you remember our first time?" I growl, pulling her body back, so she's flush against mine. I press my lips to her ear. "That first time nearly broke me, princess. Fuck, I had wanted you so bad for so long."

"I remember," she responds, and I thrust harder. "I remember you got really emotional and started crying. Then you asked if you could hold me all night."

The corner of her lips tilt up, and I know she's enjoying messing with me.

"Your mouth is going to get you in trouble," I warn.

"It usually does."

I cup her ass and spread her cheeks as I thrust deeper and harder until she continues counting once again. She lies across the arm of the couch again, but I don't let her rest. Not just yet.

Wrapping my arm around her waist, my fingers find her pussy and begin rubbing her clit. I love how wet she gets for me. The sweet smell of her arousal lingers, and I know she's going to lose herself at any moment.

I pull back and turn her around, so she's against my chest. I cup a hand around her neck and pull her mouth to mine. My fingers find her clit again as I part her lips with my tongue. It never feels like enough with her; I always crave more of her. She squeezes her hands around my biceps as she hangs on for control.

"Why do you enjoy torturing me?" she asks against my lips. I smile, knowing she's enjoying every bit of it just as I am.

"Why do you defy me, princess? Give me what I want, and we'll both be happy." I press my finger deeper inside her.

"I'm not letting you win that easy, King." She tries closing her legs, but I block her with my knee.

"Play by the rules, and we'll both win," I warn as I part her legs open again.

"I don't trust your rules." She smirks. I feel her body tensing the deeper I push inside her, and I can't wait another second to be inside her again.

"Good." I grin. "You shouldn't." Wrapping my arms around her body and cupping her ass with both hands, I lift her body up until both legs wrap around my waist. She squeals as she clings to my neck and grinds her pussy against my shaft.

"Put me down!"

"Not until you say the magic words," I taunt as I carry her over to the fireplace.

"Fuck off, Travis?"

I smack my hand across her ass cheek, and she squeals. "That's what you get for breaking the rules, princess."

"What are you going to do about it?"

I lower her to the floor next to the fireplace and climb on top of her. "That smart mouth of yours is going to get you into trouble. Are you ready to pay the price?"

"Give me your best, King."

"Carpet burn did look good on you, especially since I was the one who put it there." I lower my mouth to her neck and kiss down the length of her jaw. She arches her back as I make my way down her chest and wrap my lips around her nipple. Her hands find my hair, and as she weaves her fingers through, I swirl my tongue around her other nipple and pull it into my mouth.

"God, yes!" she cries out, pushing her breast deeper into my mouth.

I lower my hand and slide a finger inside her once again. She clenches her pussy, and I slide another one inside. I love hearing her beg for it, and I don't plan to stop until she does.

"Let me hear you, Viola," I growl, rubbing the pad of my thumb against her clit as I push deeper inside. "I want to hear you beg for it."

"I'm not begging for it. Move aside, and I'll do it myself." She shakes her hips, trying to get out of my grip.

"Defying me only makes me harder, princess." I press my hips against hers as I grip my hand around her wrist, stopping her from going lower. "You should know that by now."

"And you should know better than to deny me." She bites her lower lip, and I know she's enjoying teasing the hell out of me. She lowers her hand and palms my cock, but when I arch my hips into her, she stops me.

"*Goddammit,* Viola," I hiss, pulling her bottom lip in between my teeth. "You're going to pay for that one."

I grab both of her wrists and push them above her head. I part her legs with my knee, and once her legs wrap around my waist, I slide inside her. Her head falls back, and I thrust deeper, waiting to hear that throaty moan. Releasing her wrists, I wrap a hand around the back of her neck and pull her mouth to mine. She moans against my lips and my pace increases, feeling her clench around my cock as the intensity builds. The way her body responds to mine, and the way I can't get enough of her, lets me know without a doubt that she was made for me, and I was made for her. Everything that happened between us has built up to moments just like this. *Pure perfection*.

Our bodies speak louder than our words ever could. "I can't imagine what my life would be like without you in it."

"It'd be dark, cold, and pointless," she says, the corner of her lips tilting up.

"Always a smartass."

"Always."

"And I wouldn't have it any other way. I love you, Viola Fisher." I kiss her and don't let go until her body gives in and she releases around my cock.

"I love you too, Travis King." Her body shakes, and she screams, clawing her nails into my arms as she continues counting. And it's the sweetest fucking sound in the entire world.

We end up huddled under a blanket, and when I wake up, Viola is sound asleep at my side. I decide to put a couple of logs on the fire, so the room heats up before she wakes up. I don't plan to allow Viola to get dressed until we have to leave. This weekend is all about us, and I plan on taking full advantage.

I made sure the fridge and cupboards were stocked before we arrived. As I'm digging around for something to feed her, I feel her arms wrap around my waist. Turning around, I see she's wrapped up in a blanket, her hair a wild mess, and her eyes glassed over.

"What are you doing?" she asks, looking up at me.

Wrapping my arms around her, I pull her body into mine and kiss the top of her nose. "Looking for something to make for you to eat. You're going to need all the energy you can get."

"Mm...so your master plan is to feed and fuck me all weekend?"

"Yes." I smile. "Didn't you get the memo?"

She chuckles and nods. "Better feed me good then."

The next two days fly by, and as much as I miss Ginny, I wish we had more time. I devoured every inch of Viola on every surface of the cabin: the shower, kitchen counter, dining room table, and the hot tub.

"Well, I'd say we got our money's worth," Viola says as I carry the luggage to the door where she's waiting for me.

"Considering we broke the bed in four places, I imagine they'll be sending a bill."

She chuckles at the memory, as I wrap my arm around her and kiss her once more before taking the luggage out to the car. She follows me out, looking more exhausted than when we arrived, but I know it was exactly what we both needed.

Once the luggage is packed and the car is loaded, I lean my back against the car and smile as she stands between my legs. This was a weekend I'll never forget, and I can't wait to marry her and make her my wife.

"This was a perfect weekend," she says, resting her head against my chest.

"It really was," I agree. "However, I think we can top it on the honeymoon."

"Yeah?"

I nod in certainty. "Mile high club. Sex on the beach. Sex in the ocean. Sex in an old church."

"A church?" she exclaims, narrowing her eyes at me in disapproval.

"Why not? It's our honeymoon." I shrug casually. "Speaking of...are we going to set a date soon? Now that the firm is up and running, and Ginny is getting bigger, I think it's time. Don't you?"

She looks up at me and pulls her lips into her mouth, and I worry I've said the wrong thing. I study her face and see concern written all over, and immediately think the worst.

"Have you changed your mind?"

"No! Nothing like that," she says. "I love you, and of course I want to marry you."

"Then what is it?" I brush a strand of hair off her face, and she shivers.

"Well…" She takes a deep breath. "How do you feel about planning it nine months out?"

"I would marry you tomorrow if I could, but I want to give you the wedding of your dreams, so whether it's a month from now or nine, I'm all in."

"Good." She smiles. "Because in nine months, we'll have our hands pretty full."

I narrow my eyes as I notice the glow on her cheeks and it finally hits me.

Ho-ly shit.

EPILOGUE

VIOLA

One year later...

Once upon a time, in a faraway land, lived a young princess who awaited a prince who would give her everything she ever dreamed of...love, passion, loyalty. He'd be the sweetest, kindest, most heartwarming gentleman a girl could ever ask for. And he'd be perfect.

...And he is. Travis King, my prince charming.

I can hardly believe it's here.

But here we are, just two weeks until we say *I do*.

It's been almost two years since Travis proposed, and only three months since the arrival of baby James. Yes, we continued with our theme, even if Travis really pushed for a name from Bridget Jones. He's never winning that battle.

We finally set a date for a fall wedding in September, and even though I'm more than ready to become Mrs. Travis King, fitting into my wedding dress after having a baby has stressed me out. That led to stress eating, which ultimately led to more stress about not fitting into the wedding dress.

Travis has been amazing through it all, and no matter how crazy my hormones were, or how stubborn I was on wedding details, he's stayed by my side. I didn't think it was possible, but I love him more now than I ever have before. He's an incredible father, and watching him with our kids is a daily reminder of how lucky I am.

As I lie in bed with James on one side of me after an early morning feeding, and Ginny on the other side, squeezed between Travis and me, it's easy to see how much our lives have changed in just two years. King Marketing was named as one of Fortune's 100 Fastest-Growing Companies of the Year, which was a surprise and a blessing. The amount of exposure the company received was beyond anything we ever imagined. Small and large businesses from every corner of the map have contracted our services. Before James was born, I helped out at the firm when I could, but since Ginny is still little too, I've chosen to be the most kickass stay-at-home mom ever, and I love every minute of it. I've even started blogging about mommy stuff and books—two of my biggest passions.

Between diaper changes and constantly picking up toys, Courtney's dragged me to wedding vendor events, dress fittings, cake tastings, and worse of them all, shoe shopping. I don't mean metaphorically, but has *dragged* me out of the house, pushed me into the car, and held my hand as we walked into my last dress fitting.

"As my maid of honor, I expect you to keep all carbs away from me until the wedding. Got it?" I say as the bridal stylist laces me up. "It'll be a miracle if my boobs can squeeze into this."

Officially unable to breathe, the stylist gets me in my dress. It's not over-the-top glam like Courtney tried to make me wear, but sweet and simple. A strapless sweetheart neckline, embroidered bodice, and lace skirt. If I even look at a cheeseburger, I will bust out of this thing, but the moment I tried it on, I knew it was the dress I'd be wearing when I stood in front of Travis King to say, "I do."

"Oh, you look so beautiful," my mother gushes, dabbing a tissue under her eyes. Ginny is sitting on her lap as James sleeps in his car seat next to her feet. She loves being a grandma, even if she refuses to be called one.

"You think so? It looks okay?" I ask, chewing on my lower lip. All I can think about is the stretch marks on my boobs and the dark circles under my eyes. "I feel like a whale," I pout.

"Nothing a good facial and vagina steam can't fix," Courtney assures me, cheerfully. My face turns red as the stylist looks away, pretending she doesn't exist right now.

"Court!" I scold, frowning. "Don't make me laugh. I'll pop a button."

"There are no buttons," she deadpans.

I flash her a pointed look, and she laughs.

"Do you want to try it on with your veil?" the stylist asks, and I nod with an eager smile. The veil is my favorite accessory— a gorgeous lace that reaches my ankles but also doubles as a headband. I plan to take it off after pictures and wear only the headband piece for the reception.

"Don't forget the shoes," Courtney says as she grabs them out of the box. My feet swelled up during my last trimester, so shoe shopping was a nightmare. I ended up finding a pair of lace, peep toe heels, and best of all, they're super comfortable. However, I did size up, so I basically look like Big Foot.

Once I'm completely put together with jewelry, shoes, veil and all, I step on the pedestal and look at myself in the mirrors. I hardly recognize the woman who stares back at me. Showered, hair brushed, and even a little makeup on today, versus the sporty-spice look I've managed to nail.

Watching everyone's reactions in the mirror, I see Courtney snapping pictures of me and smiling as her fingers fly over the screen. Except she's not smiling about me. She's smiling about something else.

"Who are you sending those pictures to?" I ask, knowing she's up to something.

"Just Drew. I told him I'd give him a preview of your dress."

"He's not going to care what my dress looks like, Court."

"Yes, he does! He told me so."

Rolling my eyes, I mutter, "Doubt it." But she's too involved on her phone to notice. Ever since she and Drew became roommates, they text nonstop like a pair of teenage girls. She swears up and down that they're only friends, which I actually believe, considering Drew isn't one to sleep around, but Courtney is the one I'm most worried about. Her crush has only deepened over the years, and Drew has shown absolutely zero interest in anything more than a platonic friendship. In fact, sometimes I wonder if Drew even realizes she has a vagina. He treats her like one of the guys, or rather, as another sister. She claims to be over it, but I know better. I see the way she looks at him. I see how giddy she gets when he responds to her text messages, and I see the hope in her eyes, that one day he'll stop seeing her as his little sister's best friend.

Once the fitting is over, and I've managed to peel myself out of my Spanx, we meet up with Travis and Drew for a late lunch. My parents are over the moon about Travis and me finally getting married, and they love being grandparents but hate that we didn't move closer to them. I'm more than fine with it, considering my mother is just as bad as Courtney on the wedding planning details. Sometimes I wonder whose wedding it actually is.

"There's my gorgeous bride-to-be," Travis says with a beaming smile. He engulfs Ginny and me in a hug and then grabs James' car seat from my aching arm. "How'd everything go?"

I give him a wide-eyed look that tells him everything he needs to know.

"That good, huh?" He smirks. He takes my hand and leads us to the table he's saved for us all. Once Ginny is settled in her highchair, I unbuckle James and swaddle him to my chest. My parents and Courtney find their seats, and when the waitress comes to ask for our drink order, I realize there's still an empty chair.

"Hey, where's Drew?" I ask Travis. He looks down at his menu, and I can tell by the way his lips twitch, something's up.

"He's on his way. He had to do something quick."

Courtney leans over and speaks in my ear so no one else can hear her. "By the noises coming from his long shower this morning, I'd say he doesn't do anything quick." I shoot her a disgusted look as she flashes me a smile.

"And there goes my appetite."

She laughs and winks at me. Sometimes I wish they'd just fuck and get it over with. Whatever game they're playing is getting a little out of hand.

"So, since carbs are out of the question, looks like I can have water and lettuce."

I glance over at Courtney, wondering if she heard me, and her face is white as a ghost.

"Holy fucking shit," she mutters, looking behind me.

"What?" I turn around to where she's staring, and gasp when I see what she's freaking out about. "What the hell is he doing here with her?" I mutter, getting Travis' attention.

"Who?" he asks, turning his head. His eyes widen as the next words come from Courtney's mouth.

"Mia *Fucking* Montgomery."

COMING NEXT

This concludes Travis & Viola's story, but you'll get more of them, Ginny, & James in book 3, Checkmate: This is Reckless, a friends to lovers romance featuring Drew & Courtney!

You're cordially invited to attend the King wedding
February 2017

Checkmate: This is Reckless

(A friends to lovers romance)
A Checkmate Duet Series, book 1

Drew Fisher is the type of guy every girl wants.
Noble police officer by day, charming prince by night.
He has no idea the effect he has on women, especially me—*his little sister's best friend*. I'm the blonde Southern belle who lives up to the cliché, except I have my own quirks. I'm smart as a whip, can change my own oil, and recite The Pledge of Allegiance backward, but he doesn't see *that* girl.

It'd be easier to forget him if he wasn't my roommate and if the first thing I saw in the morning wasn't his shirtless body covered in tattoos. I've crushed on him since the day we met, but he's made it perfectly clear where we stand. *Just friends*.

I know I need to move on and accept that his feelings will never be mutual, but every day he smiles at me, I'm left dreaming of *what if*.
He has girl issues, and I've got a crush I can't deny.
We're friends, but I want *more*.

One drunken hookup leaves us with much more than a platonic friendship. Pretending it never happened proves to be more difficult than anticipated.

A crazy ex-girlfriend, a dangerous war of stolen glances, and passionate kisses leads to the most reckless battle yet. I won't be a pawn in his game, but I'll play by his rules if it will show him I'm the one worth breaking them for.

Checkmate, *Prince Charming*.

ABOUT THE AUTHOR

Kennedy Fox is a duo of bestselling authors who share a love of *You've Got Mail* and *The Holiday*. When they aren't bonding over romantic comedies, they like to brainstorm new book ideas. One day, they decided to collaborate under a pseudonym and have some fun creating new characters that'll make your lady bits tingle and your heart melt. If you enjoy romance stories with sexy, tattooed alpha males and smart, quirky, independent women, then a Kennedy Fox book is for you! They're looking forward to bringing you many more stories to fall in love with!

Places to stalk us:

Instagram.com/kennedyfoxbooks

Twitter@kennedyfoxbooks

Facebook.com/kennedyfoxbooks

http://www.kennedyfoxbooks.com

kennedyfoxbooks@gmail.com

ACKNOWLEDGEMENTS

We have so many people to thank who have helped us through this amazing journey. Grateful beyond words to everyone who has been with us since the beginning and continues to be. We have met so many wonderful readers and bloggers and adore the friendships we've made. Thank you for being on #TeamTraviola!

Thank you to our readers for giving us a chance and picking up our new release! Thank you to everyone who has left a review, sent a message, or left us a comment. It means the world to us!!

Thank you to our Checkmate Kingdom reader group (join here) for being so fun to hang out with! We love your comments, messages, and fun chats! #TheKingReturns

Thank you to our editors, Kiezha (Librum Artis Editorial Service) and Mitzi Carroll, our photographer and cover designer, Sara Eirew, and Christine Stanley from our PR company, The Hype PR. We're so grateful to have you on our team!

Thank you to our generous beta readers who read early copies, spared your time to help us work through issues, and shared your excitement with us! Jackie Ashmead, Melissa Teo, Sophie Broughton—we love you girlies!

Huge thanks to everyone who read an advanced review copy, posted gorgeous edits/images, and helped spread the love. We truly appreciate you!

Shout out to Benita from Book Beau (the original book sleeve)! Thank you for being SO sweet to us and being a part of the reading community. Your kindness shines through and we have loved working with you. (Instagram @bookbeau)

Lastly, thank you to our families for putting up with our late nights, our zombie-like appearances, and our need for constant coffee refills. We love you!

Stay tuned for more Kennedy Fox books coming your way!

Mischief Managed,
-Kennedy

Made in the USA
Charleston, SC
27 January 2017